The Gardens
of the Apocalypse

also translated and introduced by Brian Stableford:
Sâr Dubnotal vs. Jack the Ripper
News from the Moon – The Germans on Venus (*anthologies*)
by Félix Bodin: The Novel of the Future
by André Caroff: The Terror of Madame Atomos
by Charles Derennes: The People of the Pole
by Henri Duvernois: The Man Who Found Himself
by Henri Falk: The Age of Lead
by Paul Féval: Anne of the Isles – The Black Coats: 'Salem Street;
The Invisible Weapon; The Parisian Jungle; The Companions of the
Treasure; Heart of Steel; The Cadet Gang – John Devil –
Knightshade – Revenants – Vampire City – The Vampire Countess –
The Wandering Jew's Daughter
by Paul Féval, fils: Felifax, the Tiger-Man
by Octave Joncquel & Théo Varlet: The Martian Epic
by Jean de La Hire: The Nyctalope vs. Lucifer – The Nyctalope on
Mars – Enter the Nyctalope
by Georges Le Faure & Henri de Graffigny: The Extraordinary Adventures of a Russian Scientist Across the Solar System (2 vols.)
by Gustave Le Rouge: The Vampires of Mars
by Jules Lermina: Panic in Paris – Mysteryville
by Marie Nizet: Captain Vampire
by Henri de Parville: An Inhabitant of the Planet Mars
by Gaston de Pawlowski: Journey to the Land of the 4th Dimension
by P.-A. Ponson du Terrail: The Vampire and the Devil's Son
by Maurice Renard: Doctor Lerne – A Man Among the Microbes –
The Blue Peril – The Doctored Man – The Master of Light
by Albert Robida: The Clock of the Centuries – The Adventures of
Saturnin Farandoul
by J.-H. Rosny Aîné: The Navigators of Space – The World of the
Variants – The Mysterious Force – Vamireh – The Givreuse Enigma
– The Young Vampire
by Jacques Spitz: The Eye of Purgatory
by Kurt Steiner: Ortog
by Villiers de l'Isle-Adam: The Scaffold – The Vampire Soul
by Ph. Ward & S. Miller: The Song of Montségur

The Gardens
of the Apocalypse
and
The Seven Rings
of Rhea

by
Richard Bessière

translated by
Brian Stableford

A Black Coat Press Book

ISBN 978-1-935558-68-2. First Printing. December 2010. Published by Black Coat Press, an imprint of Hollywood Comics.com, LLC, P.O. Box 17270, Encino, CA 91416. All rights reserved. Except for review purposes, no part of this book may be reproduced or transmitted in any form or by any means, electronic or mechanical, including photocopying, recording, or by any information storage and retrieval system, without permission in writing from the publisher. The stories and characters depicted in this novel are entirely fictional. Printed in the United States of America.

TABLE OF CONTENTS

Introduction 7
THE SEVEN RINGS OF RHEA...19
THE GARDENS OF THE APOCALYPSE 133
Bibliography 243

Introduction

Henri Richard Bessière was born on August 20, 1923 into a family steeped in the world of show business. His father and grandfather were both directors of a local theater, and he, too, was destined for this career, but the economic conditions of the post-war period forced his family to abandon their ancestral heritage.

Young Bessière, enamored of jazz music and already well introduced in the world of the stars of French popular music, decided to become an agent. He even wrote various songs and the librettos of a few operettas. His father, Leopold Bessière, had penned a number of poems and songs, some co-authored with a friend, Francis Richard.

After World War II, Richard had gone to Paris, where he became one of the collaborators of Armand de Caro, founder of the then-fledgling popular publisher Fleuve Noir. In 1951, when Fleuve Noir decided to launch a new imprint called "Anticipation" (the term "science fiction" wasn't well known at the time), Richard searched amongst his relations and thought of the Bessières. As luck would have it, Henri had already tried his hand at writing. He had penned a detective story, which had been serialized in the press. More importantly, he had in his desk an unpublished manuscript that told of a great, epic journey of exploration through the Solar System, inspired by earlier, similar works by René-Marcel de Nizerolles (the nom-de-plume of Marcel Priollet) and Arnould Galopin, which he had read during his teenage years.[1]

---

[1] R.-M. de Nizerolles : Les Aventuriers du Ciel: Voyages Extraordinaires d'un Petit Parisien dans la Stratosphère, la Lune et les Planètes [*The Adventurers of the Sky:Extraordinary Voyages of a Little Parisian in the Stratosphere, the Moon and the Planets*] (serialized in 108 issues, Ferenczi, 1935-37).

The manuscript was divided into three volumes—two more were written later, due to the success of the series—and were published as the first three books in the new Anticipation imprint under the titles of *Les Conquérants de l'Universe* [*The Conquerors of the Universe*], *À l'Assaut du Ciel* [*To Assault the Sky*] and *Retour du Météore* [*Return of Meteor*] (the *Meteor* is the heroes' spaceship). In it, Professor Bénac, the inventor of the *Meteor*, a young French engineer, an American journalist and a young British woman, explored the Solar System, helping friendly aliens and thwarting evil tyrants.[2]

The novels appeared under the signature of "F. Richard-Bessière" which later became controversial. It was intimated that the books were written by two writers, François Richard and Henri Bessière, not unlike the well-known team of Pierre Boileau and Thomas Narcejac, who had written *Diabolique* and other successful mysteries. It is possible that Richard-Bessière's prolific output encouraged the belief that there were, in fact, two authors.

It has since been ascertained that, while François Richard exercised his legitimate role as editor, and used his greater experience to polish (and, perhaps, in the case of the earlier books rewrite) young Bessière's books, they were all nevertheless his ideas, his plots and characters, and his work.

As Bessière became increasingly successful, the "F." was dropped in 1965 in favor of the hyphenated "Richard-Bessière," and then the hyphen was, in turn, dropped in 1980, in favor of the more accurate "Richard Bessière."

---

[2] Bessière reworked the series in 1965 in the two-volume *Les Pionniers du Cosmos* [*The Pioneers of the Cosmos*] and *Le Chemin des Étoiles* [*The Path to the Stars*], updating some of the technology and his writing style, but exhibiting the same enthusiasm for space travel and the conquest of the Solar System. The book ends with: "At the end of Infinity, a new Zeus awakens in his celestial empire. The slopes of Olympus resound under the steps of the Titans. The Titans are still only men. But men who shall become Titans." Not many of all of Bessière's novels have such optimistic endings.

While Bessière's works vary greatly in terms of sub-genres, ranging from space opera to post-apocalyptic fiction, humor to horror, the author expressed a singularly unique and personal viewpoint throughout all of his novels.

The first cycle of the "Conquerors of the Universe" was, as we have seen, a traditional space opera which owed much to the would-be educational genre novels serialized in *Le Journal des Voyages* and *La Science Illustrée* before WWII, in which the manifest destiny of the Human race was to colonize other planets and bring them the benefits of our civilization as we had done to the other continents. The novel was written with Bessière's father's assistance, and tried to incorporate what was generally known at the time about astronomy and physics. The young writer's imagination shines through in the description of some truly exotic alien societies such as a race of medieval water-breathing Neptunians who have to deal with their own Joan of Arc figure! Some themes that will recur in later works, such as the transmigration of souls and the exploration of microcosmic subuniverses, make their first appearances.

Bessière's first new novel after the "Conquerors" series was *Croisière dans le Temps* [*Time Cruise*] (1952) which is very different from its predecessors. The didactic, old-fashioned style of the "Conquerors" has been replaced by action-oriented, fast-paced, often wry, storytelling; the characters are no longer 1930s clichés, but modern, believable figures. The plot centers on a scientist trying to "improve" History by preventing the assassination of King Henry IV in 1610. Instead of the anticipated Golden Age of Reason, the new timeline is on the brink of nuclear annihilation!

Vingt Pas dans l'Inconnu [*Twenty Steps into the Unknown*] (1955) explores the idea of worlds-within-worlds. The heroes are trapped inside an alien craft which takes them on a grand tour of Infinity, from the infinitely small to the infinitely large.

SOS Terre [*SOS Earth*] (1955) and its sequel, *Altitude Moins X* [*Elevation Minus X*] (1956), the tale of an invasion by "aliens" who turn out to be from an ancient Earthmen now secretly living underground, are the first novels to introduce Bessière's long-standing, recurring hero: American journalist Sydney Gordon, his ditzy wife Margaret, his catastrophe-prone son, Bud, and his scientist friends, Archie and Gloria Brent. Bessière's novels of the period read like a catalogue of all the classic themes of science fiction. This, occasionally, created problems...

Objectif Soleil [*Target: The Sun*] (1956) is about an Earth scientist forcibly recruited by the inhabitants of a Counter-Earth, located on the other side of the Sun, now threatened with ecological disaster. Bessière borrowed the themes (mostly the beginning and the end) from a novel entitled *La Planète Inconnue* [*The Unknown Planet*] by "Jean de Bizac" serialized in 1941 in the weekly magazine *Ric Rac*. What he did not know, and which was later discovered by researcher Philip Harbottle, was that that book was an unauthorized, uncredited translation of William J. Passingham's *The World Behind the Moon* , originally serialized in the British magazine *Modern Wonder* (October 1938-January 1939)!

In *Altitude Moins X*, Bessière developed a witty, first-person narrative, telling the story from the perspective of the jaded and cynical Sydney Gordon. The Sydney Gordon adventures were initially fairly serious tales of alien and extra-dimensional invaders. *Route du Néant* [*Nether Road*] (1956) described a journey through time to Earth's last days, and serves to highlight Bessière's unique blend of science and spirituality. *Cité de l'Esprit* [*City of Mind*] (1957) is about a secret city of immortals located in the African desert. *Création Cosmique* [*Cosmic Creation*] (1957) deals with technological soul transfers; *La Deuxième Terre* [*The Second Earth*] (1957) and *Via Dimension 5* (1957) with parallel universes—one of Bessière's favorite themes—; *Bang!* (1958) postulates that our universe was born from the explosion of a super-bomb in another, supra-universe.

In the 1960s, some of the Sydney Gordon novels become bleaker, reflecting the concerns of the times. For example, *Les*

Poumons de Ganymède [*The Lungs of Ganymede*] (1962) is an indictment of nuclear tests and a moving plea against nuclear weapons. Gordon becomes aware that a series of technologically advanced races just like ours have all perished in nuclear wars—is Earth to be the next? Bessière's conclusion is all but optimistic.

Bessière's other novels of space exploration also became bleaker in tone. In *Planète de Mort* [*Death Planet*] (1957), the first extra-solar expedition is sent to its doom on a desolate planet to satisfy some obscure business machinations. In *Le Troisième Astronef* [*The Third Spaceship*] (1959), the explorers of Venus confront a belligerent alien empire which has come to test a devastating new weapon in our solar system. In *Fléau de l'Univers* [*Universal Scourge*] (1957), the distant colony of Terra II suddenly finds itself embroiled in a conflict with Earth; its agents eventually discover that the Motherworld has been infiltrated by mysterious aliens who, like cuckoos, are planting their offsprings among the children of men—and their world is next. Bessière reworked the theme in *La Mort Vient des Étoiles* [*Death Comes from the Stars*] (1962), in which the Martian colony has severed all contacts with Earth, and a secret agent discovers that it has been infiltrated by aliens seeking to regenerate their dying race through a host species: mankind. In *Visa pour Antarès* [*Visa for Antares*] (1963), Earth is at war with the ruthless Antarians who plot to release a virus that will eradicate all life in the cosmos, including their own.

As a contrast to this series of grim space operas, in the 1960s, the Sydney Gordon series suddenly took a marked tongue-in-cheek turn with *Les Mages de Dereb* [*The Wizards of Dereb*] (1966), in which Sydney and his friends discovered the Land of Fiction where they faced the demented products of the imagination of a science fiction writer. In the classic *Ne Touchez Pas Aux Borloks* [*Don't Touch the Borloks*] (1968), alien toys create chaos on Earth.

A recurring opponent of Gordon and his friends became the Machine, a giant, intelligent, extra-dimensional computer with god-like powers introduced in *La Machine Venue d'Ailleurs* [*The Machine from Beyond*] (1969), which created pocket universes in which it ran fanciful simulations. The Machine tries to create the perfect world, but all its simulations fail, often with hilarious consequences. The moral of this series of playlets, in a true Theater of the Absurd, seems to be that the road to Hell is paved with good intentions, and that Man is not made for a perfect society.

If Bessière used the Sydney Gordon series as his primary vehicle for light-hearted tales of satire, in 1966, at the request of his publisher who was looking for more action-oriented space operas, he created another popular series, that of the hard-boiled Dan Seymour, a futuristic James Bond, introduced in Agent Spatial No. 1 [*Space Agent No. 1*] (1966), a somewhat reworked version of *Visa for Antares*. Seymour went on to appear in another ten novels

In *Cerveaux sous Contrôle* [*Brains Under Control*] (1966), Bessière described a *Fantastic Voyage*-like miniature odyssey inside the bodies of evil mutants created by a naïve scientist seeking to improve the species. Seymour went on to undertake a variety of perilous missions throughout the Terran Empire and beyond. His last adventure, *Les Ruches de M112* [*The Hives M112*] (1974) features a living planet capable of a thousand metamorphoses, from the most attractive to the most poisonous. The theme of a living eco-system or a life-cycle that involves all the species living upon a planet is a recurring one in Bessière's work. Seymour had already encountered a living bioverse, the deadly planet Timor, in *L'Enfer dans le Ciel* [*Hell in the Sky*] (1967). In *Le Troisième Astronef*, Venusian fruits are filled with blood, which the natives use to regenerate themselves. In *Les Prisonniers de Kazor* [*The Prisoners of Kazor*] (1970), another Dan Seymour adventure, the hostile planet Kazor is inhabited by an alien race capable of evolving from a microbial to a superhuman stage and vice-versa, never dying, only endlessly transforming. The classic *Les Marteaux de Vulcain* [The Hammer of Vulcan] (1969) depicts a band of space prospectors seeking the legendary wealth of planet Vulcan, where minerals are alive and determined to destroy all intruders. A virus that turns flesh into crystal, leaves the would-be plunderers eternally frozen but conscious.

The publication in 1960 of Louis Pauwels & Jacques Bergier's *Le Matin des Magiciens* [*The Morning of the Magicians*], with its emphasis on the secrets of Lost Civilizations and the role of the Occult in the Nazi regime, proved to be a source of inspiration to many French genre writers, including Bessière.

In *Feu dans le Ciel* [*Fire in the Sky*] (1956), we learn that Earth is periodically ravaged by a cosmic cataclysm, which has already destroyed several civilizations before ours; a handful of survivors are now forced to seek shelter in underwater cities, in the hope of restarting a new cycle of civilization, just as it had been done thousands of years earlier. In *La Guerre des Dieux* [*The War of the Gods*] (1961), an archeologist discovers a dimensional gate in Peru which opens onto a world inhabited by Olympians, benevolent supermen who once ruled over mankind. They will return to Earth to fight their arch enemies, the evil Therpians, who have awakened after millennia of sleep and want to conquer the world, or destroy it. In *Les Quatre Vents de l'Éternité* [*The Four Winds of Eternity*] (1979), the "true story" of the legendary city of Ys is revealed: it was trapped in a pocket dimension by mysterious psychic vampires. In 1983, Bessière penned a trilogy entitled *Si L'Histoire des Hommes m'était contée* [*If the History of Men Could Be Told*] which combined Gnostic cosmogony, extraterrestrial visits, Christianity and Templar mysteries. The author, being a native of Béziers in Southern France—Cathar country—brings much authentic flavor to the theme and knows how to use and blend these concepts for his reader's enjoyment.

Even more so than the mysteries of the past, the mysteries of the soul, and of survival beyond Death, is another recurring theme which fascinates Bessière. In *Pas de Gonia pour les Garkandes* [*No Gonia for the Gharkands*] (1964), men have only found one alien race in the universe, the soulless, mindless humanoid Gharkands, who are then used as hosts to receive the transplanted souls of wealthy Earthmen after their death. But the all too convenient Gharkands are nothing but an elaborate trap set up by a cosmic predator. In *Escale chez les Vivants* [*Stop Over Among the Living*] (1966), a jazz pianist who has died finds himself resurrected in a future where the transplantation of souls has been achieved and people no longer die. Again, sinister forces are at work behind that utopian facade. Conversely, in *L'Homme Qui Vécut Deux Fois* [*The Man Who Lived Twice*] (1978), the hero, also a jazz musician, travels into the past to save the woman he loves, but ends up causing the victory of the Nazis. In *Le Vaisseau de l'Ailleurs* [*The Ship from Beyond*] (1972), evil entities from the afterlife, unwilling to move on to the next stage of spiritual evolution, try to conquer Earth and replace the living. In *Les Survivants de l'Au-Delà* [*The Survivors from Beyond*] (1982), afterlife is exploited by mysterious harvesters who collect the spiritual energy of souls. In Bessière's afterlife, even minerals and animals are endowed with souls—everything is alive. Souls go through matter, conferring a spark of life to every atom, creating worlds slowly evolving towards the apotheosis of consciousness. This view of the universe owes a great deal to the philosophy of Teilhard de Chardin and physicist Jean E. Charon.

Bessière also made his mark with a number of novels that featured an original blend of horror and science fiction. These were among some of his best works. Monstrous alien entities from beyond, whose only weakness is sound, invade an Earth rendered silent in *Les Maîtres du Silence* [*The Masters of Silence*] (1965). *Cette Lueur Qui Venait Des Ténèbres* [*That Light Which Came From Darkness*] (1967) featured ghastly body-snatching parasites. *Des Hommes, des Hommes et Encore des Hommes* [*Men, Men and Forever Men*] (1968) starts like *Planet of the Apes* with a spaceman crashing on a future Earth populated by humanoids enslaved by a crystalline entity that has, over the centuries, deprived them of all initiative and pride—a world which has no more room for men like him. The image of a semi-destroyed Notre-Dame cathedral plays the same role as the Statue of Liberty in Franklin J. Schaffner's 1968 film. In *Concerto pour l'Inconnu* [*Concerto for the Unknown*] (1971), a hive-mind gradually sapping the will of humans slowly plunges the world into chaos. *Les Seigneurs de la Nuit* [*The Lords of Night*] (1973) described the triumph of the same dark powers who lurked behind the Nazi regime. One particularly original book is the amazing *Je m'appelle... Tous* [*I'm Called... All*] (1965) featuring a lone spaceman who has crashed on an alien planet and clones himself in vast numbers to escape loneliness, but in vain; he eventually succumbs to madness.

Two of the most prominent examples of this approach have been collected in this volume. *Les Sept Anneaux de Rhéa* [*The Seven Rings of Rhea*] (1962), the most reprinted of the author's novels in France, embodies all his favorite themes, from his concerns about the nature of evil and the fundamental duality of the universe to the exploration of a nightmarish world which seems truly alive. *Les Jardins de l'Apocalypse* [*The Gardens of the Apocalypse*] (1963), which is a reworked and far more elaborate version of the earlier *Légion Alpha* (1961), presents another grim view of a post-cataclysmic Earth where survivors (or, more accurately, their descendants) try to reconquer their planet. But, here, too, they are confronted by perverse, demonic visions, worthy of Hieronymus Bosch, of new forms of life, transgressing the fundamental barriers between plants and animal, who deny them their birthright.

Despite this, Bessière is still better known for his humorous and parodic novels, such as the Sydney Gordon stories and the books featuring the Machine mentioned earlier. As his career progressed, his humor became more caustic and darker, exaggerating the failings of our society, human nature, and the perils of mechanization, to more grotesque proportions.

One of the first novels in that vein was *Un Futur pour Mr. Smith* [*A Future for Mr. Smith*] (1964), which at the time was almost not published by Fleuve Noir because it departed widely from the usual criteria of the imprint. In it, a meek civil servant, who believes in automation, is transported 100 years into the future and finds a Kafkaesque world ruled by a giant computer, which has decided to eradicate humanity for its own good. *Inversia* (1966) is another classic of the absurd, which could have been written by Robert Sheckley,.. In it the hapless protagonist, sentenced to death for illegal butterfly hunting, flees to the square, anti-matter world of Inversia, a true Bizarro-like planet where everything works backwards. He eventually discovers that Inversians worship death and plan to use their anti-matter to blow up positive matter worlds. In *1973... Et la Suite* [*1973... and the Rest*] (1973), the hero also wakes up from hibernation to discover a hive world, populated by tens of billions of humans on top of each other, under the benevolent control of a computer completely indifferent to the complexities of human nature. Bessière's last science fiction novel published by Fleuve Noir, *Cadavres à Tout Faire* [*Handy Corpses*] (1985), continues to mine that vein, describing a world where the most fundamental values of Good and Evil are reversed.

We have mentioned that several novels might have been influenced by films such as Planet of the Apes and Fantastic Voyage. One interesting case is the novel *N'accusez pas le Ciel* [*Don't Accuse the Sky*] (1964) which reads as a sequel to Philip K. Dick's short story *Colony*, originally published in *Galaxy* in 1953 and translated into French the following year. Dick describes a planet where an alien lifeform is capable of mimicking human technology. Bessière goes one step further and imagines what life on that world could then turn into, with small groups of humans trapped in concentration camps, forced to perform meaningless tasks by human-looking but fundamentally alien supervisors. When they escape, they find a world littered with partial reconstructions of Earth and finally confront the protoplasmic entity which is trying to mimic and understand the human race.

During his tenure at Fleuve Noir, Bessière, using the nom-de-plume of "F.-H. Ribes," also wrote 84 novels featuring the Franco-American spy Gérard Lecomte for its *Espion-*

nage imprint. Some of these feature various genre elements, such as super-weapons, ESP powers, mad scientists, etc.; a number of these verge heavily on the satirical, à la *Our Man Flint*. Bessière also wrote several historical novels, taking place against the backdrop of the French Revolution and the American Revolutionary War. In 1953, under the pseudonym of "Ralph Anderson," he penned the novelization of the French film *Salome* by William Dieterle.

In 1984, a new editorial and management team took over the direction of Éditions Fleuve Noir and decided to let go of most of the house writers in favor of a new generation of younger authors. As a result, many of the older contributors were let go, including Bessière in 1985. This was the beginning of somewhat of an eclipse, which lasted until 1999, despite the numerous reprints and Bessière's prominence on the lecture circuit where he gave a series of conferences on a variety of occult, UFOs and other esoteric related topics.

Bessière returned to writing in 1999, becoming a prolific author of a number of non-fiction books on the same topics and even allowed Black Coat Press' French sister imprint to put out two science fiction novels originally written for Fleuve Noir which had remained unpublished to date. As he himself says, his heart is no longer into writing fiction; he has moved on to another phase of his life, but remains, as always, ever prolific and imaginative.

Rémy Le Chevalier

LES 7 ANNEAUX DE RHEA

F. RICHARD BESSIÈRE

★

★*ANTICIPATION*★

Editions
"Fleuve Noir"

THE SEVEN RINGS OF RHEA

CHAPTER I

Professor Kurt Warren stopped momentarily on the edge of the track, just at the exit of the vast aerodrome, before climbing into the fusaujet that he had parked there a few moments earlier.

The Sun was at its zenith, and a heavy, almost suffocating heat hung over the area.

The man took a brief breather, then turned his head toward the departure area. Facing him was a rocket standing upright on its fins, pointing toward the Venusian sky, bright and radiant with the promise of escape and success. He had watched it being put in place, and the final preparations being made; now it was only a question of time before the great departure.

"How beautiful it is," he murmured, almost silently—and a sentiment of pride immediately overwhelmed him: a sentiment of pride that he experienced on behalf of all his peers, for all the generations that had succeeded one another on Venus for 300 years.

His gaze still riveted to the slender and svelte silhouette of the rocket, he could not help thinking about the courageous builders of the new civilization, who, driven by invincible faith, isolated and, so to speak, stripped of everything, had climbed the steep slopes of the long calvary that the centuries had inflicted upon the virgin world, unknown and so inhospitable.

He knew, too, in what painful circumstances the terrible mass exodus of all his ancestors had occurred, just before the frightful seismic cataclysm that had ravaged and destroyed the surface of the Mother World.

The official documents spoke of a strange phenomenon that seemed to have originated in the very center of the Earth, of a sudden and inexplicable heating of the internal magma, which had given rise to pressure waves whose increasing intensity had ended up causing the rupture of the solid crust. The documents also told of the wretched conditions in which the survivors had found themselves once on Venus.

The human race, which had already reached a high degree of technological evolution, had been obliged to begin again, almost from scratch, trying to adapt itself to an utterly strange soil and struggle against a hostile nature, and then to create new mines, new factories, new industries—without any possibility, in the short term, of equaling the communal efforts obtained in a world that had been continuously technologically developed and industrialized for millennia.

Now, after three centuries, New Earth had begun to live and to get the upper hand, with all the necessary weapons, in the savage conflict that opposes Death to Life. And New Earth lived! It was the coronation of all its efforts, its sacrifices and its glory.

Such was the profound sentiment that animated Kurt Warren as he looked at the rocket standing on the plain of ochre feldspar. It had taken three centuries to reach the point of constructing such a machine, which was very nearly a replica of those that had once brought his ancestors to Venus. Now, hope was reborn, the delay having elapsed, and humans were once more ready to conquer space, as they had before, recovering their most ancient dream—the one that would finally hoist them to the pinnacle of creation.

At least, he believed so!

The nose of the rocket was pointed toward Rhea.

Rhea!

The name alone made Warren smile; he had never understood why the first exiles had baptized Venus with the name of New Earth, while they had de-baptized the Earth by giving it the name of Rhea.

To be sure, Rhea was still the Earth, and the mythological appellation had only served to differentiate, in the minds of certain reformers, the old world from the new. That was the way it had had to be—for, reformers or not, the first men of Venus remained profoundly attached, in some ways, to all the old terrestrial habits, to the extent that the first Venusian cities had been given the names of Paris, Bucharest, London, Moscow, Rome, Washington and so on. People had wanted to see in them the reproduction of all the places where they had lived.

Something similar had happened before on Earth—or, rather, on Rhea, to remain in harmony with tradition—when castaways or explorers lost in distant lands or deserts, driven by some morbid necessity, had been unable to resist giving names from their homeland to those they discovered.

But all that was also 300 years in the past...

Today, the spirit of New Earth had changed, forged and fashioned by three centuries of social, intellectual, religious and technological reforms, and if the atavistic memory of the Mother Planet continued to obsess humankind, it was nonetheless true that a new evolutionary form of thought was in the process of imposing itself—and that was what troubled the celebrated biochemist that Professor Warren was.

The scientist set these thoughts aside, climbed into the fusaujet and headed for the Venusian London, the high buildings and checkerboard blocks of which were bristling in front of him, like an immense card game laid out between two masses of verdure, which extended across the entire horizon.

The fusaujet rolled along the track between the cactenoids that grew among the rocks, then slid beneath the thick foliage bordering the northern sector of the city, racing between the trunks of giant plants, formed up like multicolored smooth or glittering columns, whose summits spread out in forked branches and gigantic leaves—rounded, indented or asymmetrical—whose cellulosic, ligneous and nucleic components still remained a profound mystery to the botanists of New Earth.

The fusaujet went into the northern sector, reaching the district for which Professor Warren was steering. That district was composed of small buildings separated from one another by carefully-maintained lawns, as well as outbuildings allotted to personnel.

The fusaujet turned into a side-road, continued for a few seconds more, and then stopped in front of a little single-story cottage, around which grew a profusion of flowers with sweet and delicate perfumes.

Warren got out of his machine and, at the moment when he intersected the invisible beam of a warning-cell, a door opened. A gleaming black form appeared on the threshold.

Warren smiled slightly, stretching his fine brown moustache, and went into the hall. "Hello, Greta," he said, as he passed by. "Call Jefferson and tell him that I need to see him right away."

The heavy mass of the household robot pivoted on the spot, and its phonic circuits reeled off without a pause: "My master is not at home, Professor Warren; I cannot do as you ask."

"All right—I'll wait."

"I fear that it might be a long time, Professor Warren."

The scientist considered the machine, uttering a long sigh. He knew that he would not obtain any precise reply unless he asked a question that required one. "Did he specify the time of his return?" he asked.

"No, Professor."

"Where is he?"

"My master sent a message from Paris, only a few minutes ago."

Warren arched his eyebrows, estimating the distance—more than 100 kilometers—that separated the two conurbations.

"Paris, indeed! But why the Devil has he gone…?"

His sentence remained incomplete, for at that moment a door opened at the far end of the corridor and a voice rang out—that of Jefferson Curtiss.

"How are you, Professor? Come in, please."

The young microbiologist came to meet Warren, who caught his breath as he saw him. "Jeff... So you aren't in Paris?"

Curtis waited until he had shaken Warren's hand before replying, addressing himself to the still-motionless Greta. "That's what she told you, isn't it? Don't pay any attention—I think her circuits are in need of a serious overhaul."

They went into the study, where they were left alone. When he noticed the young man's slightly troubled features, Warren, forgetting the slight incident, said: "Jeff, my boy, the two of us need to have a conversation before the departure. Tomorrow is the big day."

"Yes, I know."

The scientist sat down heavily on a pressurized seat and relaxed momentarily, while the microbiologist switched on the air conditioning system, rapidly expelling the excess humidity present in the room.

"Yes, Jeff, it's tomorrow—we're ready," Warren continued. "It had to come some day, and it's come."

Jeff shrugged his shoulders slightly and asked, mildly: "I still don't understand this obsession you have with the desire to reconquer Rhea." Warren knew that the *you* in this sentence was not specifically directed at him, but rather embraced the whole human community of which he was a part. He chose to ignore the allusion and let Curtiss continue. "No, I really don't understand it. It's easy to live on this world. One can even grow fat in idleness, with all that this globe furnishes to the 500 million individuals who populate it, isn't that so? What do you hope to find on Rhea that you don't have here, apart from charred, cracked and arid ground where all life is now impossible? You know that very well..."

The avalanche of *yous* and the implications intentionally developed in Jeff's words finally irritated Warren, who could not help exclaiming: "Stop, please. Once and for all, stop considering us as a phenomenon. You're a human, damn it—a human just like me...and the others."

Jeff wore a slight smile of amusement. "With a test tube and an alembic for a father and mother. I know."

"So what? You're surrounded by people who have never known their parents. Are orphans, or lost and abandoned children to be considered phenomena on that account? Come on, my boy, you're talking nonsense, firstly because the genes that produced you are purely human, as you know, and secondly because I've made a genius of you. Yes, Jeff, a genius, whom the whole world admires and respects. The four sera that you discovered last year have saved millions of lives, and they'll save many more that we in the Center would never have saved, shut up in a laboratory amid dozens of flasks and hundreds of years' worth of treatises."

He got up, marched nervously back and forth in the study, then stopped in front of the individual he had created himself, some 30 years earlier, for whom he had always nurtured a very great affection. "Listen, my boy," he went on, in a more urgent tone. "When I attempted my experiment, I wasn't unaware that I was dealing with the most important case of conscience that humankind has posed itself—but it was necessary that the experiment was attempted. We were in dire need of superintelligences to succeed in making ourselves masters of this world. It has required many generations for our organisms to readapt to this new environment, to find the first remedies against the unknown diseases of which we were the victims, and to reorganize ourselves in a better way, but the road is long and I must admit, alas, that we haven't yet reached its end."

"And your road goes via Rhea? I still don't see how that step can enhance our evolution."

"There are two reasons for this endeavor, Jeff. The first is that, as you know, in anticipation of future interplanetary voyages, the central government envisages establishing an important spatial base on Rhea. For that, we need exact information and profound analyses regarding the nature of the terrain, atmospheric conditions and so on—in sum, everything necessary to bring our projects to a successful conclusion. As for the second reason, it's…" He hesitated briefly before continuing, in a level tone: "Let's say, of a biological order, while simultaneously being…" Another hesitation. "…strictly personal, so far as I'm concerned."

"What do you mean?"

"It's for that reason that I've come to see you, Jeff."

"I'm listening."

"Well, here it is! The biological component of this endeavor having fallen to me, I've been ordered by the central government, in a legally-binding manner, to undertake certain physiological experiments on Rhea, in special cybernetic matrices that we shall set up there. It's a matter of discovering the conditions in which embryos can be developed *in vitro*, and how that world might influence them. As it will take at least a generation before we complete our reconquest of space, we shall thus have all the time we need to study the somatic mutations that might be produced in our future pioneers, whose physiology won't be adapted to the environmental conditions on Rhea."

Curtiss nodded his head, visibly interested by Warren's revelations, and the final remark, which his scientific mind gradually brought to the surface, especially when he exclaimed: "So you hope to be able to populate Rhea with supermen—is that it?"

Warren nodded his head. "Buffon said: 'Man can and must dare everything.' For my part, Jeff, I'd even dare the worst." From one of his pockets, he brought out a little box containing a few microfilms, then got up and went to a stereoscope mounted in the wall. He arranged the microfilms, pressed a few buttons, switched on the light and went back to Jeff. "Look carefully, now. The cells that you're going to see evolving have no human or organic origin, strictly speaking. They're purely synthetic. I've been working on his project for more than 20 years, and it's only now that I've succeeded in overcoming all the difficulties."

Curtiss had drawn closer, profoundly interested by these strange revelations, and not daring to interrupt the scientist—who, after a further manipulation, brought up an image of germ cells on the screen, in 3-D color, with all their complex and curious molecular architecture.

"Here's the enlargement of a nucleus, with its network of dark and light bands, where the chromosomes and the genes are situated. You can observe male and female genomes, each consisting of 24 chromosomes. Here, again, other cellular bodies and other giant molecules, with their chains of amino acids, and here, finally, enlargements revealing all the components of deoxyribonucleic acid—which is to say, cytosine, guanine, adenine and thymine. There are millions of possible combinations of those four acids that will create an ordinary human being, but to create a superman, it's necessary, above all, that the arrangement be marvelously beneficial. And what I've obtained in this picture surpasses everything one could have wished."

He interrupted himself to point at the screen, and went on: "Here, then, is the summit of evolution, the transcendence of *Homo sapiens*, the human ultimate, the superman of supermen." He was breathing hard, avoiding Jefferson's gaze. "Everything's ready. I only have to push the button for the miracle to be realized."

For several seconds, Curtiss continued to examine the picture; then, lost in thought, he retorted: "A man so perfect that he'll no longer be human. What, then?"

"Perhaps a creature with immense, unlimited powers."

"A God created by men, no? That's exactly what I've been dreading."

"And its aftermath? Is it the reversal of roles that frightens you? Come on, don't worry—there's nothing supernatural in this so-called miracle. It's not on the supernatural plane that we ought to examine this question, but only on the scientific plane, at least insofar as it concerns us, Jeff. God undoubtedly possesses powers subtler than those of men, for He benefits from a knowledge far more ancient. At an elementary level, however, man is capable of competing with Him. Look around you—our science permit us to resuscitate the dead in the course of certain surgical interventions; we suspend life by processes of hibernation; we create antimatter at will, intervening in the physical laws that govern matter; we're capable of modifying the nature of any kind of body, of conquering the Universe and of engendering Life with cells that we create ourselves—and the day will come when we finally possess immortality. What have we to envy Him, then, eh?"

"His Purity," Jeff relied, instantly.

Warren smiled, pointed at the screen again, and declared, forcefully: "There's nothing purer in our world than that simple cell, in which all the dominant characteristics of the being that will one day emerge from it are already inscribed."

"But after all, why? What do you expect from him?"

Warren cut the contacts and took a few steps, going to stand at the large bay window through which the colossal structure of the city could be seen, extending as far as the eye could see, already invaded by the mauve mists of dusk.

"Look, Jeff, I'm by no means as materialistic as you surely imagine, and yet our humankind has lost, if one might put it thus, all the spirituality that it once possessed. Our arrival here, the abolition of ancient principles, the new laws—all that has modified the human mind and destroyed our beliefs, to such a degree that our civilization has lost its faith in a divine mediator, while I have the impression that, on the eve of our conquest of space, we have a great need for a religion on which we can rely absolutely, and to wipe out all these theosophical movements that are in the process of disturbing our humankind." He turned back to Jeff, and added: "The God that our technology has killed, I want science to resuscitate."

"In order that men will end up crucifying him?" said Jeff, dully.

Warren, in conflict with himself, shrugged his shoulders leadenly. "And what if even that occurs? No religion can survive without its martyrs. And man has need of a new religion, whatever it might be, even if it consists of adoring himself. So why not offer him what he's waiting for?"

Curtiss recovered the microfilms from the apparatus and amused himself momentarily by tossing the slender reel of film up and down in his hand. "And it's on Rhea hat you intend to carry out your first experiment?"

"Let's say a first trial. I have to find out whether the embryo is capable of developing normally in an environment different from this one. In principle, it's designed to be able to develop in *any* environment."

"What you've just told me is extraordinary."

"Everything will be done in the greatest secrecy. No one except you and me is cognizant of the project. That's why I'm here."

"You know that you can have confidence in me—and, fundamentally…" The young professor held out the reel of microfilm to Warren and added, spontaneously; "…I think that you're right."

"Thank you, my boy. I never doubted that you'd approve. Look, here's the key to my strong-box. It's behind the work-desk in my private laboratory. Take it—in case I don't come back. There, you'll find all the formulas that will enable you to complete my work. Remember, Jeff, that whatever happens, it's imperative that this being sees the light of day. Nothing must stop you."

Curtiss hesitated momentarily, then said, in a formal voice: "I promise."

Warren's hand squeezed his shoulder; then the scientist headed slowly for the door. Before going out, he turned around to say: "I'm taking Mary with me, you know. I know that you'll miss her, but you'll miss both of us. Now, Jeff, *au revoir!*"

He was too emotional to say another word, and he left abruptly.

CHAPTER II

Mary Davis abandoned her sequence of calculations when the buzz of the visiophone resounded in the room. It only required a fraction of a second to tear herself away completely from the study of Euler's famous theorem, certain of whose implications were connected in her mind with Cantor's notion of the transfinite.

She pushed away her notes, made the connection, and welcomed the youthful face that appeared on the screen with a frank smile. "Jeff! I was just about to pay you a little visit."

She placed herself in the viewfield, while the microbiologist said: "Listen, little sister, you have to come immediately. You're the only one who can help me.

"Nothing serious, I hope?"

"No, don't worry—but come at once, I beg you."

She didn't wait for him to finish his sentence before replying: "I'll be there right away, little brother—right away."

She cut the link, suppressing her anxiety, and telephoned an order for her fusaujet to be brought out of the subterranean garage and prepared for use.

When the dark mass of the machine appeared at the front door, she left the apartment and leapt into it. A few moments later, she stopped outside Curtiss's cottage, just as the first stars were appearing timidly in the somber vault of the sky. Greta met her on the steps and took her to Jefferson, who seemed to be waiting for her with an impatience that he was making no attempt to hide.

"There you are, at last!" he exclaimed. "What has happened to me is both frightful and extraordinary."

"Tell me, quickly."

He knew that he could trust her, and that she was the only person in the world who could understand him and help him. Were they not both in the same situation? Did they not belong to the same species, to the élite creation emerged from the test-tubes and flasks of the celebrated Professor Warren? He drew the young mathematician to the back of the room and, without a word, switched on a tape-recorder.

Almost immediately, a voice resonated: "Jefferson Curtiss here, speaking to Jefferson Curtiss. I'm calling from Paris, booth 514, Place de la Concorde. It's 3:30 p.m. exactly. I don't feel any disorientation or sickness, merely a slight depression in nervous stimulus, certainly provoked by a drop in tension. I hesitate to prolong the experiment, for this cohabitation risks causing serious disturbances in the psyche that remained tied to the body into which I've transferred. Over and out."

She looked at him uncomprehendingly, frightened in her turn by the dolorous expression that passed over Jeff's features.

"That recording was made only a few minutes before the arrival of Professor Warren," he explained, hurriedly. "I wanted to have proof of the strange faculty that I had divined within me some time ago. I didn't want to believe it, though; I persuaded myself that it was impossible, that it was nothing but the fruit of my imagination, and that such a thing couldn't happen."

In his turn, Jeff was surprised by the strange pallor of Mary's face, and he guessed what she was feeling. "Now, I know that it's possible for me."

"How did it come about?"

He confessed all.

It had begun shortly after his coming of age, and the phenomenon had manifested itself at first in simple mental escapes, in moments of rest or ecstasy requiring the greatest neglect of physical needs. Jeff had escaped from his material body, and his thoughts had traveled beyond time and space, directed by his unconscious will, obtaining a precise vision of the places that he visited, all of whose psychic effects he felt with an extreme sensitivity.

"It was like a door opening slightly on the mystery of an unknown darkness," he explained, "but when I resumed my normal state, I always refused to allow myself to be convinced. Then, gradually, I realized the incredible truth. It was the day when I witnessed mentally a meeting organized by the central biological committee of our section, which I understood fully. On resuming contact, I was able to transcribe exactly, word for word, everything that had been said in the hall. There could be no further doubt about it. I understood then that I had the power to liberate my psyche and teleport wherever I wished, while remaining linked to my physical body, abandoned to the most complete prostration. And the experiment that I attempted today surpassed anything that I could have imagined. For the first time, I realized it over a considerable distance, by transplanting myself into the body of a person chosen at random in Paris."

"What did you feel?"

"A bizarre impression, difficult to explain, and a deceptive sensation of reintegrating myself with my own body. My will was stronger than that of the subject, and I don't think he knew what was happening to him. Perhaps he'll never understand the sudden need he experienced to dive into a telephone booth to send such a message. I called Greta, and it was she who started the tape-recorder.

Mary let herself collapse into a chair, remained lost in thought momentarily, and then came to a sudden decision. "Jeff, we're not humans like the others. I too have a confession to make."

"You, little sister?"

"Yes, Jeff. Something happened to me, but I didn't dare tell you about it."

"You're making me anxious. What happened?"

"It happened a few months ago, while I was swimming in the Great Rain Lake. I had strayed quite a long way from the shore when an undertow gripped me and dragged me under. I was struggling with all my might to get back to the surface when a strange phenomenon occurred within me. I was battling on the frontier of life and death, with an extreme concentration of my survival instinct. I didn't want to die. That was when it happened. Incredible as it may seem, after a brief moment spent in a state of total unconsciousness, I found myself sprawled on the beach, outside the liquid element, safe and sound, breathing like a damned soul. I realized then that I had been the subject of a phenomenon of complete teleportation, with third degree levitation."

Jeff grabbed Mary's hand and squeezed it in his own. "It's scary, isn't it?"

"I don't know," she murmured. "What has happened to us certainly wasn't foreseen by Warren. He was only interested in our intellectual faculties, in the final analysis—but he's made us two beings of a different sort."

"There must be an explanation, though."

"I've already thought about it, little brother. Alas, the hypotheses collide: always the duality of the thesis and the antithesis. Mathematically, at least, my case might be explained by a relativistic principle that proves the equivalence of inertial mass and weight. Situating the phenomenon at the level of the microphysical, and assuming a local deformation of the space-time continuum produced at that moment, one can find a rational explanation of my case of levitation in the total loss of the mass of my body, which thus remained under the complete control of my psychic energy. So much for the rational—but the occasional suspension of the laws of the material world also follows from certain supernatural formulas, divine or demonic. And magic, in its turn, has its white form and its black form: two aspects that oppose one another like all the laws that regulate our universe, as if the truth were inaccessible to us."

She got to her feet and continued her train of thought: "Everything rests on a perpetual struggle in both directions, and we never knock on the right door, for Truth is not inscribed on any of them. That struggle between opposed principles we find in everything that surrounds us: the True and the False, the rational and the irrational, hot and cold, death and life, light and darkness, attraction and repulsion, matter and spirit, yes and no, Good and Evil. But in all this, where is the Good and where is the Evil?"

There was a long silence, troubled only by the monotonous tick-tock of the electronic clock, which continued to spell out ponderous seconds. Jeff thought about Warren, then, and the strange revelations that he had confided to him under the seal of secrecy, which, unfortunately, he could not confess to Mary without breaking his word. He felt crushed by the enormous weight of that responsibility, which had become his own.

They talked about the imminent departure then, and Jeff did not hide his total incomprehension of the obsessive need to reconquer its old world that the whole human race seemed to experience.

"All of that passes me by and worries me," he said, "for the idea presents all the symptoms of a collective psychosis, which even Warren does not escape. Since his origin, man has never been as happy as he is on this planet. He has succeeded in vanquishing all his antisocial tendencies, has achieved an active equilibrium and has acquired the sense of an intelligent cooperation. The new society has been able to avoid the lethal and destructive tendencies of the ancient civilizations of Rhea, based in animal violence, and has finally succeeded in controlling itself. So what do they hope to achieve by returning to Rhea?" He almost got carried away, and thumped the table with his fist. "I detest Rhea. The world horrifies me...and yet it attracts us. It has never ceased to exert that morbid attraction upon us, for three centuries. It's as if successive generations have only been enabled to live and persevere here by the hope of one day returning to our world of origin."

"We can't do anything about that, Jeff. If it must be, it will be."

Jeff looked at her for a few seconds. He seemed to reflect momentarily, then declared: "I have one last favor to ask of you, Mary. No, don't ask me any questions—I'll explain it to you afterwards."

He pointed to the large bay window, through which all the brightly-lit zones of the vast megalopolis could be clearly seen. He drew her on to the terrace and said: "For now, look! Look at anything whatsoever; aim your gaze at anything you like, and concentrate on it fully, without taking any notice of me."

She formed a little moue of astonishment, and then got ready to do what he asked. She heard him go through the study, go out into the corridor and go into the living room. Then she began the experiment.

At the precise moment when her gaze fixed itself intensely on one of the tallest of the control-towers that loomed over the north sector of the city, the same image appeared simultaneously in Jeff's mind, completely isolated as he was in the closed room.

Then it was a brilliantly-lit block of buildings that surged forth in his mind; then a mass of vegetation not far from the cottage; the edge of the terrace with the somber aggregations of vegetation surrounding it; then a portion of the starry sky; Mary's forearm and hand; and finally, a circular scan of the terrace, the bay, the walls and the work-desk, as Mary made a turning movement.

All that had imprinted itself with an amazing clarity in Jeff's sensory centers, and he could not have asked for any more. He came back to join Mary, and smiled at her discomfort and embarrassment.

"Bravo!" he cried. "That's extraordinary. If we can continue the experiment over millions of kilometers, perhaps we'll be able to put out faculties at the service of humankind—for they might be able to render immense services."

"Explain, little brother."

"It's quite simple. Your brain seems to me to be an excellent relay of sorts in a phenomenon of hyperlucidity that I intend to control during the journey you're about to undertake. Obviously, there's no question of your remaining in a state of continuous concentration, but I'd like you to remain in contact with me when you can—at certain times of the day, for example. I want to check the range of the faculty." He laughed good-humoredly and added: "That way, I'll have the impression of making a small part of the journey."

"You can count on me, Jeff," she told him, spontaneously. "I'll do my best."

He took her in his arms, fraternally, gave her a big kiss on the forehead, and had a sudden desire to tell her all about the terrible apprehension he felt on the eve of her departure— but he did not feel either the courage or the obligation to alarm her without any valid reason.

And after all, why would he have done it?

CHAPTER III

It was a great day, a great departure.

A grandiose assembly watched the launch of the first space-rocket, which would open the way to the conquest of space for the people of New Earth.

A formidable tremor shook the ground of the great ocher plain, and the rocket lifted off to the cheers of the delirious crowd. It rose up slowly, atop a long column of fire, then surrendered to the dihedron of its fins and soon faded away into the cloudy sky, disappearing in an eastward direction.

It was only at that moment that Jeff decided to return to his cottage. He still had the last words of Mary and Warren ringing in his ears, spoken just outside the airlock immediately before the last preparations, and he conserved the visual memory of the joyful and confident expression of all the crewmembers at the decisive moment.

He struggled once again against the anguish that no longer left him, but it was stronger than he was, and at that moment he was still privately cursing the world of Rhea, which had finally achieved its victory.

Within a few days, the first contact would finally be made with the planet that had never ceased to haunt the minds of the men of New Earth.

Jeff returned home, where he first set about trying to put his laboratory notes in some kind of order; then, at the agreed time, he got ready to establish the first mental contact with Mary.

He isolated himself in his study, relaxed for a moment in his armchair, making his mind go blank, in order to obtain the optimum conditions for his hyperlucid faculties.

It was in this way that he was able to familiarize himself with the interior of the rocket, along with all the members of the crew and everything else that Mary's sensory apparatus sent back to him, with amazing clarity.

He saw Robert Landry, the chief pilot, watching his controls, which were humming softly in the cabin. He saw and heard Aldo Manzini, the geophysicist, who was chatting calmly with his fellow crewman Juan Sanchez, the seismologist. He also saw and heard the imposing Fred Donovan, the radiometeorologist, who had just finished sending a message to New Earth, as well as Kurt Warren, whose face appeared full on and enlarged, because he was in the process of talking to Mary at that moment.

"We've just passed through the zone of magnetic radiation," he said. "Everything is going well. A magnificent voyage, isn't it?"

He also perceived Mary's vague response as Warren drew away and shut himself up in his little private laboratory.

Jeff had the impression of really being present in the spaceship, and he closed his eyes in order that the illusion might be even more perfect. He could hear Manzini singing in a corner, Donovan joking with Sanchez, and he saw through a porthole the velvet black space in which the distant suns shone like diamonds thrown at hazard into the immense and infinite void.

Through another porthole, he saw the enormous flamboyant disk of the central star that was "radiant with all its glory." He made out the globe of Venus, haloed by its vaporous layers, which seemed to dance around it like cotton candy around a stick.

Through yet another porthole, he saw a little luminous ball that shone with a very different gleam. That was Rhea. He understood and divined that at the same time as he understood and divined Mary's thoughts. Rhea, whose strange, cold, metallic gleam attracted gazes and stirred up memories.

Then the contact was broken, and Jeff found himself alone with his own thoughts, his material body and the four walls that surrounded him. Time had fled; he had not even noticed it passing.

He calculated then that the rocket must be some two million kilometers from New Earth; that result frightened him.

What range, then, did his extraordinary power of receptivity have?

He did not stay in place until the next contact. He had Greta serve him a rapid meal, and was finishing off his daily notes when his subconscious triggered an unexpected signal. He made the effort demanded of him, and found himself suddenly plunged into an avalanche of numbers, symbols and ideograms, which filed through him with a rapid and flashing alternation, at the same time as indecipherable signs mingled with one another on sheets of paper, in a crazy and vertiginous dance. There were numbers and yet more numbers, complex numbers squared or raised to the fifth power in the space of only a few seconds, then cubes, straight lines, tesseracts, with the symbol *aleph*, in an infinite dementia that Jeff's sanity flatly refused.

Her shook himself, and divined Mary's involuntary concentration. She had resumed her mathematical work during an interval of solitude—and he understood, too, that the sequence was not intended for him. He smiled, and waited for the normal contact, which was made exactly at the predetermined time.

At that moment, the psychic contact was established at a distance of eight million kilometers, without the slightest relaxation in the nervous tension.

This time, he was granted entry into Warren's little laboratory, where the latter was checking and rechecking the orderly functioning of his cybernetic matrices, ready to put them to work as soon as they arrived on Rhea. He was showing the young mathematician the dials and biochemical recording devices arranged at the base of each matrix. Jeff could hear what he was saying perfectly.

"Two sorts of mutations might be produced on Rhea, and that's what I'm determined to discover. On the one hand, hereditary mutations that modify the germinal characteristics of a species departing from a single individual, and on the other hand, somatic mutations that only concern the individual itself, and which remain non-transmissible. The relevant dials communicate all the results obtained to us."

Jeff then "visited" the command-post, "observed" Landry undertaking his piloting maneuvers, and "participated" in the frank, good humor that reigned aboard the spaceship—which was now travelling through space more than 20 million kilometers from its home port.

The mental contacts between Mary and Jeff proceeded normally during the two Venusian days that followed, but the young microbiologist did not take long to observe that receptivity became increasingly difficult, beginning to suffer from the effects of the vast distance, which increased incessantly.

Determined to take his experiment to the ultimate limits of possibility. Jeff ended up isolating himself completely in his study, forbidding any access to his robot housekeeper until further orders. Riveted to his armchair, where he remained completely unconscious of the external world, Jeff continued to maintain the link with Mary's brain-relay—which, following the instructions she had received, continued to project telepathic messages at fixed times.

The rocket drew nearer to Rhea, whose shiny mass could now be clearly distinguished against the black background of space, with the unique satellite that it dragged along in its blind and perpetual course.

Conversations proceeded at a rapid pace on board, still in a fashion that was audible to Jeff, especially when Manzini, the geophysicist, came into the observation-room and exclaimed: "This is rather curious; I can't coordinate the reported data with the elements of Rhea that I've just checked." He was brandishing notes in his hands, which he presented to Sanchez and Warren.

"The observations I've just made," he added are in complete contrast with the data—it's inexplicable. Look, it's impossible that there's any mistake; here are the print-outs and the results furnished by the base computers. They give us an equatorial diameter of 11,982 kilometers and a polar diameter of 11,935 kilometers, instead of 12,756 and 12, 712. Thus we have an equatorial circumference of 37,642 kilometers and a polar circumference of 37,494 kilometers, as opposed to 40,076 and 40,008—which, of course, modify the volume and surface area considerably. As for the density, I think that's the sole datum that remains unchanged at 5.52. It's incredible."

Warren turned to one of the portholes and looked at the large ball suspended in the void, toward which the spaceship was plunging. "It's certainly Rhea, though, isn't it? Otherwise known as Earth, since that's what the ancient textbooks call it."

"Obviously. I still have to check the orbital velocity, but I'm already convinced that it's just over 29.5 kilometers a second.

Sanchez grimaced, visibly troubled. "Are you sure there isn't any error in your calculations?"

"Absolutely. And the figures I'm giving you are exact. I was so amazed that I carried out the calculations several times, only to arrive at the same bewildering result."

Jeff now could not help witnessing the rapid calculations made by Mary's brain-relays. Within a few seconds, she had finished checking the notes given to the geophysicist by the electronic machinery. Everything was in agreement; there could not be the slightest error.

At that moment, the conversation was interrupted by the voice of the radiometeorologist, which burst forth in the cabin, cutting off what Manzini was saying. "We've just entered a magnetic field of unknown origin; my apparatus is no longer working. Damn it! I could almost grill with that rotisserie— it's crackling all over the place."

They were about to run forward when a brutal shock threw them on to the floor, at the same time as a dull impact made the rocket's superstructure shudder.

The occupants of the cabin had the impression of floating momentarily in a weightless environment, as if the pseudo-gravity regulator had suddenly stopped working. Then every-thing seemed to return to normal—but when they stood up again, they realized that some serious damage had just been done to the compensators, for they no longer weighed as much as they usually did—which gave them an unpleasant sensation of lightness that made all their movements awkward.

That, at least, was what Jeff's alert senses perceived via the mediation of Mary's thoughts.

As she stood up in her turn, the hatchway giving access to the pilot's station opened wide, and Robert Landry appeared, his face imprinted with seriousness. "Evacuate the cabin quickly," he ordered. "There's damage to the ventilation system." The oxygen will run out shortly. Take refuge in the pilot's station. I'll get the emergency generator working right away. That will allow us to repair the circuits."

Indeed, there was already a shortage of breathable air, and they did not waste any time before joining Landry in the central post, where they were all reunited.

"But what happened?" asked Warren, anxiously.

"I don't know. Donovan detected a field of magnetic disturbance, which we tried to identify. No need to worry—we won't take long to pass through it."

They looked at Donovan, who was at the back of the cabin, in the process of busying himself with a large transparent box, in the interior of which multicolored waves appeared, while a magnetic counter was crackling in a corner, inscribing disorderly diagrams on a strip of paper, which Landry examined attentively, continually referring to the indications furnished by the radio.

It was obvious that Donovan had succeeded in capturing a few particles of the anomalous field, and that he was trying to determine its origin and exact composition in his special analyzer.

Several minutes went by in almost total silence; then Donovan shook his large warrior's head and muttered between his teeth: "It's a field of cosmic rays, offering some analogy with magnetic fields and electric currents, but..."

"But what?" Landry demanded, visibly anxious.

Donovan scratched his chin. "Well...I don't know... One might think that these waves were moving at a speed faster than light, since our apparatus can't localize them correctly. But what intrigues me is that the particles moving at the same speed as the waves don't seem to be subject to any modification of mass. That's contrary to Einstein's principle...and to all logic as well."

Mary drew closer, and the sight of the reports thus obtained became clearer in Jeff's mind. The latter sensed that the young mathematician was making strenuous efforts to maintain contact with him, for the psychic connection had already surpassed the average duration of its possibilities. Even so, he did not want her to interrupt the relay, and for his part, he progressively increased the potential energy of his receptive faculties.

"These waves definitely originate in another Universe," said Sanchez in his turn. "There's probably a rift between two continua, a sort of marginally-open portal that permits the passage of a sequence of waves whose provenance is from another dimension."

"It's possible," murmured the radio man, still not entirely convinced, "but look at these coordinates." He showed them the perforated strip that was emerging from a computer, tore it off and pointed to the data. "The point of emission certainly seems to be situated within our solar system."

He picked up a set of compasses, traced a circle, then, with the aid of a graduated ruler, drew a tangent and two parallels, and submitted the diagram to the machine. A signal-light blinked, and another came on, and the result obtained gave the exact direction.

"Saturn!" cried Landry, profoundly excited. "Saturn! There's no error—it's definitely on that planet that the point of emission of these waves is situated. What does that mean?"

"The strangest thing is that the sequence of waves seems to be aimed constantly at Rhea, without being affected by its orbital velocity." He pointed to the curves of incidence given by the radio emissions, which the surface of Rhea reflected and which corresponded with the axial displacement of the wave sequence.

"Rhea's mass seems to be absorbing them," Landry continued, after some further checks, "unless they go all the way through it—which would lead one to think that the planet is permeable to them and acts in that field like a metal ball placed inside an electromagnet. It beats me."

He was unable to say more, for, at that exact moment, a cry uttered by Manzini nailed him to the spot.

With his arm extended, the geophysicist was pointing at the large, sealed glass box in front of which Donovan was still busy. While Landry was talking, the latter had connected up the infra-red analyzer, which was sweeping its beam through the interior of the chamber containing the samples taken a few minutes earlier.

What they all saw, then, chilled them with terror.

A nebulous substance was undulating and stretching within the transparent box, crawling and sliding over the walls, trying to escape from the infra-red beam that had just revealed its sinister presence: a vaporous, ethereal, almost human form...a scarcely visible silhouette, ectoplasmic in appearance, haloed with a vague phosphorescent light.

And it was mobile...deforming, holding fast, and shifting in every direction. That lasted until the moment when the buzz of the counters became louder and a dazzling light set the cage of glass on fire.

Donovan leapt backwards, blinded, landing next to Landry and the others, who were paralyzed by emotion or dread.

That lasted two seconds, and then the fluid presence disappeared from inside the cage, and a long spark fused the side-panel, with a noise like the crack of a gigantic whip, extending to one of the control mechanisms, which collapsed in its turn.

Landry leapt forward amid the panic, trying to reach the controls, but he uttered a hoarse exclamation, staggered, lost his balance again, and crumpled like an inert mass on contact with the lever that his hand had gripped.

Donovan and Sanchez hurried to his aid, but the unfortunate pilot was already dying. The electrical discharge had doubtless been too powerful, and Landry's heartbeat was getting progressively weaker.

"Quickly!" cried Warren, utterly confounded. "Quickly, pass me my medical bag. It's absolutely necessary to attempt the impossible, or he's lost."

Jeff never knew exactly what happened in the few seconds that followed, for it was too rapid for him to follow—instantaneous, so to speak. In a fraction of a second, he understood that the effect had to be immediate in the drama that was in the process of playing out.

Liberating at a stroke all the energy he could muster, with a power whose amplitude he could never have suspected, he projected himself into the immense and terrifying void, maintaining only a thin fluidic connection with his completely inert material body, which he drew out behind him.

His extraordinary extra-sensory perceptions had allowed him to glimpse the effects of the brutal introspection of which the unfortunate Landry's body had just been the object. The horrible vaporous creature revealed in the glass cage was trying to render itself the master of Landry's lifeless corpse, around which Warren and the others were busying themselves quite uselessly.

All of that, he sensed in a fraction of a second, at the moment when he felt himself plunge into the unfathomable gulf.

He perceived the feeble distress call emanating from Landry's mind, which had already left its carnal envelope. In a strange vortex, Jeff's psyche had an impression of floating, but thanks above all to a powerful mental concentration, he understood that he had to annihilate that of the enemy at a single stroke, taking it by surprise.

And the strange psychic battle began.

The mind of the assailant, surprised by the brutal attack, clung to his own with an unexpected violence, struggling pitilessly inside Landry's body in a terrible contest for the possession of the man's material body.

Suddenly, with a stab of terror, Jeff observed that he was no longer attaining maximum concentration, and that all his efforts were diminishing by the second. Then he summoned up his last reserves of energy to mount a frontal attack on the point of contact that united him with the mysterious entity in that fantastic battle.

It was the strangest of sensations for him, as he let himself slide toward the point of contact, attacking the enemy at the vital spot, destroying the formidable attraction that it exercised upon him with a single thrust—and at the same time, he experienced an immense joy, such as he had never experienced before: a full and sublime joy, not at all comparable to those one knows in the normal routines of material life; an unknown, almost supernatural joy.

CHAPTER IV

Warren, his face contorted, turned to the other occupants of the cabin and declared: "I can do nothing more for him. He's dead."

A leaden silence reigned brutally over them, each one realizing the critical situation in which they found themselves. The controls were damaged, and the apparatus was veering dangerously, as if aspired by the vertiginous current of the wave-sequence from, which it could not extract itself.

In a blank voice, Donovan murmured: "If we can't succeed in regaining control of the ship, we're lost. We must try something, at all costs."

He was already hurling himself toward the control panel when Mary exclaimed: "Look! He's alive...he's alive...!"

Bewildering as it might seem, Landry's body, still lying on the insulating material of the floor, had begun to move. Soon, the eyelids fluttered slowly, then opened slightly, and the pilot's gaze went from one of them to another, while his lips were trying to form words that they could not quite understand.

Then Landry raised himself up weakly, and extended his arm toward the central post.

"Vector 36...twin groups...block number 2...maximum pressure...lateral nozzles 1 and 3...quickly...quickly...."

With one bound, without even registering Landry's incredible resurrection, Donovan rushed to the apparatus indicated, put the commands into action, and executed the maneuver ordered by the pilot.

There was another shock and new vibrations in the metallic carcass of the rocket, and for a moment they all had the impression that the machine was about to explode like a grenade; then, little by little, the pseudogravity returned to normal and the cluster-jets, recovering their full power, appeared to stabilize at the maximum.

With one bound, the rocket had extracted itself from the field of perturbation, and the electronic calculator that determined the duration of the ionic jet in relation to the rocket's speed was again controlling the excitation within the principal matrix. The primary generators were functioning normally, while a green light signaled the efficient conductivity of the beta tubes linked to the centrifugal injector.

It was then that, in the general relief—with which a sentiment of easily-comprehensible astonishment was obviously mixed—all gazes returned to Landry, who had now recovered al his vitality and had stood up in the midst of his companions.

Jeff immediately divined the intense emotion that was manifest in the people who still considered him to be the ship's chief pilot, whose material body he now possessed. He also understood that no one had any suspicion of the terrible and implacable battle he had fought to render himself master of it.

He had been able to recover almost all the memories accumulated in Landry's nerve-cells and he was having a good deal of trouble compartmentalizing them and differentiating them from his own, which initially translated itself as a wavering in his psychic reactions. The fact that he had been able to give Donovan all the necessary directions for the reestablishment of the rocket's equilibrium, however, and that he had recovered a part of his own personality, allowed him to glimpse the possibility of mastering the new duality that was effective within him.

He heard Warren exclaim: "You must have a damnably strong constitution to have withstood such a discharge! I've never seen anything like it."

Sanchez went further. "But for you, we'd be dead."

Jeff had neither the courage nor the desire to confess the truth. They would never understand, or be able to understand—all the more so because the dread and terror of the mysterious ectoplasmic apparition, which seemed to be the origin of these strange events, still persisted.

It was Mary who mentioned it first. "What a horrible thing!" she exclaimed. "It must possess unknown senses or means of perception. I had the impression of a motionless gaze watching us. That thing was alive, I'm certain of it."

Donovan nodded his head and murmured: "Life in the form of radiant energy: the spark of life in its pure state. Yes, that's what it was."

Warren, in his turn, hastened to object. "If these beings come from another dimension, it's possible, in quantum terms, that they possess an indivisible, inexhaustible unity of individual life in time. Do you realize the terrible superiority they possess over us, at present?"

"All this terrifies me," growled Sanchez. "I think we'd do better to abandon our voyage and turn back."

Jeff turned round. "Impossible. That might, perhaps, be the wisest solution, but I repeat that it's impossible. We need to make serious repairs as soon as possible, and we can only undertake them on Rhea. We wouldn't survive a return journey—we're too far from New Earth."

There was another silence, which Warren interrupted after a few seconds, in a tone that he tried to render persuasive. "There's no point, then, in getting overly alarmed. Since we know the exact direction assumed in space by the distortive field, let's try to avoid it—for I'm convinced, personally, that the strange fluid creatures with which we're concerned can only move inside the wave sequence." He shrugged his broad shoulders and added: "At any rate, we have to keep our spirits up."

For a moment, Jeff experienced a sharp sensation of frightful terror. He knew, within himself, that the problem exceeded human understanding. He had had an abominable revelation when the demonic creature had surged forth ahead of him, trying to drag him beyond the void, the stellar vortices, the nebulas and oblivion.

Everyone aboard had resumed their normal activities, while Jeff, for his part, continued to supervise the orderly working of the ship, calling upon the memories that Landry's mind had abandoned in his brain.

The most urgent repairs had been successfully carried out, and the ventilation system was working again, well enough that they could now devote themselves fully to the preparations necessary for landing on Rhea. That planet now appeared to them as an enormous ball swathed in cloud, only 12 million kilometers distant, at the most.

Mary had resumed her work, and several times over, Jeff had found himself on the point of confessing everything to her, telling her everything—for she alone would be able to accept the extraordinary truth. Every time, however, words had failed him and he had changed his mind.

Every time, too, Mary has seemed anxious and intrigued in confrontation with his attitude, especially when they found themselves alone in the pilot's station. He had detected a nascent anxiety in her, as well as an indefinable malaise, which she could not overcome at present, whenever their eyes met.

Eventually, he could not contain himself any longer. Taking advantage of an interval of rest, he went resolutely into the private cabin that Mary had just entered.

She turned round squarely on seeing him, and an expression of panic overtook her pretty face. "What's this, captain? What do you want?"

Jeff closed the door behind him and made a weary gesture. "Mary, I beg you—you need to know."

He saw her become even paler, and heard her exclaim spontaneously: "Jeff!"

He breathed deeply, for he had counted on the faculty of receptivity that the young mathematician possessed—and that would help him considerably in the revelations that he had to make."

"Yes, little sister, I'm Jeff. What does it matter which body I'm occupying? You have to trust me and listen to me."

Rapidly, he explained everything that had happened to him, not omitting a single detail. He told her about the decision he had been forced to make when he had realized that they had lost the game, gave her an account of the terrible battle that he had been obliged to fight in order to save all the occupants of the rocket, and explained how he came to be in their midst now, anonymously.

As he spoke, Mary became calm and confident again, for her scientific mind held sway over all other sentiments. The young woman remained lost in thought for some while, then looked at the face that was leaning toward her. It was, of course, still the image of Landry that she saw, and she had to make a forceful effort to re-establish in her mind the true personality hidden behind that architecture of flesh and bone, which no longer signified anything. In the eyes that were fixed upon her, though, she discovered a new, different gleam: the exteriorization of a soul that was familiar to her, and which reached her through the intermediary of that limpid gaze, in which a deep ocean of eternal light was reflected. It was Jeff's!

Yes, for her, Jeff's soul was immortal, for it survived of its own accord beyond time and space. That thought frightened her suddenly, although she did not know why.

"What will become of us, Jeff?" she asked, softly.

"Don't worry, little sister; for the moment, nothing can do us any harm—don't be afraid."

"Are you going to tell the others the truth?"

"No—they couldn't understand, so what would be the point? Let me do things my way, and everything will work out."

In that handsome face, she saw all the conviction, all the will-power and all the faith that she needed so badly, and she nodded her head resignedly. For the first time, she discovered in Jeff and in herself a new sentiment, totally inexplicable in human language and bearing no comparison to anything that a normal individual could experience: a sentiment of limitless scope, far beyond affection, passion and love; an enormous sentiment of purity, which surpassed purity itself; something sublime, universal and supreme.

He looked at her, smiling, delighted by the transfiguration that linked them together again—and she returned his smile.

As Jeff returned to the pilot's station, the intercom crackled and the radio operator's voice became audible. "It's done," he said. "I've succeeded in repairing the telescopic receivers, for the time being. I'm getting the first images of Rhea. It's absolutely incredible."

"Why, what's happening now?"

"See for yourself, captain. Hang on, I'll patch through the transmission."

Images danced on the radarscope screens, then stabilized rapidly, clearly revealing the configuration of Rhea's illuminated hemisphere to Jeff.

He could not believe his eyes, and called out to his companions in his turn. They immediately joined him in front of the screens.

"Great gods!" exclaimed Manzini. "Seas, continents, islands and polar ice-caps...I'm damned if I expected that!"

"It can't be Rhea—it's impossible," said Sanchez.

"And yet, it is," said Jeff, without looking away from the screen on which the images captured by Donovan continued to appear.

"But the reports are precise and irrefutable," Warren said in his turn. "Shortly after our ancestors' exodus, Rhea's crust exploded, and the entire surface was ravaged by a cataclysm provoked by the sudden heating of the internal magma. The phenomenon was checked and recorded by observation rockets and the lunar bases. Some of the images are still burning in my memory, and I remember very clearly the ocean of molten lava that had invaded the five continents, evaporating the oceans and seas. No trace remained of the ancient topography."

"That's true," Sanchez agreed, "and indisputable—and it only happened three centuries ago. It's impossible that a new configuration could be formed in so little time. Logically, we should find nothing on that planet but a surface of desiccated, cracked lava: a dead planet reduced to the state of burned, porous and bloated rock. This is incomprehensible. Look, those dark green zones are undoubtedly masses of vegetation; one can also make out streams, rivers and even lakes."

"It's bewildering," agreed Manzini, who seemed to be the most flabbergasted of all, "bewildering and demoralizing, especially for a geologist. At least, that's what I thought I was, until now…but this, truly, I don't understand. I can't offer any explanation at all."

"Many things are happening to us that we don't understand, aren't they?" Warren murmured, pensively. "Many things that surpass our understanding, unfortunately." He did not want to dwell too much on recent events, in order to concentrate on the mystery surrounding Rhea. "A planet that no longer has its normal dimensions, and which, instead of being in the most desolate state, appears to us in all its magnificence and splendor. That's a mystery I'd dearly like to clarify."

He obtained no response. Deep down, he had not expected any on the part of his companions, and he opted to continue in another tone, which he tried to render more cheerful. "My friends, I think that it's time to refresh ourselves. Let's take full advantage of our last meal aboard the rocket."

To which Donovan replied from his cabin, via the intercom: "Frozen meat and vegetable salad—the usual menu. With that, at least, there are no surprises, and no mystery."

CHAPTER V

During the hours that followed, further observations of Rhea were carried out on board, while the rocket crossed the last few million kilometers that still separated it from the majestic planet that now revealed itself to the voyagers in minute detail.

The radar soon signaled a significant swarm of rocky debris forming a sort of ring around Rhea. The received images revealed, in effect, compact masses of cosmic matter retained by the planet's gravity, orbiting masses surrounding Rhea whose thickness, in places, measured more than 500 kilometers. It was, in consequence, necessary to employ the atomic disintegrators—provided in case of encounters with meteorites—to clear a passage through these solid blocks, a collision with which would have been fatal to the spaceship.

Data concerning the configuration of the ground were gathered, as precisely as possible, as the planet rotated on its axis—but nothing, of course, corresponded to the ancient maps of Rhea that they possessed. They recorded eight continental masses, disposed in pairs to the north and the south, five great oceans, and several mountainous masses that stretched for thousands of kilometers.

The vegetation that covered the greater part of the landmasses was jade-green, its color becoming accentuated on the slopes of mountains bordering the sea, and the atmospheric recorders indicated that the climate ought to be tropical at the equator, subtropical to either side, with two large temperate bands linking them to glacial polar zones. In that respect, everything appeared to conform with the information given in the textbooks, and there was nothing astonishing about it.

Maneuvering the ship into orbit necessitated an intense effort on Jeff's part, but Landry's memories, fully recovered, permitted him to complete the delicate enterprise successfully. Then, when the atomic disintegrators were activated, the rocket descended at a vertiginous speed through the region of solid debris, items of which were pulverized ahead of it, creating the hole necessary for the passage of the spaceship, which was already embarking on the long spiral that would eventually permit it to make contact with the selected continent. Forests, savannahs, lakes, mountains and deserts filed before them on the synchronized screens.

The selection had been arbitrary, to be sure, for nothing permitted them to accord a preference to one or other continent of the globe, but the one that appeared to be most conveniently situated in one of the temperate zones had won a unanimous vote.

Thus, they were soon able to observe in detail the country in which they were about to land. The silvery ribbon of a river ran southwards between two masses of vegetation and lost itself in a cobalt blue sea whose surf, near its shores, formed around brown rocks indented with clear haloes of a sort.

"One certainly has the impression of looking at a genuine paradise," Donovan murmured over the intercom. "What a magnificent spectacle! I've never seen anything like it."

Jeff's voice cut in: "Everyone return to their places, and get ready. Fasten your safety-belts." He turned round to make sure that everyone in the cabin was carrying out his orders, then he resumed contact with Donovan.

At that moment, the rocket emerged for the third time into the day-lit hemisphere, and after a further maneuver, Jeff pointed the machine at the vast clearing that had been scrupulously located, while scanning the control panel.

Suddenly, he frowned.

The excitation of the central matrix was going awry, and primary lateral generators 1 and 3 were suddenly showing signs of weakness. With a reflexive reaction, he increased the pressure of the braking gas. The needles on the respective dials indicated a sharp deceleration—but that was by no means sufficient, as Jeff realized, to his alarm. On the screen in front of him, the verdant ground of the prairie was visibly increasing in magnification. He was bathed in cold sweat.

It was, at most, a question of minutes, and he realized that, barring a miracle, a catastrophe was unavoidable. Desperately, he pressed the switch controlling the gas again, and activated the secondary generators at full power; the resulting pressure made the ventral nozzles howl, giving the impression that they were about to explode.

The braking effect was further increased, and the noise of heavy breathing behind him clearly indicated that his companions were also following, anxiously but in complete silence, the maneuver that he was in the process of executing.

He glanced at the altimeter, which indicated 600 meters.

Jeff played his final card then. With a curt gesture, he pushed the fuel control to its maximum limit. The loud whistling became sharper still as the nozzles, heated to incandescence, violently spat out a further jet of flaming gas.

What happened then only lasted for a few seconds.

There was a violent shock, and the rocket, briefly unbalanced, listed dangerously. One of the reactors exploded with a bang, and in a flash, Jeff realized that they were irremediably lost.

He tried to get out of his seat, but did not have the time. He felt himself hurled against the control panel facing him, while a frightful noise shook the vessel. He curled up in his seat as the rocket, having rebounded dully, crashed into the ground again with unexpected violence.

Carried by its momentum, the metallic vehicle slid on its side for a further second or two, and then came to a halt with a final shudder.

Jeff came to his feet with one bound, his gaze searching for his companions. He saw Mary, who had been thrown out of her seat and was lying in the middle of the eviscerated cabin. Further away, Sanchez's body was lying in a heap against the cockpit. Warren had got to his feet, with difficulty, and was writhing in pain in his corner. As for Manzini, he appeared to be the least bruised of all, but he was pale and was trembling in every limb.

"Mary!" Jeff shouted, precipitating himself toward the young woman, who was still unconscious.

He picked her up, lifting her in his arms, and sighed deeply as he saw her come round. Then he returned his gaze to Warren, who had dragged himself as far as Sanchez's body.

"There's nothing to be done for him," the scientist reported. "Fractured skull—he died instantly."

Manzini irrupted into the cabin from the radar post just as Jeff straightened up.

"Donovan?" Jeff asked, feverishly. He had no need to wait for the geophysicist's reply; his expression said everything. He raced forward like a madman and came to a stop before the frightfully-mutilated body of the radiometeorologist, completely cut in two by a portion of the metallic wall that had been literally torn away by the crash of the rocket. He turned round, feeling sick, on the brink of vomiting.

Mary had come to her feet, while Manzini was examining Warren, whose leg wound fortunately proved not to be serious.

By virtue of a retroactive effect, a ripple of panic and terror took hold of the surviving crew-members.

"My God, it's frightful!" Mary moaned. "It's frightful…"

"What are we going to do?" lamented Manzini.

"We're alive," Jeff put in. "That's lucky, in itself. First, let's try to assess the damage. After that, we'll see what we can do."

Obedient to his advice, Warren, Mary and Manzini came to join him in the hatchway—but the spectacle that was presented to them completed their demoralization. The entire rear section of the rocket had exploded on contact with the ground, and enormous breaches had appeared in the vessel's protective envelope. One might have thought that a tornado had passed through it, ravaging furniture, instruments and apparatus of every sort as it went. All that debris was scattered on the ground in indescribable disorder, and in the utmost confusion.

Warren rushed to the little redoubt that had served as his private laboratory, and uttered a long howl like that of a wounded animal on seeing the catastrophe that had overtaken his cybernetic matrices. Nothing had escaped the effects of the crash. There was nothing but torn and shattered apparatus heaped up in his redoubt now.

Warren stood there contemplating the disaster for some time, with tears in his eyes, in complete despair. The damage was total, absolute and all-encompassing.

Slowly, he returned to his companions, shaking his head. Then, looking at Jeff, with a profound sadness in his voice, he said: "You're right, we're alive—that's lucky in itself." But deep down, his life was of little importance to him now.

CHAPTER VI

Manzini finished digging the graves while the bodies of Sanchez and Donovan were brought out of the vessel. Warren and Jeff deposited the remains of their unfortunate companions in the gaping holes; then the four survivors collected themselves momentarily while Manzini threw out the last spadefuls.

The geophysicist breathed heavily for a few moments, and then, in a voice redolent with both emotion and anxiety, said: "Rhea welcomes us with death. A charming reception, isn't it?"

Everywhere around them there was empty, glacial silence, except for a slight breeze agitating the tall grasses of the bizarre jungle that surrounded them. The trees that grew further away and the grass on which they were treading seemed healthy and vigorous. The trees bore no resemblance to those of New Earth. The dominant species had large, thick leaves and a heavy and massive trunk approximately two or three meters in height, rarely more. The nascent young leaves were as red as maple-buds, but that was only at the tips; in their normal frame they took on the strange greenish color that was surprising at first sight.

The air was light and mild, and tranquility seemed to reign over the Eden-like country.

"Eden-like" was certainly the term that came to mind... Similarly, at first glance, in its calmness and gentleness, Rhea offered the gaze the image of a veritable Eden, a marvelous Eldorado, uniquely worthy of some solitary god saturated with purity and perfection. But Manzini's words were still resonating in Jeff's ears as he finished setting up the rudimentary wooden crosses that Warren had hastily improvised. Death also had its décor, its scenery and its carnival masks... attractive and deceptive masks that Nature fabricated for it fraudulently.

He wished at that moment that he had the power to tear away the mask of this planet, which horrified him, and for which he experienced, without being able to specify the reason, an implacable aversion.

He pushed his sentiments back into the background of his other thoughts, though, in order to resume consciousness of the role that he had to play in this terrible adventure.

He thought that the best thing to do was to take an immediate census of all the important equipment aboard the rocket that had not been destroyed in the course of the accident. Certain compartments were stocked with removable equipment, and everything that was necessary for life outside the rocket. There was no lack of weapons—but was there any need to worry about that on a world as delightful as Rhea seemed to be?

They found provisions and numerous pharmaceutical products, but what amazed Manzini was to observe that the parts of the portable apparatus provided for the subterranean explosion of strata that were assumed to be still molten had not suffered overmuch from the explosion, and were still usable.

It was, in effect, a vehicle designed to gather data on the nature of the crust and the magma whose heating had produced the cataclysm that was known to have occurred, but of which no evidential traces remained. It was, in consequence, constructed of materials designed to withstand temperatures over 4000 degrees. Activated by four nuclear units, it was easily maneuverable and could move at a reasonable speed over any terrain, thanks to sets of caterpillar tracks mounted on its sides. Its equipment was state-of-the-art with respect to the most recent scientific advances in vulcanology, and the central cabin supported by gyroscopic anti-g motors always maintained itself in a vertical position no matter what he inclination of the machine might be.

As for Warren, he too was entitled to a small surprise that he was far from expecting—which was procured for him by the recovery, from the inextricable wreckage of his laboratory, of intact test-tubes containing the synthetic embryos destined for his extraordinary experiments. By a providential stroke of luck, the receptacles had resisted the destruction of the cybernetic matrices, and Jeff watched him arrange them lovingly in a little box, which he never let out of his sight from that moment onwards.

Even so, the first day on Rhea went by in a climate of general anxiety, for each of them understood that they no longer had the slightest chance of ever returning to New Earth.

Out there, obviously, no one knew about the drama that had unfolded, and the castaways could not, in consequence, expect any rescue attempt. It was thus necessary for them to envisage the situation with the resignation and courage it demanded, in spite of its gravity. The instinct of self-preservation soon took over again, fortunately, and they tried to make what provisions they could to survive on this world of which they knew nothing, but of which, deep down, they were fearful without knowing exactly why.

They were sure of not dying of hunger, for the country was overflowing with fruits and animals—whose meat was edible, if they could judge by the small mammal killed by Manzini for the evening meal, the flesh of which was unanimously deemed to be excellent.

When darkness fell and Jeff found himself alone on his bed, his first concern was to attain maximum concentration, in order to liberate the physical needs of his body and recover he psychosomatic disposition necessary for the release of the mechanisms that permitted him to maintain the links between his mind and his own body, abandoned on New Earth.

To do that, he had first to arbitrate between two tendencies, that of the promise he had given to Warren in case of the failure of the mission, which concerned the mysterious embryo of which he alone knew the secret, and on the other hand, that which made him henceforth the uncontested leader of the little group of survivors destined to end their days on Rhea.

To abandon his companions to their sad fate was unthinkable, for even though he was usually ever-ready to face the worst, he had a bizarre feeling that they were all in grave danger. Certainly, there was nothing definite to support that impression, but for Jeff, the name Rhea had something about it that was suggestive of...death. It was like the perfume of an accursed chapel that had impregnated his senses and no longer let them alone.

Did he not, however, possess the power to reconcile the two tendencies?—which is to say, to accomplish both of the imperative missions that destiny had imposed upon him. Perhaps for the first time, he understood, in the thinking part of himself, that he must go on to the end of the road that extended before him, which no other human being had ever trod.

He then considered, fearfully, the abstract and supernatural hypothesis according to which he did not belong, and never had belonged, to the normal human species, even though his mind had always tried to interpret its own supernatural stimulations in the most up-to-date human terms. He was *something else*: a being apart, a curious mixture of flesh and spirit thrown into the torment of an anticosmos that escaped him.

He knew the same impressions when he projected himself into the immense and infinite void, experienced the same dread, the same anguish, the same ecstasy and he same sublime joy until the moment when he recovered contact with his body in his little habitation on New Earth.

He felt the glacial cold that submerged it like a tide at the moment when the transmigration was completed; then, little by little, the vegetative life in which his body had remained since the abandonment gave way to a normal organic life.

The heart resumed beating with a normal rhythm, the veins and arteries inflated, the neurons re-established their synapses and the organic senses awoke, like those of a marmot in the first days of spring.

Rapidly, he made sure that he was still in contact with Landry's body on Rhea, and then he recovered his normal equilibrium.

When he opened his study door, he found himself face of face with Greta, his robot housekeeper, who seemed to be mounting a vigilant guard in the corridor.

"Why didn't you reply?" she demanded, in its toneless voice, when her visual receivers registered his presence.

It was an effect of a basic reflex integrated into the mechanism, and Jeff paid no heed to it, contenting himself with repeating the order he had given before his departure. "I instructed that I was not to be disturbed during the time I remained in the room."

There as a click in Greta's internal mechanism, and then the metallic voice replied: "The security system with which I'm equipped triggered an alarm. Your nutritive functions have not been served, and your calorie intake has been zero for 94 hours."

He shrugged his shoulders, went around the robot, but then changed his mind. "Did anyone ask for me during my absence?" He corrected himself almost immediately, in order to obtain a correct response, adding; "During those 94 hours."

"Yes, sir—an urgent call emanating from the Biological Center."

Jeff hesitated for a few seconds, then said: "Can you make contact with the Center's director?"

"Impossible, sir."

"Why?"

The reply, logical and brief, was: "The Center has been destroyed. It no longer exists."

Jeff frowned, gripped by anxiety, and then ran out of the cottage.

The spectacle offered to his sight only served to increase his anxiety and his suspicions.

In front of him, in the direction of the buildings reserved for biological research, thin columns of smoke were rising slowly into the sky, emanating from formless and charred carcasses.

Jeff ran forward at a hectic sprint, crossing the zone reserved for individual habitations, which the disaster had spared. When he finally arrived in the technical and administrative sector, he could not believe his eyes.

Around him there was nothing but smoking debris, which powerful bulldozers were in the process of clearing, while crews of security men were finishing off the battle against the fires that threatened to spread.

Nothing had been spared, not even the section reserved for Professor Warren, and Jeff realized the terrible extent of the catastrophe. He thought about the embryo and the celebrated professor's labors—of the immense loss, about which nothing could be done at present...and *something* within him reacted against his logical faculties; *something* that told him that exceedingly strange circumstances, beyond his scope, seemed to be opposed to Warren's projects, determined to prevent their realization.

Yes, that must be it: an inexplicable, incomprehensible *thing*, without any real or logical basis. A *thing* that barred his way and that of humans, which loomed up between the normal world and the other, like an insurmountable wall of unsuspected phenomena—phenomena for which the human race was evidently unprepared, for the simple reason that it had never encountered them before.

With a blank gaze, Jeff watched the people moving in the area ravaged by the fire, who could not understand. He listened with similar blankness to the vague explanations that were being advanced regarding the origin of the catastrophe. People around him were talking in empty voices, without knowledge, without valid reasons, in deaf and blind ignorance, and the world that surrounded him became, at a stroke, as empty as everything else: an immense bell that rang false, agitated frantically by an invisible hand, at the whim of its fantasy.

But all these thoughts, in their turn, were unreal, for the truth—which Jeff alone had glimpsed—was the sinister torment that had captured him, and whose current was becoming stronger by the second. He was caught in a trap, in a deafening thunderstorm, in a barrage of lightning that was making the carcass of the Universe tremble, an eruption of unknown forces whose glare outshone the light of the stars. It was a fierce battle of magical powers mounting an assault on Reason. It was a monstrous combat of Good and Evil, attaining their supreme concentration.

It was, alas, many other things—of which Jeff, unfortunately, knew nothing!

CHAPTER VII

"Well, Jeff, we were beginning to get worried. What's happening?"

He opened his eyes, with infinite trouble, breathed in deeply, and recognized the tormented face of Mary, who was leaning over him.

Warren and Manzini were already busy outside the rocket, and the Sun was shining cheerfully in the pure sky of Rhea.

Mary smiled at him when he sat up on his bunk, recovering all his normal faculties. "I couldn't tell them anything," she said, "but I'm frightened...very frightened..."

"Don't worry—there's nothing to fear." He wanted to tell her the truth, tell her what he had just learned millions of kilometers away, to confess his own fear and terror, and all the difficulty he had had in transplanting himself into Landry's body, but it was as if an invisible force were obstinately watching over him and preventing him from doing so.

Warren arrived in his turn, and exclaimed on seeing him: "You were greatly in need of rest, and you've taken advantage of it—so much the better! For our part, we haven't been idle. Manzini has already succeeded in assembling several pieces of the exploration apparatus. It will be useful for us to make a tour of the region. We'll be ready tomorrow, in all probability."

He had resumed his habitual manner, but he had been pierced by fatalism, and when Jeff asked: "What do you expect to find elsewhere that we don't have here?" he winced and replied: "Someone already asked me that question when I told him I was leaving for Rhea—and the answer I'd be able to give him now is very different from the one I gave then." He sighed, and added in a different tone: "Look!"

He opened his hand and displayed a stone ravaged by time, which he said that he had found in the vicinity, while helping Manzini lay in supplies of drinkable water. On one of the faces of the stone a little drawing was engraved, undoubtedly not due to a caprice of Nature.

"It's the work of an intelligent creature," he said. "The work has been done with a chisel, and reveals a highly advanced level of artistry."

Manzini, who had joined his companions, intervened in his turn. "That's indisputable. It's evidence of cleverly-improved tools and a second degree technology. I'm certain that, if we press on with our research, we'll discover more important and revealing vestiges."

Jeff examined he piece of engraved stone attentively, and shook his head uncomprehendingly. "Ought we to assume that we're dealing with vestiges pertaining to our own ancestors?"

Manzini scratched his head in an embarrassed manner, and opined, without any great conviction: "My God...until we have proof to the contrary, yes." Then, studying the stone attentively and anxiously, he added: "Unless it comes from a much more ancient civilization, which seems to me to be more probable." He shrugged his shoulders, tried to smile, and, in order to avoid the host of questions that he divined on his companions' lips, he hastened to conclude: "The geology that I profess is purely theoretical. Here, everything is different and I'm obliged to start from scratch. As for archeological questions, it's best to abstain for the moment—so I propose a tour of the surroundings, in order to penetrate this mystery...which rather intrigues me, I confess. What do you think?"

Everyone accepted Aldo Manzni's proposal right away. Preparations were immediately made by the little group, inasmuch as the exploratory vehicle, of reduced dimensions, was quickly put in working order.

The motors obeyed the first solicitation, and everything seemed to be working perfectly. They took their places within it, and after studying the steering mechanism with Manzini, Jeff sat down at the controls and launched the machine straight ahead into the sunlit countryside.

It did not take them long to discover a few mammals roaming free, which fled at their approach—an entire animal kingdom with the most various forms, some of which species had nothing in common with those prevalent on Rhea before the catastrophe. That, of course, could only add to the interest and anxiety that continued to increase in the hearts of the castaways.

The machine followed a course directly toward the hills, made a brief halt for the midday meal, which they swallowed hastily, and got under way again a few minutes later.

The landscape around them was still the same: bright, colorful, welcoming and hospitable. It was when Jeff was getting ready to go around the first of the hills that Mary pointed to something to his right. "There! There, look!" she demanded

They did indeed look. Emerging from a curtain of foliage, the ruins of ancient buildings loomed up, bristling with columns and frontons, invaded by vegetation.

With the aid of a rapid and skilful maneuver, Jeff steered the vehicle toward the indicated spot, and they soon emerged into the middle of a vast esplanade, on which stood several dilapidated edifices, worn away by time, in the midst of debris of every sort, swept by the wind.

They got out and, following Manzini, advanced into the midst of the ruins, not daring as yet to exchange their impressions.

In the center of a grand plaza stood the ruins of a temple, somewhat reminiscent of the monuments of ancient Greece, with numerous massive colonnades of red granite. Inscriptions, of which they obviously could not understand a single word, were visible on a large fronton.

Further away, other half-collapsed buildings offered their gazes the sad spectacle of their degradation, with their gaping orifices and dismantled walls.

Manzini set to work immediately, and soon began to make discoveries.

On a magnificent edifice of pink sandstone, black streaks altered the appearance of certain bas-reliefs in places, probably due to a migration of manganese salts oxidizing on contact with the air.

Other maladies of the stones betrayed themselves elsewhere by the action of a familiar bacterium, *thiobacillus*, whose life-cycle was effectuated in the very bosom of the sandstone, and which eventually ended up causing the disintegration of the stone, effacing the bas-reliefs and threatening the entire edifice at its base.

For a few more hours, Manzini busied himself among the ruins, studying numerous specimens, and finally, it was in a voice imprinted with lassitude that he decided to declare to his companions: "It's quite incomprehensible. These vestiges go back several centuries, if not millennia." As everyone paid his the utmost attention, he went on: "Theoretically, of course. In this case, it's difficult to admit that their origin could be anterior to the cataclysm, for nothing of that world survived. As for saying that these vestiges have a more recent origin, that's absolutely impossible and unthinkable. We must admit that we're confronted by a very curious paradox."

Jeff was on the point of replying when a slight exclamation uttered by Mary caused them all to turn round. She pointed at the ground in front of them. In the fine dust, they all saw footprints: neatly cut-out tracks; the perfectly-designed tracks of human feet.

Warren, overwhelmed by amazement, exclaimed: "Well, I'm damned!"

"Those tracks are fresh," Manzini said. "Someone has been here ahead of us."

A long, dolorous silence fell upon the little group, in the course of which each of them strove to understand the new mystery that had been set before them.

Jeff was the first to collect himself. "Follow me," he said.

With Jeff in the lead, they followed the tracks as far as the edge of the dead city, where they were able to ascertain that they faded away in the direction of the hills. There was no hesitation; they needed to be determined.

They all went back to the little exploration vehicle and, at a modest speed, they took the direction of the footprints in their turn. They soon reached the first slopes of the verdant hills, where it became increasingly difficult to guide themselves, because the tracks became less clear and less apparent in that terrain.

Scarcely had they reached the summit of a small hillock, however, when the most unexpected spectacle appeared before their eyes.

In the hollow of a little valley dotted with multicolored flowers, they distinguished an assemblage of perfectly-aligned buildings, low single-story houses bordered with flourishing lawns and dwarf trees bearing bright fruits.

Smoke was coming out of the bright red roofs and riding slowly into the calm, pure sky. Then, they finally perceived human silhouettes coming and going through the streets and across the open spaces. There were both men and men, dressed with the same simplicity as everything concerning the environment of which they seemed to be a part.

Warren was the most bewildered of all, and could not help murmuring: "Unbelievable! Absolutely incredible!" Then he turned to the others, and it was toward Jeff that his face leaned, as he murmured: "What do we do?"

Jeff shook his head, in synchrony with a deep involuntary sigh, and then took the necessary decision. "Let's go," he murmured. And he launched the vehicle straight ahead.

There was no sign of panic or amazement in the village when they arrived. All that happened was that a few of the women turned their heads on the thresholds of their dwellings, some of the men interrupted their work in the gardens or the open-air workshops, and the children briefly interrupted the games they were playing with strange little animals that seemed quite harmless. It was as if their minds had already been prepared and alerted to their coming. That, at least, was the impression Jeff had at the moment when the machine drew to a halt on the edge of the agglomeration, while a group of individuals in gaudy costumes advanced to meet them.

A tall fellow detached himself from the group; his clothing differed sufficiently from that of his peers for the idea that he must be a very important person to cross the minds of all the space travelers.

There was a long moment of silence; then the unknown man bowed ceremoniously to the visitors, who had leapt out of the vehicle, and said: "Be welcome, friends from the sky! The most generous hospitality will be offered to you in our community."

Manzini had gripped Warren's arm, murmuring in a blank voice: "He speaks our language. My God, it's enough to drive one mad!"

The gaudily-dressed individual bowed again; a faint smile was inscribed on his thin lips. "The Sage Munk awaits you in his humble dwelling. Permit me to take you to him, friends from the sky."

They could not do other than accept this strange invitation, and followed in the footsteps of their guide without hesitation, cutting through the silent crowd that pressed around them, which did not seem to be animated by any hostile intent.

They traversed a large open space and soon found themselves in front of a neat villa, perfectly constructed, whose red brick roof was surmounted by a multicolored flag. They were humbly implored to go in, and found themselves in a large room, furnished in a rudimentary fashion, but with an esthetic sensitivity and taste quite surprising in a race that did not seem very advanced.

Propriety and simplicity were the rule here, as everywhere, and the old man who stood up in front of them as they came in had a welcoming expression imprinted with an ineffable generosity. He offered then low, soft seats disposed around his carved chair, and said in a soft, slightly accented voice: "Sit down, friends from the sky—we've been expecting you."

At the sound of that voice, although it was pleasant and placid, Jeff felt a malaise that was difficult to suppress, and when he sounded her thoughts, almost involuntarily, he realized that Mary felt the same sentiment.

Then Warren's voice murmured "Who are you?"

That question seemed inappropriate, and to betray a certain egotism in the present circumstances, but the old sage did not appear to be in the least offended. Nor did he have any hesitation in replying: "Earthmen, as your ancestors once were, on this same world."

"That's impossible," said Warren, stubbornly. "Impossible. No one survived the cataclysm—and this world isn't Earth. It has nothing in common with our mother planet."

A new smile illuminated the face of the old man. "Evidently, you can't understand, and your stubbornness is quite excusable."

"Please tell us," said Manzini, who was becoming restless in his seat. "Where are we?"

The old man shook his head and replied, almost in a single breath: "On one of the numerous rings that comprise this planet. We once lived in the interior of the globe. Only yours, being exterior, found itself, by virtue of that fact, in special and entirely exceptional conditions by comparison with the others, because it placed your human race in direct contact with all the rest of the Universe. For us, it was different, for space was limited by the rocky and impenetrable barrier of your solid crust. It was necessary that the Great Cataclysm overtake the outermost ring in order to place us abruptly in the same natural conditions that had been yours. Don't believe, though, that so far as we were concerned, what happened did no damage. The new atmospheric conditions to which our people were subjected gave rise to many illnesses and many disturbances in the bosom of our humankind, and it took a long time before our readaptation was finally accomplished."

While listening to these revelations, the astronauts exchanged rapid glances, and it was obvious that they were hesitant to accept the fantastic element in that story, which they had been far from expecting.

Manzini decided to ask: "You claim, then, that the terrestrial globe is comprised of several rings, independent of one another?"

"I don't claim it; I affirm it."

"Amazing," breathed Warren. "That explains the reduced dimensions of the world, which we were able to determine during our recent observations. What do you estimate to be the thickness of the solid crust of each ring?"

"About 50 kilometers, no more—and the spatial gap separating the rings is about 300 kilometers."

Jeff suddenly recalled certain ancient terrestrial legends still maintained on New Earth, and certain old traditions linked to religious literature, which situated the dwellings of the dead and of spirits beneath the terrestrial crust: the legend of Orpheus running through the entrails of the globe after Eurydice; those of Germanic mythology exiling heroes into the depths of the Earth; Dante's frightful vision of a central Inferno; and all the crazy theories of the Hollow Earth imagined by insane visionaries.

Yes, all of that now took on the sense of an extraordinary and stupefying reality—but they had not, alas, reached the end of their surprises, for when Mary wanted to know by what strange coincidence this human race, which had no connection with theirs, expressed itself in their own language, the explanation given by the old sage completed their prostration.

At first, the earnest individual seemed to hesitate over the reply to that question; then his features creased in numerous wrinkles, and his gaze seemed to be momentarily veiled, as if he were prey to contrary impulses assailing his mind. "That goes back to very distant times," he said, finally, "when the Masters of the World decided to undertake its conquest."

"To whom are you alluding in speaking of the Masters of the World?" Jeff put in, abruptly.

"To those who reign at the very center of our globe. No one knows them, at least in their veritable aspect, for they are not human. Legends say that they are beings intermediate between man and the Powers from Outside, and that they have an inexhaustible central energy at their disposal, with which to obtain the mastery of the entire Universe. A day will come when that conquest will be realized, when they have succeeded in annihilating everything that still poses an obstacle to their project. At the beginning of Time, it is said, they landed on Earth and occupied its entrails. At the heart of the globe, they split into two groups. One followed the way of benevolence, the other that of violence, the forces of which commanded the elements and human races. It was, alas, the latter who prevailed, thus taking the destiny of the planet in hand. It is, therefore, those dark powers that currently reign over all the Rings of Earth."

"All that is quite incoherent," said Warren, nervously.

A wan smile appeared on the old man's lips. "The desire for coherence is a mortal vice, and these beings are not mortal. They're capable of changing the very nature of reality."

"It's merely a matter of popular beliefs, ordinary legends of the sort that all peoples possess. You can't say anything for sure." Warren was trying with all his might to give weight to his words, but the terrible apprehension that was buried deep within him was evident, for he was in the process of battling his own convictions. Then, admitting defeat, he broke the heavy silence that had followed his words to ask in a dull voice: "What are they?"

"What your eyes see them to be, and your minds accept them to be. But that's still only a false image; the truth is imperceptible to our human senses. All that we know is that they possess a psyche much more evolved than ours, that they unleash their powers upon one another, upon others and upon things, and that they're purely spiritual in essence."

"You imagine them as godlike, then?" exclaimed Manzini.

"Don't forget that the Devil himself is also spiritual in essence," the old man riposted.

"What relationship is there between you and these beings?" Jeff asked.

"No one can say. They have the ability to go from any point in the interior to any other, as well as the exterior; they know the secret openings that serve to communicate between the spheres placed inside one another. They know everything and are ignorant of nothing. It was they who informed us of your impending catastrophe and told us of your intention to emigrate to Venus. They told us many things about your civilization, your languages, your mores, customs and history. They dream of unifying all the humans living on this globe and throughout the universe, so as to create a single race entirely devoted to their cause, promising everyone immortality and power beyond Time and Space. Those are the sacred principles of the Black Order."

The old man fell silent, in order to give the astronauts time to assimilate the fantastic news that he had just communicated to them. It was obvious that what had been said had had a very considerable effect on the little group, and a certain malaise was evident in the glances they exchanged, without saying a word, along with a visible anxiety.

After a brief interval, however, Mary could not help exclaiming: "In sum, what do they want from you? My companions and I are under the impression that you're living a happy and peaceful existence here."

A slight nod of the Sage's head approved these swords, and once again, the old man hesitated before replying. As if to give himself time for reflection and decision, he clapped his hands twice. A somberly-dressed woman immediately came in, carrying a tray laden with bottles and goblets, which she deposited on a low table in front of the Sage.

Everyone understood that it would certainly be impolite to refuse the invitation, and, at a sign from the old man, they all tasted the delicious refreshing drink that the newcomer served to them.

Jeff examined her more attentively when she arrived next to him, pouring the amber liquid into his goblet. She was young and beautiful—extraordinarily beautiful, surpassing in beauty everything that a feminine creature could receive as a gift of nature. She was slender, with a fine bone-structure beneath her well-proportioned flesh. For an instant Jeff regretted that over-attentive examination—but it was more powerful than him, more powerful than anything.

CHAPTER VIII

The young woman looked at him in her turn, and in her large limpid eyes, in which an entire harmony of unknown colors were reflected, something was born: something like a supplication, or a distant appeal, emanating from a fabulous past in which good and evil were differently defined. It was like a powerful sentiment of unlimited confidence, which she seemed to want him to share—and Jeff, for the first time in his life, felt the strange fascination of an almost-unreal gaze that he would never be able to forget.

He came back to himself slowly when she turned away, as if he were falling from a great height.

The old Sage spoke again: "We are the only ones privileged in this world, friends from the sky," he said, with a hint of bitterness in his voice. "You're in a land where evil has no purchase, and which has partially escaped the control of the black powers—but we pay very dearly for our peace and happiness."

"How is that?" asked Manzini, frowning.

"It goes back to the first decades following your catastrophe, when our sphere finally found itself in contact with infinite space. We then had a strange revelation. Malevolent waves originating in the cosmos reached the Earth and followed it in its blind course. We identified a close relationship between that and the black powers that reigned at the very center of our globe, and understood that we could, by means of fully-consenting sacrifices, polarize our sphere, creating identical poles, as in magnetic fields. Our intention was to obtain by that means a positive pole and a negative pole, equally charged with opposite forces. We thus succeeded in creating this paradisiac place, in exchange for a country destined to become a sort of collector of the malevolent waves, whose origin escapes us."

Jeff took advantage of a pause to ask, feverishly: "Should I infer that every happy individual in this country corresponds to an unhappy one at the opposite pole?"

"Yes. The balance must not be broken at any time, or grave repercussions would ensue for our race. Volunteers offer themselves every day to perpetuate this equilibrium and accept suffering in order that others may live in peace in this beneficent land."

The old man fell silent, allowing his visitors to assimilate the strange words that he had just spoken. The astronauts looked at one another, profoundly moved by what they had just learned, which surpassed their human understanding.

The old man, who seemed increasingly troubled and embarrassed, was about to resume speaking when the young creature who had just sat down next to him spoke in her turn: "It's as well to admit the truth now," she said, "although it will cost me personally to inform you."

The old man's hand clenched on hers. "Wait, Marka…"

"No, it's impossible—you know that." She turned to Jeff and his companions. "You understand that it's impossible for you to stay here. You're strangers, and no one will sacrifice themselves for you. No one will accept it, for the risk is too great. If you prolong your sojourn among us, the equilibrium is at risk of being broken, and we cannot go against our principles."

Jeff thought he could read pain and infinite suffering in her eyes, and internally he admired the courage of the beautiful Marka, which cut straight to the heart of that embarrassing question.

They got up with a single movement, understanding that it would be futile and impolite to persist, completely disorientated by what they had just heard.

The old man told them that he knew about their difficulties, for they had obviously been aware of the accident that had occurred when the ship landed, but the planet was vast and the continents numerous. They could leave their country for other lands—above all, never to return. That was the promise that he obtained from Warren, whom he considered to be the leader of the little crew.

As they said their goodbyes, however, Jeff decided to ask the question that gripped his heart, and which had not ceased to haunt him since the beginning of the conversation. "Do you know the secret passage that will permit us to reach the interior spheres?"

A shake of the Sage's head left the question unanswered. He did not know; no one in this world knew.

Jeff did not press the point, and took his leave, while Marka joined the escort that conducted him and his companions back to their vehicle. Once again, Jeff turned round before climbing into the apparatus, and contemplated her lovingly. He suddenly divined that it was her who had provoked the imperious thought demanding that he turn round one last time.

He saw her come forward to stand in front of him, almost touching him. Then she spoke, very rapidly: "Go to the accursed continent; there you will find someone who will help you to find the secret passage, since that is your desire. Goodbye."

He wanted to ask other questions, but Marka had already vanished into the crowd, and he abandoned any thought of following her. He took his place in the vehicle and started the engines.

It was only when the township had disappeared over the horizon that Warren decided to open the discussion.

"Great gods, all this is terrible! What are we going to do now?"

Manzini ignored the question to ask Jeff: "What did that Marka want of us? The old witch spoke to you before leaving. What did she say to you?"

Jeff wrenched himself from his own thoughts to hear Mary add: "That horrid woman horrified me. I couldn't tolerate her presence a minute longer."

Jeff turned round, livid. "What? Who are you talking about?"

"Marka, of course—the old servant."

"Old and ugly, was she?" he murmured, dully.

"As to that, yes," Warren put in, "But why did you say that?"

Jeff did not reply, and his fingers clenched on the controls. An atrocious fear had invaded him, and he understood the strange phenomenon of which he had been the object, and which had affected no one but him.

But why? For what reason?

He tried to expel Marka's marvelous face from his memory, but did not succeed. He might have tried, if only for a moment, to recover the real image of the old woman from his memory, but that was impossible, for at no time had she appeared to him in her true aspect...unless the contrary were the case, and her youth and beauty had assumed the appearance of old age and ugliness in the eyes of his companions. Even in the inverse of the paradox, however, he could not glimpse the reality, and the hidden meaning of that mysterious imposture.

"Well, Landry, answer! What did she say to you?"

Manzini was posing this question for the third time when he finally decided to answer it.

The vehicle rolled, dived, veered, flew through the air, rolled again, bounded and stopped. As if by the effect of a magic wand, the landscape had changed abruptly, and dead terrain appeared around the vehicle.

There was nothing comparable to the aridity and desolation of the spectacle that confronted their eyes. The vitrified soil, congealed in tormented and chaotic forms, extended as far as the eye could see. A few sparse blades of grass appeared here and there, stubbornly resisting the hot blast of a violent wind sweeping the rocks and the dust that drifted at the edges of gigantic crags, whose sharp ridges seemed ready to bite a low, heavy and colorless sky.

The cruel perfection of the landscape had something horrible and terrifying about it, and Jeff hesitated before moving forward again.

Further away, clouds the color of lead moved aside to give way to ferocious sunlight, reflected by the cracked and bloated ground. A tortuous heat rose from the superheated soil, and Jeff had to switch on the vehicle's air conditioning.

They continued on their blind course, however, in a desert where there seemed to be no life, and where death seemed to reign as master.

They soon had to call a halt to get a few hours' rest, remaining on their guard in the meantime and keeping watch on the functioning of the apparatus, which seemed to be suffering from the brutal heat prevalent in the country.

Finally, in the early morning, they distinguished within the light mist that enveloped them the structure of a vast city built in the rock, in the middle of a sinister landscape swept by the winds and drowned in the howling of the unleashed elements.

At low speed, the little vehicle moved between steep rocky slopes cluttered with stones and debris of every sort.

Silhouettes moved between the decrepit and dilapidated buildings, which constant maintenance could not protect from the fury of a hostile nature—and the first faces that came toward them made them feel nauseous.

Men and women were walking through the fissured streets, shamelessly displaying the wounds and frightful stigmata that were eating into their flesh. In a crack in the rock, a young boy was tearing apart and devouring the remains of an animal caught in a trap. Further way, a human skeleton, half-covered in dust, was directing its round, empty orbits at the little group.

The further the machine advanced, the more horrible and repulsive the spectacle became.

Half-naked individuals were squabbling around a meager pool of water, trying to recover the slightest drop—down to the last molecule—but the avid earth sucked in its share, and the thin trickle of water was lost in the superheated sands, which the wind striated with fine, bizarre and abnormal undulations.

On the threshold of their dwelling, two leprous old men were crouching down, frozen like statues, waiting for death to bring the deliverance for which they had probably never ceased to wish.

Death reigned as master in this place. It dictated its laws to the people, who only tried to survive by virtue of a natural and unconscious instinct.

The voyagers got out of their vehicle, but no one addressed a single word to them. One might have thought them phantoms on the frontier of life and death, incapable of distinguishing between the two states, insensible to everything, sparing of the slightest gesture or movement. An acrid, fetid odor saturated the dead city and clutched at the throat, like some monstrous witch's ointment.

While his companions hesitated to continue walking amid the smoky shadows of the sandy street, Jeff advanced at hazard, straight ahead. Marka's words were resonating in his head like strokes of a gong punctuated by the howling of the wind. It was as if thousands of serpents had combined their hisses in a hallucinatory chorus rising from abandoned Syrinxes.

Jeff went along the sordid side-street, stepped over collapsed bodies stripped of flesh, went around human debris projecting from the sand and shoved aside a leprous individual whose horrible nudity interposed itself momentarily between him and the deserted open space, like a fleshless scarecrow agitated by the breath of torment.

He stepped over a miry patch where a few vermin-laden pieces of detritus were rotting, then stopped suddenly, cocking an ear toward groans that had just reached his ears. He adjusted his direction, took a few more paces, and reached the doorway of a collapsed building. There, on the threshold, a creature huddled in a fetal position was moaning: "I'm thirsty… I'm thirsty… Something to drink… For pity's sake… Something to drink…"

Jeff bent down rapidly, took up the gourd that hung from his belt, and, without caring whether the supplication was addressed to him or not, found that his soul was telling him what to do.

The gourd that he held out was snatched by two avid and skeletal hands, and when the withered face of the old woman emerged from her rags, he felt a terrible internal blow. The vitreous eyes that fixed themselves upon him suddenly took on the gleam of the same unknown colors that he knew so well.

There was no noise around him at that moment: no howling, no whistling. It was as if, at a stroke, nothing more existed of the external world but him…and *her*.

The creature drank a long draught and gave the gourd back to him with a gesture of thanks. In that emaciated face, eaten away by old age and infinite suffering, he was able to read the striking beauty and marvelous youth that were hidden there, as if beneath a carnival mask that a simple gesture on his part might tear away and throw to the wind. But the gesture was unnecessary, because he knew now that he had reached his goal. When she leaned toward him, he scarcely had the strength to pronounce: "Speak, I beg you—tell me where the passage is."

He wanted to shout her name and beg her again: "Marka!"—but the sounds would not emerge from his throat, and he waited for the reply.

The moribund woman's thin arm pointed at the rocky spurs.

"At the summit… At the end of the gully that leads to the brown rocks… behind the curtain of vapor that no one has dared to go through… but with your vehicle you can… go, then… that's where the orifice is."

This time, the name reached his lips and he murmured: "Marka!"

She replied, once again: "Go!"

CHAPTER IX

Before the curtain of vapor, Jeff stopped the vehicle, in response to Manzini's demand. Floods of scorching yellowish fumes were escaping from a large fissure, masking the sky and the landscape behind them.

"This is madness!" exclaimed the geophysicist. "We have no right… and anyway, it will do no good."

"Perhaps," Jeff murmured, "but we're doomed anyway, so we might as well go on to the end and discover the truth, if we have the chance."

"He's right," Warren agreed. "For my part, I'd rather die and know than live in doubt and uncertainty. When we accepted this mission, didn't we make a gift of our persons? So?"

"I'm in agreement too," Mary added.

Manzini made a weary gesture, sinking back into his seat. "Let's go," he said, simply.

The vehicle plunged into the vaporous sheet, leaping over the crevasse and sliding over the porous soil, eventually to each open air a few hundred meters further on.

Fine droplets carried by the wind were falling incessantly on the brown moss-covered rocks, and in the surrounding humidity crawling insects clung to the rocky alls. In places, their number was so great that there were compact viscous masses covering the rocky outcrops, which seemed to move and change shape as the vehicle continued its course through the gully.

They soon found themselves in front of a sheer rock-face in which, to their right, a gaping dark orifice appeared. Jeff steered the vehicle into the dark vault, immediately switching on the photon projectors.

A long corridor strewn with boulders presented itself ahead of the machine, with a ten-degree slope, and Jeff modified the maneuver, in accordance with the instructions given in the manual. The corridor appeared to become narrower after 100 meters, but it soon resumed its initial form; then a vast hall appeared, colossal and imposing.

Guided by the anti-shock radar, the monobloc engine continued its slow progress, while the floating cabin sustained by the gyroscopic anti-g motors always maintained its horizontal position no matter how steep the slope became.

The vehicle's instruments soon indicated a depth of 1500 meters, while the corridor widened again to increase its slope by several more degrees. The needle continued to sink on the dial, and it was when it reached the figure 10 that Manzini emerged from his silence to allow his enthusiasm to burst forth. His scientific mind had regained the upper hand, and he marveled momentarily at the fantastic aspect of the situation that was permitting the apparatus to attain depths never envisaged by its constructors. The external temperature had increased, but not in the proportions one might have expected— scarcely 30 degrees.

Finally, the Geiger counters became operative and revealed the presence of radioactive elements in the stratum. The clicking accelerated as the monobloc engine went deeper. The external temperature increased further, but eventually stabilized between 60 and 70 degrees.

Amazed, Manzini never ceased stirring in his seat and repeating joyfully: "Fifteen kilometers... It's unimaginable. We should already have encountered molten matter... It's absolutely inconceivable."

Fundamentally, he was right, but the absence of internal magma invalidated all the data and all the theories that had been supposed to be irrefutable.

Having reflected for a long time, Manzini was soon able to offer his companions the most rational explanation that he was capable of formulating. The gallery the vehicle was following presented itself, if one could believe the graph of its base, as a sort of serpentine coil, and the spiral in which they were moving was hollowed out in matter resistant to the terrible heat and formidable pressure that must reign at the same level in other peripheral strata. He obviously could not make any pronouncement on the nature of the unknown rocks that formed the gallery's floor and walls, which defied all the laws of geophysics.

They had to be content with these vague explanations, and continue their expedition with all the necessary precautions.

Long hours passed in this way, rather monotonously, for the spectacle offered to them always remained the same, and they soon began to feel the effects of fatigue. It was, however, necessary to go on to the end, for the thickness of the solid crust, according to the old sage's estimates, could not be greater than some 50 kilometers.

The spiral descent continued, therefore, and it was when the needle reached the figure 50 that they all prepared themselves. Indeed, after five supplementary kilometers covered at the same inclination, the monobloc seemed to stabilize gradually, as the angle of inclination decreased, and they soon found themselves in a vast hall, where Jeff stopped the vehicle's motors.

He consulted the instruments, darted a rapid glance over the little screen of the radioscope, and checked the sounding apparatus.

"Opening at 500 meters," he announced.

No one said a word as he got under way again, but a terrible apprehension was gripping their hearts.

The vehicle moved forward slowly, then reached an elevated section that lifted them almost up to the rocky vault. They came through the narrow passage thanks to a clever and audacious maneuver on Jeff's part, then abruptly found themselves on a vast arid and deserted plateau, where no wind blew.

A pale luminosity haloed the jagged ridges, and the spectacle they were granted at that moment surpassed in majesty everything that human eyes could have wished to see.

Above them, the rocky crests appeared to fuse with the compact mass composing the extremity of the solid crust of the world they had just quit, and which formed a sort of infinite vault above the gaping and unfathomable gulf that extended between them.

The summit of the gigantic mountain on whose side they had just emerged overlooked a world that still escaped them, and of which they could not, for the moment, have any notion, for it was invisible, drowned in an opaque and luminescent mist.

The shoulders of Atlas supporting the world! Such was the first thought that came into Mary's head with respect to the mountain on which they found themselves, but her mathematical mind quickly rejected that elementary comparison, for the sole viable rationale to explain the unsupported maintenance of the solid crust of the external world found its solution in the direct relationship of the presumably-identical velocities of rotation of the concentric spheres. The inertial forces of each of them nullified those of gravitation, and the hole maintained itself like a filled ball, in accordance with an equilibrium of evenly-distributed forces.

Around the machine there was empty space, a complete and total void, and Jeff took account of that by darting a glance at the atmospheric analyzers, whose indicators remained mute. The external temperature was close to absolute zero. He had no hesitation, therefore; it was necessary not to prolong the halt if they wanted to reach the surface of the new world as quickly as possible.

Jeff steered carefully, and allowed the apparatus to slide down the gentle slope of the mountain, skillfully avoiding the hazards of the terrain that presented themselves in front of them. As they descended, the ambient luminosity increased, to the extent that, after a few hours, the vault above them seemed to be radiating a bright glare.

Manzini offered the hypothesis that this phenomenon must originate in a source of photonic particles retained in the stratum above by a sufficiently strong magnetic field. It followed that the radiation became brighter as one penetrated the layers of air, by reason of the vibrations produced by the electromagnetic particles. Indeed, the first gaseous molecules were registered by the instruments, and a blue-tinted layer of atmosphere soon enveloped the landscape, its upper layers obscuring the highest parts of the compact mass of the exterior solid crust.

The world that they had just reached could not, therefore, experience any alternation of day and night, and an eternal light must undoubtedly bathe all the points of the sphere that the machine was approaching.

Soon, the attentive eyes of the astronauts perceived the configuration of a new surface, with large verdant portions where, in places, other patches appeared, steel-blue in color.

There were no other colors—just green and blue, as far as the eye could see...blue and green, extending to infinity, as if this world only knew two colors, and was ignorant of the rest.

Signs of life appeared gradually around the vehicle; the first tufts of grass were visible in the cracks in the rock—wild, coarse, bright green grass with sturdy stems, undulating softly in a light breeze.

Jeff decided then to fly over the region, in order to find terrain suitable for landing, and the monobloc leapt into the velvety sky, rapidly losing altitude and plunging toward the green and the blue, whose shades were strangely confused in places.

They flew over a large lake, a vast continent, an archipelago, a sea, an island, and then another continent attached to the island by a slender isthmus, on which the vegetation, as everywhere else, seemed to be disputing every inch of ground to conquer it with its vital expanse.

It was Warren who spotted a large grassy area: a prairie isolated within the enormous and colossal vegetal mass that surrounded it, and which offered a perfect landing-ground.

Jeff did not hesitate for another second, and delicately settled the monobloc on the thick grass, cutting the contacts with a sharp sigh of relief. He was exhausted, as were his companions, and it was deemed appropriate to get a few more hours sleep before setting off to explore the unknown world that they had just reached.

"It would be prudent to take turns," Jeff decided. "One never knows."

"You're right," Manzini agreed. "I'll take the first watch with the Professor. You and Miss Davis have the greatest need of sleep—make the most of it, and don't worry; we'll stand guard."

Warren took two blasters out of one of the storage-lockers, and patted the butt of the weapon that he appropriated. "With these, we'll be able to defend ourselves—don't worry." He got out of the vehicle with Manzini, and they began chatting outside the airlock, while Mary and Jeff installed themselves comfortably on the pressurized couchette-seats.

Mary relaxed momentarily, then turned to Jeff and murmured softly: "How are you doing, little brother? I can sense your torment, but its cause escapes me. What's happening? Why are you so unhappy?"

He did not even hear her words, and his lips remained mute. The powerful memory of a marvelous face was still engraved in Jeff's mind, blotting out all other thoughts. There was something like the icy sparkle of millions of stars within him, like the immemorial communication of a distant force that came to him from an anticosmos, whose subtle caress he felt. The desire to drink that enchantment from its source was so strong momentarily that he forgot everything else, even the crucial role that he was playing in this strange adventure.

Then, he suddenly plunged into sleep, and oblivion.

CHAPTER X

A few hours later, when Jeff took his watch with Mary, he waited for Warren and Manzini to install themselves in their turn on the couchettes before drawing the young woman to one side.

"Mary," he said, "since our arrival on Rhea, the two of us haven't had an opportunity to speak freely, so it's necessary that you know now."

Rapidly, he confided to her what he had learned on the subject of New Earth in the course of his transmigration during the night after their arrival. He told her about the fire that had ravaged the Biological Center, and the immense loss represented by the destruction of Warren's secret files concerning the famous synthetic embryo.

He had, in consequence, no more hope on that subject, and he did not hide it from her, even though he was far from approving of Warren's experiment, which he considered, in spite of everything, as a sacrilege against the entire human species.

Mary reflected intensely, then told him what she thought. "In that case, we ought to tell Warren the truth, even if we don't share his point of view. That which God refuses to men, a mere mortal might perhaps accomplish. Yes, Jeff, all this surpasses us and is beyond our comprehension. A boat drifts this way and that when deprived of its rudder, and our human race finds itself in the same situation. Why should Warren not succeed?"

Jeff shook his head forcefully, chased away a few somber thoughts emerging from the depths of his unconscious, and then replied: "Perhaps you're right, after all."

"Nothing is lost. Warren can confide his formulas to you, and you can realize them after recovering your true body on Venus."

"I fear that might be impossible," he sighed.

"Why?"

He smiled faintly, looked at Mary covertly, and then made an abrupt decision. "Because I tried while I was resting, and I couldn't. I can no longer travel back to my own body. Something is preventing me—I can feel it... And I can't do anything about it. It's too strong for me."

An extreme pallor overtook the young woman's face. "But then, Jeff, what will become of your body on Venus?"

"Don't worry; I'm not completely separated from it—but the nervous tension will end up relaxing some day, and then there'll be no more hope. But that's not important for the moment, is it?"

They remained thus for several minutes, motionless and silent, glad to be together and to be able to exchange their ideas and opinions freely. Then, Mary's hand suddenly gripped the young man's. "Jeff," she murmured, "something moved over there, in the trees."

He straightened up, took hold of his weapon, and looked in the direction indicated.

"Between those two giant tree-trunks, behind the bush shaped like a sea-urchin."

"I can't see anything."

"Yes, I'm sure of it. The lianas you can see suddenly moved to the right; the large leaves parted to let them through."

"Probably the wind?"

"It's not strong enough."

To soothe his conscience, Jeff made a circular scan around the vehicle, and took a few steps through the soft grass, but could not see anything abnormal. A few large insects were flying back and forth, but everything seemed calm and reassuring.

He put the trivial incident down to Mary's nervousness, but decided all the same to remain on his guard. As nothing untoward occurred, however, they recovered their confidence until it was time for their companions to wake up.

It was now a matter of beginning the exploration of this vegetable world and trying to find out whether human beings lived here, with a view to attempting to make contact with them. Nothing thus far had given them any hope of such an eventuality, for the first observations they had been able to make had given no indication of the presence of human beings.

First of all, it was necessary to check certain items of apparatus and ensure that they were in working order before undertaking a long excursion, as there was some urgency about renewing their supplies of drinking water, which had diminished considerably in the course of their recent voyage.

Jeff and Manzini took responsibility for these rapid tasks, and decided to inspect the immediate vicinity in the hope of find the liquid element that was in danger of running out. The first priority was to determine whether any water they found was drinkable and posed no danger to their physiology.

Armed with the necessary instruments of verification, the two men headed for the nearest point of the forest and began their search.

The humidity of the soil increased toward the edge of the thick woodland, and pools of water appeared between the mossy stones that they crossed warily, guided by the slight splashing sounds that became increasingly distinct in their ears.

"Over here," said Manzini, who was leading the way.

Jeff followed him to the bank of a stream meandering between aquatic plants anchored in cracks in the rocks, inside which they deployed long fibers bristling with long hairs, which bathed idly in the running water.

Further away, other plants with fantastic forms were growing on the banks of the stream, some of them reminiscent of motionless wax candles and others of giant insects, whose large translucent leaves recalled the wings of dragonflies.

Others seemed to be crouching at the feet of massive gnarled trunks, seemingly supported by paws of a sort, which served them as roots. That, at least, was the impression that

Jeff experienced on seeing them, and that vision made him frown slightly, while a vague apprehension insinuated itself into his heart.

Now, everything that his eyes perceived took on frightful and hallucinatory proportions. The grandiose and marvelous vegetal spectacle suddenly showed its true face, unleashing an insurmountable fear and horror in Jeff—but it was too late. The cry that he uttered did not permit Manzini to avoid the brutal attack of which he was the object, as he leaned over the edge of the stream with his analytical apparatus.

From the invisible depths of the forest, a long muscular stalk had emerged, like an immeasurable neck, coiling tightly around the geophysicist's body. The shock caused him to lose his balance and howl.

The burst of fire launched by Jeff made the green pulp burst asunder and cut through the enormous stem, the severed section of which writhed in a spasm of agony. With one bound, Jeff precipitated himself toward his companion, who was trying to get up, while another plant, flexible and hideous, coiled around another trunk, extended itself with a loud noise of rustling leaves. Its roots and stems were also tongues and whips, which set about thrashing the air violently, with an angry buzz that chilled the blood in the two men's veins.

Vegetable filaments surged forth from a nearby bough, joining in the attack with sinister hissing sounds. Just as Jeff prepared to open fire again, the stem that was lashing him ferociously snatched away his weapon and hurled him against the rocks. That tumble saved his life, for he instinctively rolled sideways, behind the improvised shelter of a rock, while his unfortunate companion was seized by a tentacular sucker with saw-like teeth, which enveloped him completely. Fibrous rootlets contracted in order to reinforce the grip, and in the space of a second, the long tentacle lifted the struggling Manzini into the air and drew him into a cone of shadow, where he suddenly disappeared. There was a horrible scream, abruptly stifled, a frightful noise of breaking bones—and that was all.

Momentarily at a loss, Jeff tried to get to his feet and reach the weapon that he had dropped during his fall, but the muscular dart that struck him full in the face drew a cry of pain from him and knocked him out.

Completely unconscious, he fell to his knees and collapsed full length on the ground, insensible of the drama that was unfolding around him.

When Jeff recovered consciousness, he recognized the faces of Warren and Mary, who were leaning over him. At first, they were only imprecise shapes that were dancing before his feverish eyes, but they soon assumed their real consistency.

Jeff found that he was lying on one of the berths inside the vehicle, and the excruciating pain that he felt in his cheek reminded him of the horrible fight.

In front of him, Warren was still breathing hard, his shirt covered in green stains, whose peppery odor was polluting the cabin. He understood all that he needed to when Mary said to him: "God be praised—the professor got there in time. Oh, Jeff, it's frightful!"

Slowly, he raised himself up on to his elbow and looked at Mary, astonished to hear her pronounce his name in front of the professor—but she continued almost immediately: "I've told him the truth. I had to, Jeff."

Warren placed his hand on Jeff's arm and added: "Yes, it's better that way now." He stood up, took a few steps within the cabin, and shrugged his shoulders heavily. "And to think that it will all be for nothing! It's all my fault…everything!"

Jeff got up with a single movement and made a nervous gesture, which he quickly repressed. "Don't say stupid things—let's try to get out of this, instead—if there's still time."

He headed toward the pilot's station, but came to a sudden stop in front of the large porthole that was facing him. "Great gods!" he thundered. "Is it possible?"

Climbing plants were mounting an assault on the vehicle, and some of them had already succeeded in weaving a tight net around the cabin. The vegetal torrent soon covered the metal, obtaining leverage from vigorous dwarf trees that had appeared, encircling the machine with slow but precise steps. Roots were digging into the soil and anchoring them deeply, while the attacking lianas were visibly swelling to become enormous cables, slick but resistant.

"We have to do something, at all costs," cried Warren, taking up his weapon, ready to rush through the airlock.

"No, don't move!" howled Jeff. "If you open it, we're doomed. Leave it to me."

He raced to the gas taps, and Mary immediately guessed his intention. The first scorching flames that shot out of the nozzles literally carbonized the roots that were beginning to grope beneath the vehicle; then the lianas caught fire in their turn, like torches, behind the portholes. Others were slowly consumed as the intense heat reached them.

Jeff started the motors. The machine trembled, then brutally tore itself free from the network of vegetation, carrying aloft shreds of plants clinging to the metal, which soon disappeared, dispersed by the wind and the displacement of air.

The three survivors felt a sharp relief, but they did not take long to start wondering what would become of them now, on this inhospitable world in which the human species probably did not exist.

Indeed, the plants reigned over all the continents: organized and intelligent vegetables that even humans were powerless to battle. It was, however, necessary for them to find a solution at any price, firstly to finish the repairs that the machinery required.

After due reflection, Jeff decided to set the monobloc down on a moderately wide beach over which they were flying, where, with the aid of active surveillance, they would be able to avoid a surprise attack. There was a risk, but Mary and Warren approved without discussion.

The machine settled gently on the fine sand, a few meters from the waves, which erupted into foam in the breakers.

In front of them was a further deployment of the verdure. Ranks of trees bordered the beach, and in places, veritable walls of living wood held back a parasitic vegetation that was trying to infiltrate itself between the roots and stems of the higher plants.

Leaves fluttered when they came out of the vehicle; some snapped like the jaws of caymans, while others sent their stinging tentacles whistling through the air, or clawed the sand with their toothy roots. But no plant ventured on to the sand, and Jeff had set down well out of their reach. He set to work rapidly, flanked by Mary and Warren, who were ready to make use of their thermic weapons.

After two hours of patient effort, Jeff was finally able to reassure the professor and the young woman. In a few minutes, they would be able to attempt the return journey—but neither he nor the others saw a sticky green streak emerge from the waves and creep over the moist sand like a clumsy snake. The alga had scented its prey and become bold enough to leave the liquid element, extending its length further and further, guided by its instinct of nutrition.

It slid along, crawling cautiously, then accelerated its motion when it was certain of its victory. The long sticky filament stretched itself out and wound around Warren's legs, trying to topple him.

When Jeff and Mary turned round in response to the professor's cries, the long green tentacle was already pulling its prey toward the water's edge. Jeff understood immediately that his thermic weapon would not be any use, for he risked hitting Warren in his present situation. He leapt forward then, promptly pulling the knife from his belt, and threw himself desperately upon the hideous muscular tentacle that had wrapped its green flesh around the professor, cutting through every last fiber.

The noise and odor of the battle had, however, excited the plants that bordered the beach, and when Jeff heard the bursts fired by Mary crackling behind him, he understood that there was no hope this time.

Agile vegetal carnivores plunged over the sand in the direction of the still-palpitating debris of the audacious alga, and sharp jaws set about devouring that unexpected pittance.

Jeff found himself abruptly separated from Warren, who was running along the beach in an attempt to avoid other rapacious plants that were mounting an assault. With one bound, he leapt over a spiny bush, which tore off a few strands of cloth as he went by, then ran toward the vehicle in order to cover Warren's retreat, and also to help Mary in the terrible combat that she was waging all alone in confrontation with a group of gaping mouths, gnarled stems and forked roots.

Jeff wanted to recover his weapon, but could not find it—nor Warren's—because the branches of giant lichens had already invaded the places where they had fallen.

He could see Warren, who was still trying to reach the vehicle, avoiding the brutal assaults of his pursuers as best he could, and, as he launched himself forward to help Mary, what he saw next surpassed in horror anything that he could have imagined.

An urn-like flying plant with frayed edges was beating two muscular leaves ponderously above the young woman's head, able before she could make the slightest gesture, it settled heavily upon her, gripping her with its sinewy roots, lifting her from the beach and trying to drag her away into the crown of one of the large trees. But Mary was struggling furiously, fighting desperately against the sinister vegetable, whose awkward flight seemed to become even more drunken.

Horrified, Jeff saw the flying plant deposit Mary on the gnarled branch of a huge mangrove-tree, and understood that he must act very quickly, or the young woman would be doomed.

It was impossible for him to reach the vehicle. So, impelled by a will superior to his own, he plunged forward, howling with rage and disgust, his long cutlass in his hand, animated by an invincible and almost supernatural strength.

When he passed between the first thick trunks, he saw the flying plant resume its heavy flight overhead, and disappear into the lianas and stems—but he could not see Mary.

Suddenly, he realized his imprudence, his lack of reflection, and the futility of his action. He took account of his situation by turning round and aiming his gaze at the beach, where he saw the young woman, liberated, running to rejoin Warren. He suddenly remembered the strange faculty of teleportation that Mary possessed, and which, once again, had permitted her to extract herself from a delicate situation with no harm done. But what could he have been thinking, to make him forget the ultimate chance that Mary had at that tragic moment?

He shuddered, sensing that he was caught in a trap in the midst of all the surrounding vegetation.

"Don't be afraid; so long as I'm with you, nothing can do you the slightest harm."

He turned round abruptly at the sound of the strange voice that had just resounded behind him. A few paces away, a half-human, half-vegetable creature was swaying gently on its slender stem, in which long tapering legs were fused together. The indescribable silhouette seemed to be enveloped in a cloud of green gold, which simulated hair, and which extended along a corolla whose widespread white petals revealed the delightful sketch of a magnificent face: a face whose eyes, like drops of dew, shone with *unknown colors*. In her large vegetal eyes, where mirages and symphonies were woven together, billions of stars were sparkling with an infinite softness.

"*Marka!*" Jeff howled the name rather than pronouncing it, and he felt love and death delivering themselves to a furious combat within him.

Marka! The pink gash that took the place of her mouth stretched, and an imprecise vanilla-like odor floated into the air around Jeff, annihilating almost all his other thoughts.

A slender and graceful arm lifted him up and held him up beneath the thick vault.

"In that direction, beyond the forest, from high in the air, you'll see a diamond-shaped clearing; the entrance can be found between the rocky masses bordered with fire-plants, but your vehicle will pass over them easily. Go, then, since that is your desire."

Jeff retreated slowly, his eyes riveted to the soft and velvety face that continued to smile at him, and it was not until his feet touched the fine sand of the beach that he came back to himself and turned round. Mary and Warren had cleared the area adjacent to the apparatus, and when he rejoined them, out of breath, in the airlock, Mary murmured: "God be praised, Jeff—you're safe and sound."

He had neither the strength nor the courage to reply, but in Warren's gaze he read the question that the latter was addressing to him. It was also legible in Mary's face, pale and transfigured. He let himself collapse in front of the controls, and confessed: "I know the secret of the passage, but I don't have the right to make the decision alone."

It as Warren who took it upon himself to reply: "There's no reason for us not to continue, as you know full well."

And Jeff started the motors.

The machine landed just in front of the gaping opening of the dark cave, facing the neatly-aligned fire-plants that seemed to be guarding the entrance with a ferocious jealousy.

As soon as the monobloc slid over the wild short grass, it revealed the presence of intruders, and the large transparent leaves pivoted and orientated themselves toward the apparatus, concentrating the luminous rays through their silica and launching an attack.

Around the monobloc the wild grasses were scorched, then burst into flames under the action of the burning rays, but the steel of the machine did not suffer the slightest damage.

Jeff increased his speed, and the metallic mass broke through the vigilant guardians of the cave as it passed.

They found themselves once again complete darkness, but the photon projectors cut through the blackness to reveal a long, sloping rocky corridor similar to the one they had used to reach the world.

It was obvious that the required procedure was identical to the previous one, and once again, Jeff began his maneuvers.

CHAPTER XI

The long spiral tunnel emerged once again on the steep slope of a gigantic peak, where darkness and a complete vacuum reigned supreme.

Here too they found the low temperatures of sidereal space above an unfathomable gulf completely masking the new sphere, which still conserved all its mysteries for the three survivors. The only thing that was different was the absence of luminosity as they descended toward the surface.

The grey obscurity that surrounded the machine conserved its consistency for more than 200 kilometers, and it was not until they came close to the ground that a feeble luminescence began to float around them, without succeeding in dissipating the darkness completely.

This world knew neither daylight nor its burning brightness. A heavy and humid atmosphere surrounded the globe, a few kilometers thick at the most, and those first estimations caused Jeff to furrow his brows. "To go outside the vehicle, it will be wise to equip ourselves with oxygen masks."

"And our thermostatic suits," Mary added, beginning to prepare all that equipment.

The descent continued, still warily, and they finally landed on the surface of the unknown and mysterious world: a hard, arid, almost level ground, with neither cracks nor protrusions, bleak, deserted, gloomy and sinister. There was not a breath of wind, merely a heavy, thick atmosphere that would be difficult to breathe. There was not a sound: nothing but a terrible, distressing, eternal silence.

The monobloc rolled forward, skidded and stopped, while its passengers wondered whether they might be able to go. In every direction there was the same spectacle, devoid of odor, taste, light and sound. It was nothingness materialized.

Jeff, Mary and the professor emerged from the vehicle, still on their guard, and saw broken lines in the soil, which deformed according to the angle at which one looked at them, and which acquired, in the course of their progression, the aspect of bizarre geometric figures with no consistency and no meaning.

It was absurd. Warren bent down to gather a sample of the soil, but his fingers encountered a hard, smooth and rigid material that was impossible to grip.

Jeff tried to reflect and find an explanation, but he did not understand at all, because there was nothing to understand.

With Mary, it was different. For her, this world was even more terrifying than the others, for it refused to remove its mask, and she felt an immense disgust and hatred growing within her, along with the impenetrable mystery that enveloped this nightmare world.

And suddenly, the world exploded. It exploded in all its fury and violence, liberating all its maleficent power and wrath from its entrails. Geysers of vapor sprang from the abruptly heated ground, incandescent lava from the cracking surface. Columns of purple, yellow and blue flames rose up from zigzag crevasses, which set fire to the entire sinister region. And all of it seethed, crackled, whistled and hissed, awaking echoes in a dazzling glow of Dante-esque colors.

Jeff, Mary and the professor huddled together, terrified, fortunately sheltered by their protective suits. They had to get back to the vehicle at all costs, and escape this new trap that had been set for them.

Around them, the soil became mobile, swelling up in numerous bubbles which exploded with a sinister "plop." It was a festival of fire, a satanic unleashing of the flames of the Inferno.

Before the three companions had reached the vehicle, however, the *thing* arrived. At first, it was a sort of compact and formless white mass, which surged forth from beyond the circle of fire, catapulted by an invisible force, violently projected from the dark zone, falling on to the fiery geysers. There was a fountain of vaporous debris, which rebounded from the bloated crust and evaporated in the blink of an eye.

Gripped by panic, the three survivors retreated, but gigantic flames interposed themselves between them and the vehicle. They were like tongues of dazzling fire with human silhouettes: an infernal ballet of flamboyant spectres, so to speak. The fire-creatures undulated in fountains of polychromatic sparks, whipping the air with the burning appendices that served them as arms. And they were all moving, dancing, contorting, gliding over the charred surface with the evident intention of encircling the humans.

An arm of fire lashed out at Warren's protective clothing; he recoiled in terror.

It was then that other phantasmal silhouettes made their entrance on to the stage amid that Luciferian scenery: white forms with massive trunks and thick limbs, which emerged from nowhere and rushed toward the fire-beings. A fantastic battle was joined before the humans' horrified eyes. In the space of a few seconds, the entire flamboyant zone was invaded by creatures of ice, which hurled themselves on their incandescent enemies, attacking from several directions at once.

It was a hallucinatory struggle of ice and fire, in which each of the combatants was sacrificed in advance in the implacable hand-to-hand fight to which the contrary forces delivered themselves.

The ice-creatures launched themselves at selected adversaries, each one hurling the entire mass of its crystals at the base of the flaming vital link that connected a fire-creature to the ground. There was a loud crackle of superheated vapor, as the icy mass liquefied and the flamboyant silhouette was extinguished, vomiting a flood of acrid fumes in one last gush, which poisoned the atmosphere.

Further away, a riposte was produced within a group of flame-beings. Suicidal creatures dispersed, attacking the enemy in force and by surprise, combining in twos or threes to fall upon and ice-creature, which melted rapidly, mingling its vapors with those that continued to float over a battlefield that was as absurd as it was terrible.

The arrival of the ice-creatures, however, saved the humans from certain death, and Jeff dragged his companions behind him when he realized that the fire-beings, precipitated into the conflict, were completely uninterested in their presence and had evacuated the vicinity of the vehicle. They plunged forward then, splashing through a noxious black mud, which the porous soil seemed to be absorbing avidly—but they suddenly ran into two ice-beings that had emerged from behind the machine, and were advancing in their direction.

It was Warren who fired a lethal blast of fire, scything through the massive creatures, which writhed under the bite of the blast and came apart, seething—but others were arriving at a run, surprised by this unexpected attack, which must have seemed to them to be abnormal.

Jeff gave the order to fire, and the thermic weapons were activated. Attracted by the strange and unknown fire, however, 20 flame-creatures plunged in their direction, and Jeff realized that he and his companions had made an error. He understood confusedly, realizing that their true enemies were not the inhabitants of the glacial world, as he had imagined, but those who reigned over the infernal country. He became certain of that when he felt the hot and violent breath of a strange and inhuman thought inside him, which bit into his flesh and soul simultaneously.

He stopped firing and retreated, at a loss, before a fire-monster that glided towards him smoothly. Two dazzling tongues reached out toward him as if to seize him. Jeff saw that the long moving arms were attempting to wrap themselves around him. He also saw the oval and distinctly-outlined head, haloed with a sparkling plume that formed something akin to golden hair, and little blue, red and white flames assembled to form eyes, cheekbones and lips.

The hot thought reached him again, clearer than before, originating from the volcanic creature that met his gaze with its fiery eyes. "It's in the frozen world that you'll find the secret of the next passage, so avoid attracting the wrath of your new allies."

A cry of rage rose from Jeff's throat, but did not escape his lips. Unconsciously, he made ready to launch himself upon the odious creature in a savage and bestial leap, perhaps dictated by hatred...or love, given that it was sometimes very difficult to differentiate the two sentiments. In any case, he could not do it, and while he realized the futility and imprudence of his action, the flamboyant apparition of Marka vanished, coiling like a fiery serpent around the dying column of a geyser.

The avid earth absorbed all of it, and nothing then remained on the surface, except for three panic-stricken humans who were running toward a metal apparatus that was ready to receive them.

The ground continued to unravel beneath the three companions with the same bleak desolation they knew so well. No one in the vehicle spoke, and utter exhaustion was legible in every face.

In the end, Mary could stand it no longer, and when Jeff became stubborn once again in his determination to find the icy world which would be the voyage's terminus in the fourth ring, she raised the subject of Marka. It was stronger than she was.

"But what goal does this creature have in mind? Where is she taking us?"

"Exactly where we've decided to go," Jeff replied. "To the center of the Earth."

Warren furrowed his brows slightly. "On whose orders is she acting, and for what reasons is she acceding to our desire?"

"We'll surely find out before much longer," Jeff said, as if to himself, "when we reach our goal."

"If we get the chance," Mary sighed.

Jeff shook his head with conviction. "We'll get there—that's not what worries me. It's more a matter of what we'll find there."

There was a heavy silence, troubled only by the noise of the softly-humming motors. Then Mary said: "Is she our ally or our enemy?"

To which Jeff replied, without taking account of the ambiguity of his words: "Perhaps both—that's the most terrible possibility of all."

At that moment Warren uttered an exclamation, as he rose from his seat and pointed at the porthole in front of him.

"There! There! Look...the frozen world!"

Indeed, he was not mistaken. The region that they were in the process of overflying had taken on a brighter hue and, after a vertiginous descent, the whiteness of the ground became significant for the three observers, who immediately discovered a new landscape, entirely different from the one they had just left.

Here, ice and snow combined to describe chaotic arabesques on the undulating ground, from which emerged a few masses of compact matter bristling with spikes and fine needles, which the monobloc brushed as it passed by.

The machine set down on a thick, soft layer of loose powdery snow, unagitated by any breath of wind. Around the three survivors, the sad and bleak spectacle of a world frozen to the limits of cold appeared, in all its lugubrious desolation.

Phantasmagorical creatures emerged from their formless shelters courageously, not manifesting the slightest bellicose intention when Jeff decided to get out of the vehicle. Once again, he had to rely on Marka's initiative and allow himself to be guided by events and circumstances, for they had no precise data regarding the opening giving access to the fifth ring.

The curious creatures, endowed with an embryonic sentience, only reacted to an opposing action, and apart from the ice-fire duality, nothing else had any normal significance for them. Thus, it was without the slightest dread that the little group advanced into the midst of those nightmare creatures, whose population had to be very large, to judge by the numerous groups scattered around the apparatus.

The cold was intense and they had to adjust the thermostatic apparatus of their insulating suits. They were convinced that something was going to happen at any moment, and a further incident would provoke the discovery of the secret passage. But nothing happened, and when Jeff, Mary and Warren arrived at the foot of an enormous glacier, they stopped indecisively, hesitating as to which way to go—and yet, they were close to their objective; they knew it.

Creatures dragged themselves ponderously in front of them, passing by without even noticing them; others crouched in crevasses and cracks, becoming immobile and insensitive to everything.

Then a vague light appeared at the base of the glacier, seemingly coming from a crevasse; the phenomenon attracted Jeff's attention, and he made a sign to his two companions. All three accelerated their pace and rapidly reached the faintly-lit section, which opened into a narrow passage in the side of the glacier itself.

They ventured into after a slight hesitation, and suddenly found themselves in a sort of grotto, the vault and floor of which were bristling with enormous stalactites and stalagmites of ice, like cruel and pointed teeth ready to bite them and tear them apart.

In the middle of the grotto, a fire-being was undulating between the frozen ridges, displacing itself with precise and measured movements. They followed it in silence, intrigued by its behavior, and Jeff soon recognized Marka's flamboyant apparition. She immediately attacked the stalactites and stalagmites at the back of the cavern, and the icy needles started melting at her contact. Then tongues of fire licked the ground, which began to liquefy rapidly in the intense heat. Jeff observed the stubborn ardor that Marka devoted to her strange work. It did not take him long to realize what her goal was.

By degrees, she proceeded to clear the orifice of a secret corridor obstructed by the ice, and a small opening soon appeared in the midst of the compact blocks that were melting and deforming beneath the repeated assaults of tongues of fire.

After a few minutes, the passage was entirely liberated, and a large dark opening was sketched out in the depths of the cavern, at the same time as the scorching breath of Marka's thoughts reached Jeff's brain.

"The passage is free now. Take it, since that is your desire."

The dazzling apparition faded in its turn, the flamboyant tongues dying on the edge of the orifice and vanishing in an ultimate splash of multicolored sparks.

CHAPTER XII

At the exit from the serpentine tunnel, Jeff braked the propulsion motors to guide the monobloc carefully through the gaping orifice that plunged vertically above the upper layers of the fifth ring.

What did this unknown world have in store for them? They dared not think about that, conserving in spite of everything the hope that they invested in Marka, whose true intentions still escaped them.

This time, the situation presented itself differently, and when the monobloc came to rest on the rim of the orifice, they saw no solid support linking the limits of the crust to the surface of the world on which they had to land, and which remained invisible to their eyes, drowned in a consistent violet mist.

The three humans remained indecisive for a moment, Jeff hesitating to propel the machine into the void. Then, suddenly, something emerged from the nothingness: a gigantic mass whose colossal proportions frightened them momentarily.

The thing was moving through the void with extreme slowness, seemingly licking the solid vault of the fourth ring, advancing n the direction of the orifice.

It seemed to Jeff, Mary and the professor that, this time, it was the mountain that was moving, without and fixed support, offering them its moving link between two strange worlds, precisely executing the maneuver necessary to take charge of the apparatus.

When the dark mass came level with the monobloc. Jeff started the motors and the vehicle slid over the strange flexible and rugged matter presented by one of its edges, in the form of a canal, and descended a gentle slope toward he invisible surface.

When the descent began, they estimated that about 200 or 300 kilometers of empty space separated them from the solid crust. A strange luminosity enveloped them as they advanced along the moving canal, which was sometimes tinted mauve, sometimes violet, sometimes dark red or indigo—but all the colors ended up melting together and combining to form a purplish hue, whose sickening viscosity drew a grimace of disgust from Mary's lips.

The air became breathable, although laden with fetid vapors that stung the eyes and gave rise to nausea.

The heart of the Earth was opening up, increasingly mysterious and menacing The humans required a strong dose of courage to continue their route, which brought them closer to the new stage with every passing moment—but Jeff continued to remain master of himself when he realized that the soft canal had made contact with the surface.

The monobloc rolled on for a few hundred meters more, over a few hillocks bristling with long, hard and rigid stalks, which presumably constituted the vegetal species of the interior planet. Abrupt crests were surmounted; damp valleys and sticky plains were crossed, and then, as he had done in the superior circles, Jeff brought the vehicle to a halt.

In the place where they found themselves, the landscape conserved the same absurdity and the same atrocious color, which seemed to cling to the ground like the heavy mists above the marshes of Venus.

Without forgetting their thermic weapons, Jeff and Warren got out of the machine, but deemed it more prudent to leave Mary inside. She was perfectly familiar with the operation of the monobloc, and would always be able to rejoin her companions in case of danger.

The two men ventured slowly to the summit of a small, bloated hill, and inspected the surroundings.

As far as the eye could see, there was desert, solitude and desolation, but when Warren went down the slope in order to reach another protrusion, Jeff heard him shout: "Come here, Jeff! Quickly!"

The young man left his observation-post and rejoined the scientist, who was pointing at the ground at his feet. Jeff felt faint tremors, originating from the ground, and frowned. The rhythm appeared to be regular, although very feeble.

They walked on, their senses alert; then the tremors became clearer and me perceptible. One might have thought them the effects of a distant pulsation: the beating of a gigantic heart, whose regular rhythm was making the entire surface of the soft ground vibrate.

Warren looked at Jeff for a long time before making up his mind, and then took off his protective gloves. With a trembling hand he felt the rough and flexible mass of the porous ground into which their feet sank slightly. When he raised his head again, Jeff saw that he was pale. The expression that passed over the professor's features caused a trickle of cold sweat to run down the young man's back.

"Well, say something," he said.

But Warren seemed terrified, to the point of being unable to reply. Then Jeff repeated the gesture with his own hands, and realized in his turn the nature of the unknown ground.

His fingers touched a supple, warm and quivering mass, and that hideous contact drew a dull moan of disgust from him. The matter composing the ground was purely organic. They had reached a world whose surface was nothing but flesh...living flesh: the flesh of an enormous creature whose body constituted the entire planet.

When they were back aboard the vehicle, Jeff and Warren bought the young woman up to date with their strange discovery, and a momentary hesitation overtook the three companions, who did not know what to do next.

This time, they had the impression of finding themselves in an inescapable impasse, and a sentiment of despair overwhelmed them.

On Warren's advice, the vehicle took off again and flew over a considerable part of the living, quivering sphere, saturated with mauve radiations and warm vapors—which, according to the professor, must constitute the sole elements of nutrition indispensable to the colossal and solitary creature.

Enormous moving tentacles emerged from the gelatinous spheroid and reached up into the air, loin themselves in the somber colors of the sky and continuing untiringly to lick the vault that kept them prisoner.

The enormous entity had reached its extreme limits, and its sensitivity had become almost non-existent. It had not reacted at all when the reactors had spat out their flames at the moment of take-off, charring a few square meters of its soft epidermis. Similarly, nothing happened when the vehicle landed for a second time between two large pores in the form of basins.

All three of them got out, their weapons slung over their shoulders, and Jeff pointed to a fatty crease that formed a ledge between two valleys bristling with long hairs reminiscent of enormous steel needles. The opening was large enough to allow them passage, and for a moment Jeff thought they had found the escape route.

"Let's take a look," he proposed, taking the lead.

They had to switch on the little photon-projectors fixed on top of their helmets in order to orient themselves inside he dark tunnel, whose walls were covered in blood-red encrustations.

They advanced further, to emerge abruptly into an immense gallery that probably measured more than fifty meters across.

Jeff, who was leading the way, felt his heart skip a beat in his breast, and instinctively took hold of Mary's arm to stop her moving forward.

A faint light was flickering within the space; the air was thick, sticky and suffocating—and bathing in all that, eggs as large as beer-barrels were heaped up pell-mell, held together with the aid of an adhesive secretion.

Further away, some of these eggs had broken shells, and the monstrous creatures that had hatched out were lurching weakly on a multitude of tiny feet.

Although they were not in danger, the three humans took a step back before the spectacle that presented itself to them in all its horror.

They moved along the uneven wall of the chamber and came into another, even vaster, cluttered with more eggs, this time speckled with red and green, some of which had already liberated larvae reminiscent of giant worms. A round mouth opened at one end, where two globular organs of an unknown kind hung down.

"We're in an incubation chamber, that's undeniable," said Warren, "but where can these eggs come from, and what's the point of all this?"

As Mary opened her mouth to reply, the movement that Jeff made, pivoting on his heels, made the other two turn round. "Look out!" he cried, in a muffled voice.

In font of hem, emerging from a dark tunnel, an enormous caterpillar undulated in their direction, its antennae quivering. A large and powerful horny beak began to click dryly, and bushes of multicolored eyes gleamed intensely.

Warren was not mistaken. It was indeed an incubation chamber, and the creature that had appeared before them was the female that had laid her eggs in the body of the nutritious entity.

The deep wound excavated in the living flesh appeared to present some analogy with the life-cycle of certain insects that had existed on the surface of the Earth before the cataclysm—a cycle that consisted for the female of paralyzing the nutritive organism and depositing its own eggs in the inflicted wound in order that the carnivorous larvae, once hatched, would have an abundant supply of fresh meat.

Without hesitation, Jeff fired, and the head of the caterpillar exploded in the middle of the immense hall—but the rest of its ringed body blocked the corridor, and Jeff, for reasons of prudence, decided to avoid employing the terrible caloric rays.

"First, let's try to determine whether there's another exit," he said to his companions, while trying to get his bearings.

In the next chamber they went through, other amorphous and legless larvae were clinging to the encrusted walls with the aid of a ventral foot, which served them as a sucker.

In yet another chamber, a dozen small animals with abdomens striped with green and yellow silks, clicked their jaws as they devoured the living flesh of the walls where they clustered with sickening avidity. Their bodies were soft and tender, and gave off a strong chlorinated odor that was utterly horrible. A few, disturbed in their meal, flapped around in fury and fear as the Terrans passed through their midst to reach another gallery that might perhaps lead to the exterior—but they fell between Scylla and Charybdis, for the large chamber at the end of the tunnel was occupied by two enormous monsters standing guard over their clutches.

As they entered, the jealous and watchful females leapt up on their long legs, revealing large, staring eyes beneath their vertical eyelids, as red as the living flesh of the walls.

They advanced threateningly, weighed down by the enormous seminal vesicles they were dragging along the ground. Their beaks clicked, and the noise brought forth an echo in Jeff's brain. Without pausing for thought, he fired several bursts, although his weapon was almost empty.

There was a fountain of viscous entrails, half-charred, which spattered the walls while the body of the first female exploded like a pricked balloon. The armored head of the second met the same fate, and noxious shreds rained down on the humans, who were on the brink of nausea.

The bursts of fire, however, as Jeff had feared, also reached the palpitating flesh of the nutritive entity, splitting the walls and opening new wounds. A rush of thick blood sprang from a gaping wound, a torrent of blood that soon expanded as far as the feet of the three humans, semi-paralyzed by horror and terror.

"This way!" cried Jeff, turning round and dragging the young woman behind him.

Their only hope now was to clear the cavity that was still blocked by the remains of the caterpillar, but the flood of viscous blood was already pouring into the gallery, and they were beginning to wade through a noxious mire. Panic-stricken, they cleared a way through the hungry larvae that barred the route, using their weapons in the attempt to gain precious time.

Abdomens were split open, and soft feet dislodged by the sanguinary current that continued to pour out of the wound. The bursts of gunfire crackled, killing and killing without respite anything that stood between the humans and the external openings. The larvae died, writhing and thrashing. Shells exploded; beaks clattered.

When they finally arrived, wading thigh-deep through the bloody pulp, at the charred remains of the caterpillar, Jeff and Warren soon succeeded in clearing the tunnel, and they all raced desperately toward the surface.

Two caterpillars and three other monsters of various species were running through the valleys, evidently attracted by the odor of the battle.

"To the vehicle, quickly!" Warren cried, leading the way while Jeff supported Mary, who was completely exhausted and out of breath.

They reached the monobloc in record time, and Jeff launched it into the air with a rapid maneuver. They observed then that they were in a lamentable state, covered in blood, with fragments of flesh clinging to their garments. Their first concern was to devote themselves to a thorough wash and a complete change of clothes, which they did by turns, one of them always remaining on watch over the progress of the machine.

But where were they going now? What would happen next? There was still no clue to point them in the direction of the next exit.

Below them, there was still the same frightful spectacle of living flesh extending to infinity.

The monobloc was completing its third circumnavigation of the fifth ring when the contours of the surface suddenly attracted Jeff's attention. Seen from this height, the region over which they were flying, with its vales, depressions and chaotic encrustations, gave the collective impression of the body of a gigantic woman lying on her back.

Mary and the professor made the strange and rather surprising comparison in their turn. The two depressions with multicolored glints that formed the eyes were staring eternally at the sky, with an expression of immortal patience. Two perfectly-rounded mountains formed the harmoniously-shaped breasts. The roundness of the arms and legs was represented by neatly-curved folds, and when the monobloc swerved slightly to go around the extraordinary sculpture, the curve of an admirably slender thigh was revealed.

A whole host of other details was gradually revealed, in a gigantic and monstrous beauty, with a well-developed torso and a slender neck...and still that face was looking up at the sky, its limpid eyes staring at the machine.

Fascinated, Jeff had already understood that the eyes were Marka's—a Marka whose grandiose beauty he was now able to admire, which she offered to him without shame, on the immeasurable scale of her passion or hatred. He was trying, however, to maintain his self-control and repel all the absurd and inhuman thoughts that rose up to assail his mind when he heard Warren exclaim: "The right hand! Look!"

Indeed, one sole finger was not curled over: the index finger, which seemed to be pointing, with precision, at something that they could not yet see. No more was required, however, for Jeff to understand the mute message addressed to them.

Marka was indicating the exact direction of the secret corridor.

The monobloc drew closer to the surface, almost brushing the twin mountains of the colossal statue's breasts, and flew along the long arm to the extremity of the extended index finger.

When they landed, all beauty had disappeared from that swollen appendage, which formed a scaly and encrusted pleat, and they preferred to turn their eyes away so as not to be gripped by nascent horror again.

A few meters away, a moderately broad fissure opened in the palpitating flesh of the entity, and they were immediately sure that it was the escape route.

The monobloc plunged into it, and was engulfed in the fold, which swallowed them immediately...

CHAPTER XIII

The thermic rays made a considerable contribution to drilling the living cylinder appropriated by the machine, opening large breaches when the way became too narrow, inflicting wounds on the insensible monster. The solid crust finally appeared, and the usual procedure led the vehicle to the ultimate limit of the rocky rind.

A deep sigh of relief was exhaled from their oppressed lungs when the exterior orifice was reached, but they wondered privately what this new stage had in store for them.

Beyond the orifice, a dazzling light greeted the monobloc when it emerged from the dark corridor.

The grandiose and magical spectacle presented to them surprised them, so completely unexpected was it.

There was no mountain or connecting link between the two worlds, nor any rocky escarpment, dark void or immeasurable vacuum.

Beneath them, a planet resplendent with light and sparkling colors was perfectly visible, scarcely veiled in places by a few masses of light cloud.

Warren's scientific mind rapidly revealed the mechanism of this little universe in miniature, equipped with its own "sun"—if one could give that name to the round and blinding mass suspended in the void, whose proportions were fairly large.

The molten mass maintained itself in the circular space scarcely 30 kilometers from the outer edge of the solid crust from which it had just emerged, and completed a slow revolution around the sixth ring, procuring that world an alternation of days and nights: an inverse mechanism within a constant relativity, since it was, in the case of this world, the sun that was a satellite of the planet around which it rotated.

There was, in consequence, no reason why the vehicle should not employ its usual means to reach the welcoming surface presented to it, and Jeff promptly decided to do so.

The monobloc described a slow spiral through the clear sky and came closer to the ground.

Vast quadrilaterals appeared, with other curious checkered assemblages within them. It was as if vast grids were marked out in the ground itself, each gap disappearing into the interior of a rind. They extended as far as they eye could see, separated from one another by strips of land of varying width.

Finally, a vast city appeared, spread out like a chessboard, bristling with high buildings, massive and compact, which conferred a certain grandeur on the whole. A human, or humanoid, civilization obviously existed on this world.

Although that observation reassured the survivors somewhat to begin with, it was not long before a disturbing suspicion gripped their hearts. Was the presence on this world of people, or at least of intelligent creatures, really more desirable than that of monsters like those encountered in the superior circles?

They dared not explore the deeper implications of that question, all the more so because the monobloc was settling gently on to a wide strips of land on the fringe of the vast megalopolis.

Human forms appeared outside the nearest buildings, seemingly ignoring the machine's presence. When Jeff got out of the vehicle on his own, none of the creatures appeared to notice his presence. There were men and women, scantily dressed, making precise and regular gestures, with no superfluous movements, with no sign of confusion or disorder.

Jeff called out to some of them, but none replied to his appeals. Irritated, he turned to Warren, who had joined him. "They don't even hear us. What might that signify?"

"They don't see us either, that's for sure," he professor observed, with a frown.

At an exclamation from May, they turned to see a group of humanoids approaching the vehicle, but before Jeff and

Warren were able to intervene, the most fantastic event occurred. The creatures passed through the machine, like vaporous phantoms, and continued their progress without appearing to pay any heed to the strange phenomenon that had just transpired.

The three companions understood then that no interaction whatsoever was possible with this human race, with whom they could not make any contact.

When Jeff had the idea of steering the vehicle through the building that stood at the end of the track, he felt Mary's hand clench on his shoulder—but he was not mistaken. The machine penetrated the stone construction without the slightest damage, passing clean through it without any hindrance.

"This is quite incomprehensible," Warren whispered. "And the alternatives that present themselves to us are rather disturbing—which is to say, whether we still exist, or whether it's his world that has no real existence."

In front of them, the life of the city continued before their eyes, and a shudder of panic shook the humans at that thought—but the real and concrete presence of the vehicle they possessed, as well as all the objects belonging to them, permitted them to look at the question from another angle.

In effect, the fundamental difference was between that which existed on this world, and that which was foreign to it: that was the barrier. But the problem was by no means as simple. When they landed again on the border of the city, the little mammals with doglike bodies and ratlike heads that they encountered fled rapidly, frightened by their approach. That was utterly confusing and beyond all comprehension.

All three of them left the vehicle and repeated the experiment on a couple of little animals, which looked at them fearfully and prudently beat a retreat on seeing them, while the same animals seemed insensible to the presence of the phantom creatures that were all around them.

Mary reflected intently, then issued a hypothesis: "These animals are the true masters of this world, I'm certain of it," she said, "and it's all the rest that's false and unreal. That's why neither they nor we can make can make any contact with this fake civilization."

Her reasoning seemed sound, and he two men agreed. "Now we need to discover what all this is hiding," Jeff added, "and I'm determined to figure it out. Let's avoid exposing ourselves unnecessarily—stay on board and don't worry about anything."

He picked up his weapon and added: "I won't be gone long; I'm just going to cast an eye over the surroundings."

He leapt lightly to the ground, and headed for the phantom city.

Marka was waiting for him in the city center. He had an intuition of that as soon as he had crossed the city limits, and the route he followed seemed to be indicated by a will superior to his own.

He had been familiar with the effects of that supernatural force since his first encounter with the mysterious creature, so he was not astonished to see the marvelous image of Marka appear to him. She was waiting at the entrance of an enormous building, austere and rigid, which contrasted in its coloring and symmetry with the surrounding edifices.

She was human this time—terribly human—and in her true proportions. "I've been waiting for you," she told him, simply, with a profound smile on her shapely red lips.

She came forward, almost making contact with him, and he took an instinctive step backwards.

"Have no fear," she said, reassuringly, placing a material hand on his arm. "Come in—it's time."

He followed her, fascinated, going with her into the building, which appeared to him to have lost its immateriality to become, like Marka, real and substantial.

They went along a bizarrely decorated corridor, ornamented with geometric figures that were too esoteric for his human senses, and finally went into a large room in which a vague sugary odor floated. She sat him in a chair whose sculpted feet were enormous claws, and whose wood was as black as the unfathomable voids of the cosmos.

She looked at him for a long time, and strange gleams danced in her fiery eyes. Then she said, simply: "You and your friends have reached the terminus of your voyage. That's what you wanted, isn't it?"

He nodded his head slightly, and continued staring at her intently. Then he asked: "Who are you?"

The question brought a cruel smile to the creature's carmine lips. "I belong to another world—to another universe—and I rule yours."

"You?"

"Yes, me, and those of my race. We can adopt any form or appearance whatsoever, at will. We're symbiotic beings, as you've had the opportunity to observe."

"That's what the old sage said on the continent of the Happy."

"He told the truth."

"Why do you cling to this world?"

Marka did not appear to comprehend the meaning of this question, whose implication escaped her. "This world belongs to us. We have been its masters since the beginning of Time, since we defeated the opposing Powers."

Jeff blanched suddenly, still hesitant to accept the horrible truth. "Those of God?" he asked, weakly, with a slight movement of recoil.

The maleficent creature seemed shocked by his attitude, and shook her head slightly. "How dare you speak of something of which you know nothing, and which you cannot even imagine? What image do you have, then, of the Superior Powers?"

"Good and Evil, Witchcraft and Sanctity, Purity and Perversion—those are the only images I know."

"But you're incapable of locating where Good resides, or where Evil resides, for you're only contradictory creatures. Good and Evil surpass the natural limits of the mind and escape your consciousness. You're scarcely capable of discriminating between Good from Evil, on the grounds that each hates the other—but that's purely fortuitous. There are perverted gods, and virtuous demons."

She took a step in his direction and added: "Even the Devil can appear chaste on occasion."

"For love of Good or dread of obscenity?" Jeff replied, dryly.

"I'm simply playing with ideas. Above all, don't be scornful of the names I employ, for they belong to human language. We have other terms to symbolize the superior Powers of which you know nothing, and there's nothing supernatural in the spiritual domain with which, unknowingly, you have coexisted since the beginning of Time. Do you *really* know whether it exists? Does a spider or fish know that humans exist? Absolutely not—and you're in the same situation."

Slowly, she went toward a heavy and massive door occupying the center of a paneled wall, and said: "Now, open your eyes and mind. Try to understand and accept."

He drew nearer as she opened the door, utterly fascinated by the demonic gaze that remained riveted to his own; then Marka's image seemed to dissolve, and he suddenly found himself confronted by an unfathomable gulf, which plunged into a void beyond the dark opening.

Then an assemblage of multicolored geometric figures sprang forth, which began to rotate around a sort of dot that was more luminous still. The whole abruptly took on the appearance of a mirrored sphere with an almost intolerable glare.

Jeff felt himself drawn toward mystical illumination and absolute contemplation, further than religious, poetic or musical ecstasy, toward the malefic sources of the infernal powers of an anticosmos that exploded in all its spiritual horror. He had the impression of yielding to the sublime and superhuman, and of having opened a door on the mystery of an unknown darkness that he had never yet suspected and to which there was no longer any logic.

A gigantic maelstrom submerged him, and moving images unraveled within him in a vertiginous dance originating from the "transfinite instrument" that he sensed being animated by the Superior Wills.

Jeff felt the glacial breath of the void and the torrid heat of distant suns. He saw metallic and phosphorescent oceans, ecstatic shadows, rivers of stone and fire in which multitudes of serpents with scales of steel battled one another.

Processions of the dead, emerging from the depths of centuries, bore with them the dampness of graves.

He saw the scintillating ring of Saturn, gigantic emitter of maleficent waves, and he saw the long corridor which linked that world to the Earth—and in that corridor he distinguished he damned shades of the dead drawing away in time and space, rendered more-or-less transparent.

And the horrible and atrocious Truth appeared to him simultaneously.

The masters of that world were entities of formless gas, infiltrating the environment that suited them, nourishing themselves on souls and not on flesh and blood, and they were ready to do anything at all to obtain it. He saw in them the specters of the victims they had destroyed: faces and silhouettes borne away through the darkness and the void.

That was the fate of all the human beings who still lived on the surface of the sixth ring—and he understood that it had been identical for the people of his race, his distant ancestors of the seventh ring, destroyed in the catastrophe...ever since the origin of humankind.

Jeff also took account of the terrible struggle that opposed the powers of Evil to those of Good for the conquest of this world, although Evil was rooted there with all its demonic power. He understood the Machiavellian plan conceived by the extraterrestrial entities, who had never ceased, throughout the centuries and millennia, to influence the minds of humans, inciting the latter to fight atrocious, destructive and terribly murderous wars. He was conscious of epidemics, cataclysms, massacres and all the scourges that had struck humankind since its emergence.

The immeasurable appetite of the gaseous entities had no limits, and the supreme attempts conceived by the adverse powers had all resulted in complete failure, in spite of the sacrifices imposed on their delegates.

The Fall...*the terrible Fall*, extrapolated to infinity, and annihilated in the absurdity of the Great All.

Jeff also knew that the cataclysm that had destroyed the seventh ring had been a desperate move by the forces of Good, thus giving surviving humankind the hope of an eternal safeguard on the soil of Venus—for Venus was still inaccessible to the infernal creatures, who did not have any installation in the core of that planet appropriate to their needs.

He saw these installations in the transfinite instrument that continued to function at a vertiginous pace. Psychic receivers carpeted the ground of the ultimate sphere, on which he had just landed. It was like an immense checkered network, each orifice of which captured the psychic substances originating from the human victims of death.

The strange apparatus drew that immaterial nourishment through the concentric spheres, subsequently to direct them to the central nucleus, which operated as a colossal energetic core responding to the needs of the gaseous entities. The surplus was transmitted along the wave-tunnel linking Earth to Saturn, and the Saturnian base, in its turn, communicated the precious vital energy toward the directorial centers of another Universe.

As for the phantasmal beings encountered on this sphere after the monobloc's arrival, Jeff finally understood why there could not be any possible contact between them and human beings. They were creatures called to develop their faculties of mimicry: the terrible shock-troops initiated to human appearance, of which they only possessed the immaterial image as yet, but which would eventually become consistent by virtue of patience and perseverance.

Suddenly, the rotating luminous ball vanished; everything became blurred, faded, diluted, melted and extinguished.

When Jeff resumed contact with reality, he found himself confronted once again by the image of Marka, whose false angelic purity horrified him. He could only see her eyes: eyes that could do anything, and which penetrated him like icy blades, to his innermost depths.

"Now I know," he said. "I know…but why have you revealed all these secrets to me?"

She made a tired gesture, and said, in a dull tone: "Because you belong to me and I don't want to lose you."

He felt himself blanch, and still refused that which his soul accepted. "Marka," he murmured. "It's impossible…"

He was under her spell, and knew it, but there was such supplication and sincerity in those eyes! At that moment, there was nothing terrifying about her, but a great deal of warmth, generosity and attractiveness.

"I beg you, accept or you're doomed—eternally doomed. Do you understand?"

"But I'm a human, Marka—I'm a human."

"I can save your soul. There's still time."

He suddenly experienced a mad desire to embrace her and to liberate, at a stroke, all the burning passion that had been seething within him since the first day he had met her—but that was beyond his strength. He could not do it.

She—not she, but *it*, he told himself—had tears in her eyes, and when he straightened up before her there was a sort of religious terror in the gesture that she made. "I'm not your enemy," she stammered. "I don't wish you any harm…"

That surpassed human understanding. He felt the horror of that sacrilegious love and murmured dully: "How dare you?"

"I don't know…I don't know… For the last time, I beg you, accept. If you don't, we're both doomed. I won't be pardoned for my weakness."

Jeff suddenly understood that time was precious, and that he had to respond.

"I surrender myself to you, Marka," he said. "Dispose of my soul as you see fit; I abandon it to you—but on one sole condition. Save my friends and permit them to return to the surface—you have no rights over them."

She smiled palely. "It will only be a stay of execution. Sooner or later, they'll be condemned."

"Let them live for a while yet."

He saw her struggling against her rules, her laws, her principles and her nature. Then she said: "Go, and assure them of my protection until they return to the surface. But hurry...if my superiors ever learn of this treason, that would be terrible. Quickly, I beg you."

Without hesitating for another second, Jeff raced outside the building, plunged through the phantom city and soon arrived within sight of the monobloc, still stationed in the same place.

He sensed the anxiety of Mary and Warren when they saw him again, but neither of them asked him any questions when he told them to leave without him.

He was short of time, and he contented himself with acquainting them, in a few sentences, with the plan contrived by the extraterrestrials, and then he confided to hem: "Soon, other ships will come from New Earth to land on Rhea. A new human race will be founded on this world, for without being aware of it, we're subject to the attraction of the maleficent powers. They must be told...and must liberate themselves by destroying the Saturnian installations. And there's no one but you who can transmit the secret of that deliverance—no one but you! Go! The way is open to you. Accomplish this supreme mission."

He shook the hand that was extended to him, effusively, then turned to Mary. There was an infinite sadness in her smile, and an atrocious dolor.

"Jeff..." she breathed.

"No," he said. "It's impossible..."

And he went through the airlock.

CHAPTER XIV

The monobloc reached the rocky vault of the outermost ring.

It was at that moment that Warren, to his consternation, observed that, during a mistaken maneuver which had almost thrown the vehicle against the solid mass, the little test-tubes containing the experimental germ-cells had been broken inside their case, destroying their precious contents forever. All except...ONE: that of the synthetic and universal germ-cell, whose cracked tube had partially resisted the shock.

But that was only a question of hours—perhaps minutes—and the life would be snuffed out sooner or later, when its prison of glass gave way.

"There's no more hope," he said. "And yet I'm certain that this is our humankind's only chance."

He felt the pressure of Mary's hand, which was placed on his shoulder. "No," she said, "nothing is lost, since I'm here. That being must live, and he shall live. Conduct the experiment on me. It's the only thing I want, now."

Warren looked at the young woman for a long time, and nodded his head. "Yes," he said, finally, with force and conviction. "He shall live...he shall live..."

A few minutes later, everything was ready for the delicate experiment. Warren hesitated for a fraction of a second longer, and looked at Mary, happy and confident. She had just lain down on her berth.

Then, resolutely, Warren's syringe plunged into the interior of the test tube.

When Jeff came back into the room Marka was waiting for him. Wall-hangings with gold embroidery emanated perfumes of amber and iris. She was savoring her victory.

"Now I belong to you. What do you intend to do with me?"

"To make you immortal, as I am and as our love is. Our souls will become one, but for that it's necessary to separate you from that material pelt of which you have no further need. Only your spirit can reach the final stage—which is to say, the central nucleus where all our energies are concentrated."

"Marka, I fear that might not be possible. Our souls will never fuse. They're too different from one another. You've forgotten that."

"Why do you say that? Sanctity demands too great an effort. You're only a human, like all the rest, and that effort is not within your scope."

She laughed, for the first time, very sure of herself; then a gesture swept aside a purple wall-hanging, revealing a large opalescent rectangle that Jeff initially assumed to be a mirror.

It was a mirror, but not an ordinary one. The material of which it was composed was fluid, and the interior of the rectangle seemed to extend to infinity in a pale off-white coloration.

"This mirror doesn't reflect matter at all. It's a psychic mirror. Come forward and look at the image of your consciousness and your soul."

He went forward and looked.

He could not see anything—nothing but the eternal fluid off-white coloration.

What could he have seen, *since there was nothing to see?*

His soul was too pure and transparent to be reflected in the mirror—and the scream that Marka uttered as she realized that was terrible.

"No," she moaned. "No...it's not possible. So that's why I never succeeded in fathoming your thoughts...but what kind of being are you, then?"

She was the one who recoiled now, frightened—even horrified. "Where have you come from? Who are you? Why do you have the image of our eternal enemies?" He looked at her uncomprehendingly, but she continued, absolutely terrified: "No, no...it's impossible...you can no longer enter the final sphere. That would be terrible...terrible..."

He went toward her slowly, frowning. "Why? Come on, answer me!"

"The slightest element of contrary force might provoke a catastrophe and disrupt our energetic equilibrium."

He was almost holding his breath. "With you or without you, Marka, I shall enter."

"*They* won't let you through the barrier. No, they'll prevent you from doing so."

"I'm the one making demands of you now, Marka. Guide me. Guide me!"

At that moment, he was sincere. No longer caring about Good or Evil, beyond the most violent hatreds and passions, he wanted and desired her presence, an intimate and eternal union with an implacable power."

Beyond Good and Evil, Love carried him away.

She ran to him and threw herself into his arms, vanquished and transfigured.

It was at that precise moment that Professor Warren, in the monobloc, injected the synthetic germ-cell into Mary's flesh.

Jeff had the impression of a experiencing a terrible blow, which bruised his soul and his flesh simultaneously. He suddenly became conscious of the frightful reality. The last link that still united him with his own body, left behind on Venus, had just been broken. He felt its tension ease and abruptly relax, and he understood that death had already done its work on his body on Venus.

He tried to recover his equilibrium, but in spite of his efforts, none of the muscles in Landry's body responded. The heart ceased beating and the inert mass of flesh and bone fell on the soft carpet of the room at Marka's feet, while Jeff experienced the same sensation he had felt before during his projection into the immense void of the cosmos.

Death had struck him for a second time, and he realized that while he tried to overcome the profound malaise that gripped his mind. He did not understand the reasons for the brutal coincidence, for they escaped him, and he was only conscious that he now had to do what he had decided to do.

He saw and sensed Marka's mind, also completely liberated, drawing him into the vertiginous gulf in which it was united with his own.

The sensation was simultaneously intoxicating and terrible. It was a plunge into the incredible, immemorial world of a race that had succeeded in vanquishing death itself.

Black whirlwinds sprang from the gulf, thunder roared in the midst of fiery lightning-flashes. A biting wind blew violently, but those sensations were purely human and Jeff interpreted them unconsciously as he had had always known them while alive.

Then the décor changed; the black became grey and the noises faded into silence. Marka and he were walking over a moving ground of dust and heavy vapors.

Other entities set foot in their turn on the moving ground, projected toward he energy centers: cargoes of souls poured out by the receivers of the sixth ring, which would swell the psychic reservoirs of the nucleus. Shadows were coming and going, some still bearing the imprints of the bodies they had possessed, which were rotting somewhere in damp soil, eaten away by vermin. But vermin were also eating away this infernal world, which seemed to be bathed in bloody moonlight.

On the purple horizon outlined in the distance, hallucinatory forms were jostling one another, winged clouds with grimacing faces, unraveling only to appear in other, even more hallucinatory forms. They were the Masters of this world, and Jeff saw them for the first time, with their long smoky figures, faceless, celebrating the mysteries of their worship, busy with multiple tasks, guiding and directing the newcomers, in the immense enjoyment of a power that they knew to be inviolable and invincible.

At least, it had been—until today…

Jeff's mind perceived the directives given by Marka's.

"Let's go on," she demanded. "We're still only in the external fringes. Let's cross over."

They arrived there without hindrance, and at the moment of the crossing, Jeff felt all the pain and suffering that Marka was experiencing. It was that of thousands of generations, the sum of all the human races that the globe had engendered since Genesis. It was…"

But it was too late.

Of what happened then, neither Jeff nor Marka was conscious—especially Jeff.

Just as Marka had foreseen, the contact of opposed forces disrupted the fragile equilibrium. There was a chain reaction, which was propagated through the nucleus with blinding speed. The colossal energetic center exploded, liberating unsuspected forces, incredible torrents of energy, fantastic spiritual concentrations, swept away by a powerful blast that made the cortex of the other concentric spheres comprising the hollow planet tremble.

In an infinitesimal interval of time, an entire demonic and maleficent past vanished. The world of Lucifer returned to oblivion.

And in that same infinitesimal interval, a single immortal soul, pure and transparent, rose up again to the sources of Life, directed by a Supreme Will, impregnating itself in a fetus of synthetic origin, the first sketch of a Being that would finally bring humans to the Light that they had never known.

GOD HAD WILLED IT THUS!

LES JARDINS
DE L'APOCALYPSE

F.RICHARD
BESSIÈRE

★

★*★**ANTICIPATION**★*★

Editions
"Fleuve Noir"

THE GARDENS OF THE APOCALYPSE

CHAPTER I

The plump, soft *thing* behind the window stretched itself. It clung to the fine mesh, like some improbable creation escaped from a diseased brain.

Hallucinatory.

Karen considered it disgustedly, until its glaucous mass finally tore itself away from the protective trellis to hurl itself into the air with the sly nonchalance that seemed to characterize its strange and mysterious species.

Staggering.

Several of them were floating in the deserted and abandoned street. That was considerably fewer than before, but the approach of spring always caused them to surge forth anew, more highly-colored and more luminous—and also more alive. The spheres were like great transparent balloons, with a density equal to that of the atmosphere, devoid of mouths, eyes, noses or ears—nothing but a delicate quivering membrane, incessantly deforming to take on the most varied appearances.

Repugnant.

Karen had always been familiar with them; they were a part of the narrow little universe in which she had floundered since her birth, whose limits she continually bumped into 24 hours a day. She remembered the long mornings she had once spent in front of the window watching the *things*, counting them and studying their fantastic metamorphoses, becoming ecstatic about the dazzling gleams of bright, almost unreal color that the delicate membranes emitted.

Frightful.

But children did not understand what was horrible and atrocious about those *things* floating majestically in the middle of the street, variegated by the sunlight like dewdrops in the first glimmers of dawn.

For Karen, now, the veil had been torn away, and she knew. Only the street had conserved the same absurd significance for her: a broad expanse of dust and stone; an empty frontier between two distant worlds, hers and the other—the opposite one, where bright lights shone every evening behind other windows, in other universes, where there was another living world, perhaps another Karen!

She saw red-tinted clouds gathering over the horizon, forming tongues of fire in the distance, between the façades constructed in the majestic style of the third world war.

Terrifying.

It seemed to Karen that something fleshless was moving in the part of the horizon scarcely visible between the façades, just where the grey landscape pockmarked with dark shadows appeared. One got used to that, however.

But the things...those impalpable, light, multicolored, quivering beings that floated in the air and could suck a living organism dry in a matter of seconds...what were they?

Abominable...maleficent...demonic...

They were, however, the all-powerful masters of the agonized world that was still surviving after nearly a century. A century, already! One morning, all of a sudden, the *things* had appeared. Undoubtedly, the world had not understood what had happened to it.

But Karen did not know that. It was so long ago!

Karen turned round at the noise that the door-slab made as it slid into the opening of its niche. At the back of the room a silhouette emerged from a dark round opening, like an animal leaving its lair, and Karen immediately recognized Pat.

He stood in front of her, half-naked, brushing off the dust soiling the smock that he wore instead of trousers, with a gesture that was more mechanical than attentive.

"Hello, Karen…"

"Hello, Pat…"

He caught his breath momentarily, looked at her for some time, and then sketched a circular gesture with his hand at breast-height. "It's your father, Karen," he said, simply. "He's dead."

Just as simply, she said: "Oh!" Then she repeated Pat's gesture, with her back to the window.

That was the Rule. Adults died in order to hollow out other excavations, other tunnels, other corridors, in order to open up another breach into another world. Karen's parents, like Pat's, had not escaped the Rule. Were there not cybernetic nurses to raise children?—vigilant guardians of human produce, virtuous machines nurtured on scruples and benevolence.

The Adults lived in another sector, further away…where life was maintained, where people worked for the survival of a race that refused to die.

That was the Rule.

Past also said: "Tomorrow, our sector will join up with sector eight. There'll be a celebration, Karen."

She smiled, and her eyes shone intensely. She smiled because Pat was tall and handsome, and because she knew that one day they would couple. That decision was Pat's prerogative. Only he could take the initiative.

Then she frowned—because she thought about Peggy, who was older than her, and who had already offered Pat pleasures that she divined in herself, but which she had not yet known.

Mira and Peggy would also be at the celebration. Pat would dance in front of them, carried away by his excitement, laughing and shouting at the top of his voice. Mira and Peggy would leap to their feet and start dancing in their turn, joining in with his capering. Naked, entirely naked, right down to…

It was like that every time, in the more distant tunnels, on days of celebration.

Karen turned her head and looked through the window. Little glaucous masses were drifting slowly past. Some flattened themselves out, others became frayed. "Pat," she said, abruptly. "What was it like before?"

He stepped forward and placed his hand on his young companion's shoulder. "What do you mean?"

"People lived in the open air, didn't they?"

"That's what they say."

"They exposed their bodies to the rain, the sunlight, the snow and the wind."

"So they say."

"How funny that must have looked! What else did they do?"

"How should I know?"

"Father said that in summer, people went into the country to make bouquets—bouquets of...flowers. Yes, flowers—that's the word he used."

"Flowers?"

"Yes, Pat. They were plants with colored leaves, all scented. He said that it was a gift of nature, after the rigors of winter, and that flowers were a symbol of freshness, youth, strength and love. It's curious isn't it?"

She laughed naively, amused by the interest she had momentarily awakened in Pat's mind—and Pat laughed in his turn, as he laughed at all of the legends handed down from the ancient generations.

Karen suddenly stopped laughing, and Pat suddenly realized that she was nervous and overexcited, while she pointed to the multicolored patches that were dancing chaotically between the somber façades. Each of them was now a formless confusion of green, red, yellow and blue stripes, imprecise and unhealthy, vaguely rectilinear, with ill-defined contours.

"Do you really believe that we'll be able to rid the world of those *things* some day? And that the world will be as it was before?"

"The world you're talking about is foreign to us, Karen; it's no longer ours. It's possible, but I don't believe it. That's

136

what we've been supposed to believe for generations, though, and the visiophones continue to reel off comforting promises. Always the same—and intended for us, of course, for the Adults ceased to believe it themselves a long time ago. But it helps to make our miserable existence bearable, it seems."

Karen stared at him with wide eyes. "Come on, Pat—you're talking like an Adult."

"I'm almost a man, Karen. The difference is determined by the Adults; it's only a question of legal majority."

There was a certain grandeur in his words, but as much disgust and rancor. Scarcely emerged from the mists of childhood, Pat was conscious, like all those of his age—who often matured precociously—of not having the same rights as others, and bumping into the distinct line of demarcation that exists between childhood and maturity.

He took a few steps across the room, and stood in front of the dusty old visiophone mounted on the wall. "The day when this apparatus stops working will be the end. The broadcasts are already becoming increasingly spaced out. One day, we'll listen to the last. The screen will light up and the bald little man, all puffed up, will appear with the same confident and persuasive smile. He'll reel off the same words: 'Victory is near, it will be soon...our scientists are on the right track. Nothing can prevail against human intelligence. Nothing can prevent our victory. Have confidence...have confidence...'"

Negligently, he picked up a fragment of a biovitamin tablet that was lying on a shelf and started nibbling it, as he turned to Karen. "And then it will be the end," he said. "The last reserves of energy will be exhausted, and nothing will work any longer. Gloom, darkness, silence and death."

"Give me a tablet, Pat."

He rummaged in the distributor outlet, brought one out and handed it to her.

"If I die with you, that's all right by me," she declared, "since we'll be together in the Unity."

She pressed herself against him, savoring his warm presence.

Outside, the vile creatures continued to stir gently behind the windows.

Hideous!

CHAPTER II

In the disused tunnels, a celebration was in full swing. There was a stifling, abnormal warmth in the large round space, while faint shadows danced along the rocky walls.

It was the great celebration of the junction, which furious and implacable youth was celebrating in a sealed vessel—one of the forbidden sanctuaries that the Adults were wary of entering: one closed world within another, more mysterious still, where impossible joys overflowed abdication and resignation.

What did the pretext matter? Today, people drank, danced and shouted because two hands had clasped through a thin layer of dirt, and a face had appeared in a gaping orifice.

A face...another face...and then another. And another, and another...

The Adults had also experienced that delight, and the moment had been moving and solemn, full of pathos.

That had been the way of things for long years, since humans had refused solitude and defeat, and complained of their distress and misfortune in the face of an excessively cruel destiny.

They had been anxious to know what had become of the other survivors, had wanted to become acquainted, to join together, to rediscover one another, to bring all their ideas and thoughts together—the very same ones that the visiophones sketched out in the voices of a few select individuals, in the course of the rare broadcasts that still reached the unfortunate survivors.

Then, some day or other, there was a new junction, which pushed the frontiers of their ancient prison—which, sooner or later, would become the tomb of a slowly-dying race—a little further back. That was the way it was. Humans refused to die alone—as if the law of numbers might help them accept their own fate more easily.

And these young people, who were letting themselves go in the overheated room, did not accept their fate either. For them, the passage of time did not matter; only the present had any real significance.

When Karen came into the room, a kind of insulting chatter was rising from the crowd, emphasized by the noise of one group; the most excited were singing a refrain that was simultaneously obscene and obsessive. Couples were dancing at the back of the room, while lamplight was reflected from the boxes of *kaola* brandished by hundreds of hands. There was a lot of drinking, and a lot of laughing—as if alcohol and laughter might provide antidotes to death.

Karen threaded her way through the crowd, between hot, frenetically-agitated bodies. She avoided an enlaced couple who were struggling silently in a corner, and tried to reach Pat, whom she could see in the middle of the arena. She went around a podium, from which a voice was trying to be heard over the racket. It was that of the group's intellectual, the gang's orator, Doc. He was quoting Ronsard, like an echo of a fabulous past, which he had probably discovered while riffling through a few old books that had escaped the ravages of time.

"The valley of Tempe will one day be a mountain.

"And the summit of Athos a broad plain,

"Neptune will be covered in wheat some day,

"Matter remains but form is lost..."

The remainder of his speech was lost in the din. Karen reached the arena, disdaining Mira and Peggy, scenting as she passed by the reek of jealousy aimed at her. She only had eyes for Pat, who was standing in the middle of a group engaged in animated discussion. Then she mingled with the participants in a vocal debate that was in progress, fixing her gaze on a young boy wearing a metal plate attacked to his tunic, bearing the symbol of a blood-group: the letter B.

She guessed immediately what was happening. In this debate, Death played a leading role, but no one paid any heed to it—not even the one who bore the insult on his breast: the malevolent B that legend held to be partly responsible for the human nightmare.

That prejudice dated from the third world war—the one that had pulverized and devastated three quarters of the globe. At that time, a bold hypothesis had attributed temperamental differences to different blood-groups, thus explaining the mode of adaptation that conditioned the tendencies inscribed in the blood-flow. To confirm the thesis, the continent that had unleashed the war and sowed death over the planet had, unfortunately, proved to have a population with a relative predominance of group B—one of the four groups into which all human blood is divided.

The boy in the middle of the arena belonged to this group—the accursed group, according to the ancient superstitions—and, like everyone else, he had to accept the rules of tradition, as well as the customs of evenings of celebration. His group had chosen him to fight the duel, and Karen's gaze soon found the supporters of the elite, who were taking their places on the tiers, while the As, the Os and the ABs jostled in their turn for the positions reserved for them.

An odor of aggression and ferocity suddenly filled the large room—but Doc's voice resounded from the podium. "It's the Rule," he shouted. "The Law of the Unity. Our Law. Matter remains but form is lost."

Karen detested this kind of spectacle, and her hand squeezed Pat's momentarily.

Pat turned round, smiling wanly. "I can't do anything," he told her. "I have to obey the Rule. I can't accept their insult."

She knew that nothing could change the present minute, and when Pat launched himself into the arena she felt herself gripped in her turn by a strange excitement. Once again, victory would go to Death, for the duel would be implacable, devoid of mercy or pity, and the enthusiasm of the audience, in any case, testified that they would not be short-changed.

Knives in hand, the two adversaries began to study one another, searching with their gazes, then feinted a few times in order to weigh one another up, urged on by the shouts of the excited crowd.

The representative of group B was a tough adversary for Pat, whom the Os had selected, and his agility had something feline, cunning and disconcerting about it. His ardor for battle came to the surface, confirming the psychobiological tests of the previous century. His aggression was perhaps an aspect of natural function, but the idea did not occur to anyone that self-defense might also be a simple human response—the one known as the survival instinct, which overrides any psycho-biological contingency.

The B was seen as nothing but a rigid, impermeable, wild and bellicose creature, haloed with all human calami-ties—and when he hurled himself on Pat to strike unexpected-ly, a howl of indignation went up from the As, Os and ABs.

Pat sidestepped and attacked in his turn, grazing his op-ponent's left arm. For a moment they fought hand-to-hand, in a ferocious struggle, rolling on the ground to the acclamations of the audience.

Karen closed her eyes, and the seconds that followed seemed to last for centuries. She heard the shouts of the crowd, the encouragements, the insults, and especially the mockery directed at any awkward or unfortunate move.

Then, all of a sudden, the shouting grew louder and be-came unified, like a tide overflowing a dyke, flooding the overheated room.

She opened her eyes again, and saw Pat standing in the middle of the arena. Group B blood was reddening his knife and dripping on his feet. In front of him, the body of his ad-versary was writhing in the dust. It twitched a few times more, then stiffened and did not move again.

Thus was the triumph of the Law affirmed. And once more, Death was victorious over Death itself.

Music burst forth, sudden and aggressive, and Karen saw Mira and Peggy, still inseparable, quit the tiers together to join the victor. She could do no more, and did not have the courage to watch the terminal celebrations; it was beyond her strength. Then again, there was Mira and Peggy...

Karen wove her way through the crowd, left the large room, and headed into the deserted tunnels. As she drew away, she accelerated her pace to flee the atmosphere and the spectacle that had become odious to her.

She soon found herself at home, stunned, her head still buzzing, and even slightly feverish. What did the rest matter now? Pat was alive; that was the only thing that counted. She remained thus, lying on her bed, lost in her thoughts, forgetting any notion of time, until the moment when she finally realized that Pat was in the room.

He was standing there covered in blood and dirt, smiling and embarrassed. He had become an awkward, inexperienced adolescent again, incapable of finding the words he needed to soothe the pain of a feminine heart. And Karen's was so different, so incomprehensible!

She got up and knotted a handkerchief round his arm to stem the blood-flow, murmuring: "Why must things be like this? It's atrocious..."

Pa frowned. "I couldn't get out of the duel, Karen—the boy insulted me. He challenged me. I've put my life at risk as he put his at risk; the fight was legal, just and fair. And don't forget that he was a B."

"Why this hatred? Why?"

He looked at her with some bewilderment. "It's not just a question of blood. The Bs have remained faithful to old religious traditions. For us, they're the perpetuation of an evil and error-strewn past, and their ridiculous rites are a sacrilege against the Unity. Come on, Karen—we're the ones who are in the right, and we don't have the right to renounce our cause."

"Do we also have the right to hold a grudge against them because they're in the wrong?"

Pat suddenly felt that he was being crushed by an immense weight, beyond his strength, because he feared that he had not employed the words he needed to translate his thinking accurately. "You have to understand, Karen," he said, finally. "The god of the ancients is dead, because he was meaningless, and we've revived him in his true form. How can one adore a divinity capable of rancor, and of transferring the faults of a few to future generations? And doing so in the name of the Unity? That's what happened, though—the ancient texts confirm it. For millennia, human beings were persecuted in the name of a false and absurd religion; people explained the human condition as the cost of an original sin, and predicted for our species the most frightful punishments engendered by the anger of that vengeful god."

He shook his head forcefully. Carried away by his own conviction, he continued: "No, no, that's impossible, and I refuse to believe it. The Unity is incapable of such horror; those prophecies are merely the work of those who thought they were able to judge a god by the state of the terrestrial world. One cannot imagine the Unity deprived of generosity and mercy; the rest is unthinkable. That's why we fight, Karen—to rehabilitate the Unity to which we all belong, in spite of the old traditions that still subsist." He clenched his fists and concluded: "*We* have no need to nail anyone to a cross."

There was a heavy silence in the room, troubled only by the soft hum of the electronic apparatus with which the apartment was equipped.

Outside, dawn was breaking, and the first light of morning caused the vile creatures appear, with their incessant, eternal dance. Karen looked at them momentarily, and a cold shiver ran down her spine. Were they not the concretization of that ancient belief, that millennial prophecy, which had never ceased to haunt the human mind: the final, dreaded Apocalypse?

She did not have the courage to confess her own thoughts to Pat. What good would it do? He would never accept them. For him, the end of the world had nothing to do with the laws of the Unity; it was merely an accident, a fault imputable solely to human stupidity.

Then Karen's gaze went back to the street, and the exclamation that she uttered made Pat spin around. "Look, Pat!"

He ran forward and saw in his turn.

In front of them, in the middle of the deserted street, there was an object lying in the street: an object that had not been there the previous evening; an object that had never been there in the street.

It was a shiny object, made of metal, in the form of a cube.

It was a box.

CHAPTER III

For several minutes, Karen and Pat stood by the window, prey to the most profound amazement.

There was not the slightest breath of wind outside—nothing but a fixed and rigid nature. It could not, therefore, be the wind that had carried the object, and that unexpected presence amid the morning mists had something disconcerting and abnormal about it.

"That object wasn't in the street yesterday evening," Karen repeated, "I'm sure of it."

"Then how did it get there?"

"I don't know."

"The *things*?"

"They don't have any power over metal—and that box looks quite heavy to me. Look how its base is disappearing into the dust." She guessed Pat's next question, and shrugged her shoulders. "No, no one would be crazy enough to open a door or a window. Why would they?"

"What, then?"

Karen leaned on the window-sill and remained silent momentarily, lost in thought. Her eyes never left the mysterious object.

"If only we could find out what's inside it," she murmured, as if speaking to herself. "But no, that's impossible. We'll never know. We're condemned until we end our days to look at that box, all alone in the middle of the street, without having the slightest chance of discovering its secret. What can there be inside that box, eh, Pat?"

He too was staring in fascination at the strange metal object, around which the monstrous creatures were dancing, doubtless attracted by the unusual presence. "Anything the imagination can put into it," he replied, smiling. "An entire universe might be contained in a box, with all its secrets and fabulous treasures. Perhaps, also, nothing—emptiness, with a little dust and nothing more."

She laughed, amused by these suggestions, but he sensed that her natural and very feminine curiosity had been pricked to the quick.

"All the same, that box didn't get here by itself," Karen said, abruptly. "Someone or something put it there. Who or what?"

"You're crazy."

She sighed. "Do you really think that I can go on living without trying to find out? There's no more than four meters between the wall and that box. I'm going to find a way."

"I'm not mistaken—you're crazy, completely crazy. Crazy or not, though, I forbid you to commit the slightest imprudence. Have you really thought about what you just said?"

"But, Pat..."

"You're just a silly girl—a brainless child—and I refuse to listen to you."

She lowered her head, mortified, and stepped away from the window. "All right, Pat," she said. "I won't ever mention it again, I promise."

She stood in front of the automatic distributor, pressed the buttons of her choice, and obtained some concentrated foodstuffs, which had formed part of the ancient reserves. They were very nourishing synthetic products, which only had to be suitably prepared in an appropriate oven to give them a pleasant taste and a consistency acceptable to the body.

One day, those reserves would be exhausted; that was inevitable—but for the moment, Karen did not care about that at all. Many other thoughts were stirring in her head.

She put the plates on the table and turned round to call Pat—but Pat was asleep on the bed of moss.

When Pat woke up, he lay there for a moment with his eyes half-closed before recovering his senses completely; then his attention was abruptly attracted by what Karen was doing in the other room.

He could see her through the door, which stood ajar, in the process of trying to fix a copper coupling between two flexible wooden rods, which she had probably unearthed from some corner of the cellar. At present, she was attempting to consolidate the apparatus with a piece of steel wire, with an urgency that suddenly awoke Pat's interest.

Suddenly, he understood. He knew what Karen was trying to do, and the use she intended to make of the improvised fishing-rod.

He bounded to his feet and shouted: "Karen!"

For an instant, their eyes met; then Pat saw the end of the rod. She had already fixed a hook to it, with slightly flattened edges.

"It's insane, Karen—you can't do this."

She made a weary gesture. "It might very well succeed. It's just a matter of opening the door slightly, just enough to get the rod through."

"The spheres won't give you enough time. Our bodies attract them. They'll fall upon you, and you'll…"

"No, Pat—I tell you it might easily succeed. There are none of them in front of the house at the moment."

He made no reply, but broke the rod into several pieces, thus giving free rein to his anger and his exasperation.

"Very good," she said, without turning a hair. "Rather admit that you're scared."

"Take back what you just said, Karen."

"No, I stand by it—you're a coward."

A red tide of wrath abruptly colored the young man's face. He roared: "I ought to tear out your tongue to render you mute until your dying day—you deserve it. But the punishment would be too much for you, wouldn't it?"

She turned her back on him, furiously—and it was then that Pat perceived the footprints in the dust of the street.

"I'm seeing things!" he cried, taking hold of Karen and obliging her to look in her turn. "Tell me that I'm not dreaming!"

The tracks were clear, neatly excised. They were like the imprints of large, heavy shoes and their spacing was mathematical in its regularity.

"Someone has walked down the street," Pat went on, feverishly.

"Look—the tracks head toward the plaza."

He nodded his head, looking in the direction indicated. "Come on," he said. And he drew her behind him toward the access tunnel.

Running breathlessly, the two young people now plunged into the central tunnel, which they soon abandoned in order to take another side-branch. Their mad rush through the interior of the subterranean maze continued until they finally reached a small ground-floor room, where there was a spiral metal staircase which seemed to fade away at the top of a curious circular edifice.

They climbed up, passing several landings, and eventually found themselves at the summit of the tower, beneath a semi-transparent plastosteel dome, in the midst of a multitude of optical instruments, with which Pat and Karen were very familiar.

Everything was there that the City's survivors had been able to recover by way of magnifying-glasses or binoculars, and ingenious combinations had even allowed the improvisation of a little telescope, which the Adults sometimes used to make the unvarying horizon that bordered the city like an impenetrable wall seem as far away as possible.

It was a troubling revenge of a hostile and capricious nature that had restricted human ambition to narrower limits, and that greenish line drowned in mist would always hide its secrets. No one would ever know what lay beyond it. They could scarcely imagine it by the referring to the ultimate visions that were obtained from the top of the tower. There began the reign of vegetation and solitude; there, also, began an unknown, mysterious world, of which legends and old traditions spoke in ambiguous terms, without anyone being able to tell how much was true and real.

Pat maneuvered a large telescope, which swiveled on its mount, and whose large orifice was tightly fitted into the plastosteel shell. The transparent dome slid in its turn until the young man had caught sight of the footprints. He had a very clear view of them, and the magnification that he obtained allowed him to make them out at the far side of the triangular plaza that Karen had mentioned.

They extended thereafter in the direction of the arsenal—or, rather, what still remained of that ruined building, situated on the edge of the city in one of the abandoned sectors. On the other hand, their provenance was much more obscure, for the tracks disappeared in a large avenue bordered with tall buildings that blocked the view.

"We have to tell the others," Pat said. "They need to know."

They left the tower and retraced their steps through the labyrinth of subterranean corridors.

As they reached the tunnel giving access to Karen's residence, they bumped into Doc. "Pat," he said, "We've been looking for you. We've convened a tribunal at Karen's. Come quickly."

They followed him without asking any questions, and found their companions in the main room on the ground floor. In the middle of the group, a man—an Adult—was being securely held. His face was covered with bruises, and he was drooling and panting like a damned soul. With his habitual discretion and amiability, Doc pointed at him and said: "We caught this fellow at Moustache's, in the process of stealing food from his cellar. He claims that his distributor is no longer working. That's hardly an original excuse, don't you think?"

Pat's gaze settled rapidly on the metal insignia that the Adult wore on his tunic: a ruddy B on a copper plate. He shrugged his shoulders, though. "Let him choose whether to go to his Devil or his God. We've got other things to worry about—which are much more serious, believe me."

Voices within the group complained and grew louder, but Pat went to the window and extended his arm to point to the mysterious object.

CHAPTER IV

When Pat had finished speaking, the heavy silence that followed was soon broken by Ferret's voice.

"If there's a mystery, ask the Adult about it. He must know."

All heads turned toward the man, whose surprise was manifest in his features.

"He's right," added Peggy, always the most excitable. "The Adults always know everything, and that gives them all the rights—even that of stealing girls from the tunnels and raping them—and the Bs aren't the last, you know! I'm sure that he knows."

A brief tumult filed the room, and Pat tried to re-establish silence.

"Please!" he shouted, over the din. "Let the Adult speak."

But the Adult had nothing to say. For him, too, the mystery remained complete. What could he tell them? "I don't know," he ended up saying, in a dull voice. "I swear that I don't know."

"You swear on what?" demanded Ferret, in a mocking tone. "On your shoddy god? Look Pat, he's sure in the process of saying his prayers. I'd like to hear him saying them aloud. That would be amusing, eh? What do you think, friends?"

The excitement within the company increased, and sonorous *yes*es filled the room, while two boys forced the Adult to his knees in the middle of the group, in response to a signal from Ferret.

"Come on, Papa—and loudly, for we're listening! Quiet, the rest of you!"

The man became livid. "Vile—you're vile!"

"Recite your prayers, thief!" howled Moustache.

Tears formed in the corners of the man's eyes, but he contained himself, still clinging to a few shreds of dignity. "I stole because I was hungry. That's what awaits you some day—all of you…"

"That's not what you were asked," said Ferret. "Are you praying, yes or no?"

The man scented the odor of the fever that was gripping the group and obeyed. He lowered his head, put his hands together, and his voice, still trembling, reeled off the first syllables: "Our Father, who art in Heaven, hallowed be thy name…"

But Pat was not listening. He only had eyes for Karen. She was pale and mute, completely petrified; the distress that he sensed in her made him feel ill.

Karen… idiot… brainless silly girl… don't you understand? What was she thinking? What value did she attach to this incense, this speech, to the words that the man added to the end of his prayer: "God forgive them."

Forgive what? And *who* could forgive? Certainly not the proud and overly vengeful god that the Ancients had imagined. No, an absurd being could neither hate nor forgive. All that was false, unjust, specious. And the filthy creatures capering outside the window—were they, too, God's creatures?

Mira's voice suddenly snatched Pat from his reverie. It rose above the mockery and the jeering, like a whiff of cunningly-contrived Machiavellianism. "We want to know. In consequence, I propose to the tribunal an excellent means of retrieving that box."

"Go on," said Doc.

She pointed at the Adult. "Let him go out and fetch the object. His liberty in return for his sacrifice. Four meters to cross—that takes two seconds. Four seconds in all, in both directions."

Doc smiled, looked at his companions, and then turned to the man, who was now trembling in every limb.

"No, it's impossible—you can't do something like that."

"Difficult at his age to break with old habits," said Ferret, sarcastically, addressing Doc with a conspiratorial wink.

"Yes, I see—the man's a neophobe."

"Bravo, Doc, that's the right term. Now, who'll take charge of opening the locks?"

There were several volunteers, and it was Peggy who was finally granted that favor. She took her place beside the security mechanisms, and put on a show of studying them for some time before declaring: "I'm ready."

"You have no right... you have no right!" howled the man. "What god do you serve, to do such a thing?"

Pat stood squarely in front of him. "Unfortunately," he said, "we don't speak the same language—but I'll try to answer you anyway."

"A simple mental heterogeneity," Doc put in, sententiously. "Go on, Pat."

"This god of which you speak, sir, you are a part of Him, like all the atoms that compose the Universe. You're a parcel of the Unity, that's undeniable. Good and Evil are merely human sentiments and have no significance for the Unity, which is far purer, without addition or mixture. So, don't judge it according to our image, for we too are only human." He pointed to his companions behind him, and went on: "Not as vile as you say, for no one here has ever had any intention of pushing you outside. You merely needed a stern lesson."

A scornful smile was painted on Pat's lips as he added: "You're nothing but a coward." Then he turned to Peggy and said: "Open the door."

There was a heavy and glacial silence, a brief moment of suspense. Finally, it was Mira who cried: "That's it, Pat—show him what you are. Show this coward that you can do it yourself."

The security mechanisms were already grating under Peggy's manipulations. Karen tried to run forward, but Pat held her back.

"No, Karen," he said. "It's necessary." He gestured to the others to be quiet, and said to Peggy: "Go on!"

For the first time in 100 years, the heavy door opened slightly. Then, suddenly, in response to another gesture from Peggy, it opened wide and Pat dived out.

He plunged forward like a bullet, through the yawning gap, and did what he had to do with lightning rapidity—confusing, even, for none of the vile creatures patrolling idly in the warm and humid atmosphere had time to react.

When the door closed again, heavily, Pat stood in the middle of the room, clutching the metal box in his hands. He set it down on the table, took a few deep breaths, and then said to Karen: "There—that's what you wanted, isn't it?"

Outside the window, a compact swarm of multicolored spheres was agitating feverishly, sticking to the protective grille with an unaccustomed rage and determination.

CHAPTER V

For two days, the box that Pat had recovered had resisted every effort to open it.

It was made of a strange alloy of steel and vanadium, and offered an unbreakable resistance. It would have required an instrument much more adept than those the group had at their disposal to prevail. That caused the most distress to Doc, who had taken the initiative in the operation since they had all taken refuge in the main hall to investigate their discovery.

"It'll take a molecular disintegrator to break into it," he said, pensively, trying to give more weight to his remark.

"A what?" asked Moustache.

"Yes, I've read about it—a machine used by the ancients."

"Oh..."

"There must, however, be another way," Pat put in, advancing in his turn.

"Ferret promised to find us a blowtorch—we'll see. Heavens above, what can there be in this strongbox? It's heavy."

They all fell silent, hanging on Doc' words with the greatest interest. The clownish fellow with the shock of red hair knew many things—far more than he could have learned from the cybernetic nurses, whose pedagogical resources were rather limited. To be sure, they taught people to speak and to read, and furnished a body of general knowledge, but that was all. Doc, on the other hand, was something else. He also knew what he had learned from the old books he had discovered in a trunk in the cellar, the valuable inheritance of some distant ancestor—probably a disciple of Aesculapius, to judge by the essentially medical character of the books in question.

They were pleased to listen to Doc when he found, as usual, pompous scientific terms that had a fine ring to them.

When Pat made allusion to the footprints discovered in the dust of the street, thus raising a further problem, Doc reflected and declared: "The person who lost his box knew a means of going out in the open air—that's obvious—but with what purpose? What mystery might be concealed behind all this?"

"Personally, I think it's an experiment," said Peggy, abandoning Mira to her reading when she saw that her young companion was utterly disinterested in the conversation. "Yes, an experiment. Let's assume that this box was deposited in the open in order to study the behavior of the *things*. In that case, it might provide us with information on their..."

"Tropism," Doc completed. "No—you're putting the cart before the horse."

"What did you say?"

"It's an old expression. I'll explain its meaning later."

"Doc," Mira put in, looking up from her book, "can you explain what this sentence means? *Frankie went into the bistro to drink a Cinzano.* I haven't understood anything since I started reading this book."

"Where did you find it?"

"In Moustache's cellar. There was a pile of them. What does *drink a Cinzano* mean?"

Doc grimaced. "A medical term, presumably—I've forgotten it."

"Further on, it says: *Poor Frankie was crippled by taxes.* What are taxes?"

Doc smiled. "It's just as I thought. The ancients must have called some sort of rheumatism *taxes*, and making him drink a Cinzano confirms that it must be a matter of a remedy or medicine. That's obvious."

"Thanks, Doc—you're great. How about this?"

"What now?"

"I don't understand any of it. It's some chap who says to Frankie: *Spill the beans, ugly mug—tell us where you stashed the loot, or we'll work you over, and be quick about it, you lard-bucket.*"

Doc pulled a face, took the book from Mira's hands, and glanced at the faded yellow cover. "*Drugs Galore,*" he read, aloud. "An old language, certainly very ancient, like Hebrew or Latin. A pity we don't have a translation."

He was about to say something else when Karen and Ferret irrupted into the room. Their faces reflected the most intense emotion, and the piece of synthetic fabric that Karen was brandishing caused Pat to frown.

"Why, what's happened, Karen?"

"Pat, Pat—our experiment has succeeded!"

"What experiment? What are you talking about?"

"Ferret and I know how we can go out in the open air."

There was a deathly silence in the room. Everyone drew closer to the new arrivals, their faces suddenly serious.

Pat was the first to recover his composure. "Go out in the open air?" he queried.

Karen held out the piece of red fabric to him. "I've suspected it or a long time," she affirmed, "but I didn't dare mention it—I wanted to be sure first. This color makes the *things* retreat. They're afraid of red."

"What do you mean?"

"A sort of chromophobia, perhaps," Doc put in. "Very interesting. But what allows you to make the supposition?"

Ferret was about to reply, but Karen interrupted him. "It's not a supposition, it's a certainty now. Look—I noticed it one day when I'd put one of my garments near the window. It was as if the spheres were gripped by alarm—panic, even. Then they moved away, and none of them reappeared at the window while the red garment was still there. Afterwards, I had the opportunity to see the same phenomenon recur several times over."

"So they're capable of fear," Doc murmured, pensively. "A very intense panic reflex, followed by a violent increase in the motor faculties. The explanation is valid. Continue, Karen."

"So I wanted to obtain proof before talking to you. This time, the experiment is conclusive. Come along, quickly."

They all followed Karen and Ferret out of the room, not forgetting to bring along the mysterious box, which still refused to yield its secrets, and soon reached Ferret's residence. The latter immediately steered them toward a barred window overlooking a rather large interior courtyard surrounded by high somber walls.

In the middle of the courtyard, a curious animal was prancing on its four legs, its body entirely swathed in strips of red cloth. One might have thought it a creature from a nightmare, and he little group stood watching it for some time, incapable of saying anything.

Suspiciously, Pat asked: "What is that animal?"

Karen smiled. "It's a cat."

"A cat?"

"Yes—I thought it best to try the experiment on an animal first. Ferret helped me by procuring the little beast."

"That's true," Ferret confessed. "I stole it from the Reserve while Karen distracted the Adult who was on guard. No one saw anything. Oh, if you'd seen it, my friends! I've never been in the Reserve before. There are all sorts of animals there—large, medium and small—with fur, feathers, beaks and mouths that could swallow you in one go." He pointed at the quadruped that was continuing its capers in the courtyard. "The word *cat* was written on that one's cage. But the dirty beast doesn't seem very friendly—look how it scratched me."

"Me too," said Karen, displaying her hands. "It did that when I was putting the bandages on. Nasty cat!"

"How did you get it into the courtyard?" Pat asked.

"It was quite simple," Ferret admitted, pointing out the orifice of a conduit, formerly used for the expulsion of household waste. "We opened the inner access-hatch and threw the cat down the chute. And from this window, Karen and I saw something incredible. The spheres were immediately gripped by panic, and fled. Look—none of them has the courage to approach."

What he said was true. The few stray globular creatures that appeared over the courtyard fled immediately at the sight of the cat swathed in red bandages—which confirmed the assertions of Karen and Ferret. The *things* were afraid of redness. They fled from that color, without seeking, in their panic, to know the cause of the insurmountable terror to which they were subject. For them, it must be frightful... horrible... terrible... utterly incomprehensible!

"Extraordinary!" Doc exulted. "Sublime! The experiment is a work of genius—worthy of the greatest minds that our wretched humankind has produced. For the first time, we can see with our own eyes a living creature moving in the open air without running the slightest danger. What audacity, eh? What audacity!"

"Bravo!" cried Moustache, suddenly excited. "Hurrah for Karen and Ferret!"

The enthusiasm was general; hands were shaken and claps on the back energetically exchanged. Someone burst out nervously into thunderous laughter—but it was necessary to discuss the matter calmly, and after a few minutes, Pat succeeded in re-establishing silence, cutting short the projects that were being elaborated on every side.

"Let's not go mad, please," he said, firmly. "For greater certainty, it's necessary that the experiment be attempted with a human being. Only then will we have absolute certainty."

They all volunteered, but the honor finally reverted to Pat, who was the leader. Feverishly, they helped him to cover his body with the red strips of cloth that Mira and Peggy had hastily cut up from pieces of cloth recovered from Ferret's residence.

Soon, without the slightest dread, Pat opened the door and went into the courtyard in his turn, joining the animal— which did not seem to know which way to turn. It did not understand what was happening; this was obviously far beyond the comprehension of a cat.

Behind the window, the group saw Pat pick the animal up, and fill his lungs with the pure air of *the outside*, which no one had breathed for a century.

How sweet and delicious it must be—revivifying, even! What a strange feeling it must produce!

Pat waited for a few more minutes, and then came back in. His head felt heavy, and it was buzzing, but his breath was fresh...marvelously fresh.

For him, as for the others, he was coming back from another world—a world to which he had opened the way, and which would one day belong to everyone.

"For the moment," Pat said, tapping the box, "this must remain secret...at least until we've discovered what the box contains, for it's probable that the Adults have a significant advantage over us."

"We're as capable as they are of succeeding," Peggy affirmed. "We'll succeed."

"Very well," Doc added, "there's not a moment to lose. It's necessary to collect all the pieces of red cloth that we possess and make clothing and hoods for each of us. The girls can do that. Any objections?"

There was none—and the following day was entirely devoted to the work in question, with all the ardor and determination that animates enthusiastic and excited youth in confrontation with a problem that is within its compass. They were experiencing, without being aware of it, an imperious passion for discovery and an atavistic urge to exploration: a kind of prefiguration of the millennial curiosity that gave impetus to science.

It was a new hope and a new victory that shone for them in darkness of a nightmare that threatened to be eternal.

When everything was ready, their thoughts returned to the box, and the blow-torch located by Ferret convinced them to return to work in the main common-room.

And it was while they were working doggedly on the metal of the box that an imperious voice resonated in the room.

"Stop, I command you. Don't touch that box."

The man who had pronounced these words was tall and well-built, with a harsh, authoritarian face devoid of expression.

It was an Adult.

CHAPTER VI

The Adult came out of the tunnel entrance and took a few steps toward the group.

"My name is Greene," he said. "I've come from Sector Four."

His words cut through the heavy silence that reigned in the room, like whip-cracks.

He only had eyes for the box sitting on the table, and Pat guessed what had happened. It was the other one, of course—the cowardly Christian, set free on his orders—who must have talked about the box. He had hurried back to his own people, the Bs, and had told them what had happened. Yes, it could not have been anyone but him. But what did this man want from them now? Why was there so much harshness in his words?

"I want you to give me that box," the Adult went on. "You have no right to touch it. Give it to me."

"Are you, perhaps, the object's owner?" asked Doc, calmly—but it was more an expression of opinion than a question.

The man looked at him. "Let's say that I'm one of its owners. I've been sent to collect the object. Give it to me."

Pat stepped forward. "Just a moment," he said. "We're not refusing to give you the box, but we'd like to know what it contains."

"You'll never be able to open it."

"Perhaps we won't—can you?"

Pat's audacity caused Greene to frown. "I'm sorry, but I'm not authorized to do that."

Pat placed his hand on the metal box, abruptly. "And I'm not authorized to obey you. Youth is stubborn, as you must know, sir."

"I admit that, up to a point," the Adult retorted. "Come on, let it go. You don't understand."

"Understand what?"

"For the last time, give me that box," the Adult said, coming forward to grab it—but Ferret, Moustache and Doc had moved forward, ready to pounce at a signal from Pat. Greene stopped, understanding that he was about to do something gravely imprudent. "Very well," he said, in a dull voice. "Since I have no choice, I'll have to do as you wish. But you'll regret it."

He took a small device from his pocket, comprising a small wheel inserted between two flexible and movable roads. Then he hesitated. "I'm offering you one last chance," he said. "Think…"

Without taking his eyes off him, and without saying another word, Pat handed him the box.

The Adult shook his head, sighed and started sliding the little antimagnetic wheel along the external edges of the box. Gradually, the upper part of the box was raised up, and the interior became visible.

There was a curious collection of pieces of metal, a dense tangle of cogwheels and connecting-rods, levers and insulated wires.

"Well, there it is," said the Adult.

"What's the significance of all that?" Pat asked.

"You really want to know? As you wish. It's the major component of a detonator that we've spent many years developing, each part of which has been separately assembled, in the greatest secrecy, inside the old arsenal—which still exists in the northern suburbs of the city. To do that, we had to invent a remote-controlled robot obedient to our instructions. The operation was carried out by night, when no one was aware of it, and a faulty maneuver was doubtless responsible for the loss of the box. I only regret the zeal and temerity that drove you to take possession of the object—we didn't expect such folly."

"What use are you going to make of the detonator?" Doc put in, visibly interested.

The Adult hesitated again. The conflict going on within him was obvious, but the hostility he read in the faces of those surrounding him overrode his desire again. "We're doomed," he said. "Although you know that. In a few months—a year at the most—nothing within the city will be working. Our machines aren't eternal, and we don't have the means to repair them and keep them going. Already, at several places in the city, we're observing numerous breakdowns, sudden deteriorations in every domain. Our food reserves aren't inexhaustible, and famine is lying in wait for us. One day, everything will stop, and that will condemn us to a slow, agonizing death—a terrible agony in the darkness of this subterranean prison, in which we've only survived thus far by a miracle." He looked down at the box and added: "The group to which I belong has taken the necessary decision. This will cut short our suffering and hasten our end. I'm not hiding anything from you, you see. This evening, at nightfall, the detonator will trigger our giant bomb, whose elements have been completed thanks to a few old isotopes that our robot discovered in the ruins of the arsenal, which date from the last war. Everything is ready."

He shoved Doc aside in order to take possession of the mechanism—but Pat leapt forward to block the move.

"No!" he cried. "I'll never let you do it."

"Are you afraid of death?"

"I think it's absurd when it isn't necessary."

"Unfortunately, it's not up to you to make that decision. Come on, children—show a little dignity, I beg you. I demand that you give me that box."

Pat acted then on a violent reflex. Picking up the box, he hurled it violently to the ground and stamped on it uninhibitedly, thus giving free rein to the fury and anger that he had felt boiling within him for some time.

Professor Greene had become livid, and he uttered a kind of groan as he stared at the scattered pieces that were lying at his feet, bent and broken, completely beyond use. It had all happened so rapidly that he had not had time to intervene.

"You're mad!" he howled. "You're mad! That was our only hope…"

But Doc had thrown himself forward. "If only you'd consented to listen to us!"

Greene did not even look at him.

Doc went on: "Hope, of which you speak as an impossible thing, is what we possess. We're the ones who…"

Greene shoved him aside violently. "Let me go. You don't know what you're saying."

"But we have proof."

Greene stepped back, white with rage. He was no longer listening, blinded by hatred and the impotence in which he found himself. "May your souls be cursed forever!" he cried. "And I'll see to that myself!" He turned around abruptly and disappeared into the access tunnel, after having freed himself from Doc's grip.

There was an instant of suspense in the little group; then Moustache and Ferret launched themselves outside in their turn, running at top speed.

When they reappeared, after a minute or so, consternation was painted on their faces. The end of the tunnel was guarded by three Adults, and any flight would henceforth be impossible for them.

Pat frowned, and drew Karen to him. "I can guess their intentions," he said. "They're going to kill us because they fear that we'll divulge their plan." He looked around, sweeping the circular room with his eyes—but he knew that there was no other exit. He only wanted to give himself time to think.

It was at that moment than a faint voice resounded from the direction of the tiers. "This way, quickly—follow me."

With a single impulse, they all rushed forward, climbing the tiers of the semicircular arena, almost running into a vague form crouching in a dark hole that had appeared between two superimposed rows.

"Don't be afraid. My name's Fats. I heard everything, and I can help you."

Pat looked down at the unknown person. He had a pleasant, sympathetic face and his smile radiated loyalty and sincerity. "What are you doing in that hole?" Pat asked.

"It's a disused tunnel, and I'm one of the few people who know about it. We block it up during meetings. It's our secret."

"Where does it lead?"

"Into the ancient stores of chemical products, near sector five. Hurry, before they find out that you've gone."

No one thought of asking further questions, and they all slid as best they could into the narrow tunnel, moving through the rubble and the dust, guided by Fats' voice as he set off on the march. The darkness was complete, and they had to grope their way through the gloom, breathing with difficulty and stumbling at every step. The tunnel was so narrow and low, all the way, that they were obliged to bend down to be able to make progress.

That blind march continued for several hundred meters, and then Fats' voice rang out again. They had just come out in the ancient store-rooms, and a bitter, fetid odor floated in the heavy and humid atmosphere. "We're safe here," Fats affirmed, breathlessly, "but it's best to be prudent. There's an exit at the far side of the cellar, which opens on to the central tunnel. I know it."

"Thank you," sighed Pat, "but we're condemned anyway."

"Yes, I heard."

"They won't forgive us for what we know."

"I suspect so."

"What about you? Aren't you afraid?"

Pat obtained no reply, and it was in a different tone that he addressed the group. "I don't believe we have any choice," he said, firmly. "Henceforth, there's no place for us in the city. Given that we have a means of going out into the open air, the only solution that remains to us is to run away."

"Come on, Pat, that's impossible," said Ferret. "To live in the open is unthinkable. We'd never survive."

"I'm wondering why," growled Doc. "Our bodies are no different from those of the ancients. They could live that way easily. For my part, I agree."

"Me too," said Peggy and Mira, speaking in unison.

"I'll go with you," said Moustache, in his turn. "Imagine—I've dreamed of this since I was born."

Only Karen's voice betrayed an intense emotion. "All the same, we can't run away without trying to warn other people about Greene's intentions."

"Our sacrifice would be futile," Pat murmured. "The alert must have been raised, and we'd be apprehended before we could do anything." He turned to Fats. "What about you? Will you go with us?"

"Of course, if you'll let me. Oh, I know what's going on—I overheard your conversation. I know your secret."

"Well, so much the better. We have one spare set of clothes—it's yours."

"Thanks, Pat—but I'm thinking about what your companion said. Why did the Adults refuse to listen to us?"

Pat sighed in the darkness. "Because we're rebelling against their reactionary attitude; because we want to open new windows on new horizons; because our behavior is unacceptable to the Adults; and because we're becoming conscious of a world they no longer understand. For our generation, time has ceased to be the ally of youth, and our hours are numbered. It's no longer permissible, in those circumstances, to hold our breath and choke. We're the ultimate *bêtes noires* of their nightmare."

He stood up, and addressed himself to the others: "You stay here while Ferret and I go to get the protective clothing. Above all, don't move. We'll consider our next move then."

Karen grabbed his arm in the darkness and said: "I'm going with you, Pat."

CHAPTER VII

The trio went to the back of the store-room and slipped into the central tunnel, already deserted at this hour.

For the sake of economy, only a few lamps were shining weakly in the corridor, and all three of them were therefore able to make their way through the side-shafts that led to Karen's, Mira's and Peggy's homes without being spotted.

They were finally able to collect the precious red fabric clothing, and got ready to return, their mission accomplished.

On the return journey, however, they passed the entrance to the tunnel giving access to the Temple of the Unity. After a slight hesitation, Pat plunged into it first. They did not feel that they had the right to leave the city of men without rendering one last homage to the Unity.

They came into a low-ceilinged room that was entirely empty, the back wall of which bore nothing but a curious geometric figure. Two secants emerging from a common point formed a V inside a perfect circle.

Two figures; two symbols. The origin and apogee of the Unity. Everything was summarized in that divine symbolism, denuded of all grotesque and gaudy artifice, conceived in the image of a self-enclosed people.

They went forward slowly, as if fascinated or dazzled, vanquished by the nascent ecstasy that they felt within them, suddenly drawn toward mystical illumination and absolute contemplation, perhaps yielding to the sublime and the super-human.

A symbol of purity and innocence, Karen abruptly undressed, offering her complete nudity to the Unity, repeating the gesture of the first monotheists, and thus according to nudism an immoderate, almost absolute, religious value. The profound meaning of the gesture probably escaped her consciousness, by virtue of the fact that her action was unreflective and spontaneous.

She stayed there like that, on her knees, mingling her prayers with those of Pat and Ferret, prostrate to either side of her.

Pat got up first, resuming contact with reality. "It's time," he breathed. "Let's go!"

Scarcely had they reached the central tunnel, however, when they suddenly ran into two Adults, who attempted to oppose their flight. They were presumably dealing with men who belonged to Greene's group.

Turning back, Pat, Karen and Ferret tried to reach a secondary branch, but a pursuit was already being organized behind them. A thermic blast suddenly crackled, sweeping the rocky wall and causing stony debris and charred earth to rain down into the tunnel.

"Faster!" cried Pat, dragging Karen along. "Faster!"

There was then a mad dash through the subterranean maze—but the Adults were gaining ground and the noise of their footsteps echoed lugubriously in the deserted tunnel.

The little group of three young people went through several rooms at a run, and soon found themselves at a right-angled intersection offering access to several directions. Pat stopped in mid-stride and made a gesture, obliging Ferret and Karen to flatten themselves against the low-ceilinged wall.

Ferret understood immediately what Pat intended and gathered himself. They both leapt forward with one motion, like wild beasts on their prey, plunging at the moment when the two Adults appeared.

It was rapid, almost instantaneous. The two men, surprised by the unexpected attack, uttered hoarse cries and rolled on the round, trying to make use of their weapons—but neither Pat nor Ferret gave them the time.

The Adult at grips with Pat was uncommonly strong, but the arm that held the thermic pistol cracked with the noise of breaking bone. Then the man lost consciousness and rolled to one side, inert.

Ferret got up in his turn, wiping away the blood that was trickling from his lip—but he had come out of it very well; his opponent was unconscious, having been knocked out with the butt of the weapon that had been torn from his hand.

Pat took possession of the other pistol, and looked curiously at the terrible weapon. He had never had an opportunity to study one. It probably originated from a stock dating from the last war, which had escaped the catastrophe by some miracle or other. Greene's robot had almost certainly discovered the weapons in the arsenal's store-rooms. "These could be useful," Pat whispered, slipping the weapon into his belt.

They drew away rapidly, their senses alert, abandoning the two Adults in the tunnel, and soon rejoined their comrades in the dark room in which they had left them. There was no more time to lose now. At any moment, someone might discover their retreat and raise the alarm. They had to flee: to abandon the city in which they felt themselves to be strangers, and which no longer accepted them.

Their only objective was to reach the open air and make contact with the only world that could still help them to live.

In minutes, they were ready, molded into the skillfully-tailored protective suits. In response to an order from Pat, they were leaving the room to go to the exit, when an object fell out of one of the forsaken garments that Doc was carrying and rolled into the cone of light originating from the central tunnel.

They all recognized it immediately, and looked up, while Doc picked it up and handed it to Fats. "Why didn't you tell us that you were a B? What prompted you to act as you did?"

"Easy enough to understand," Mira put in. "He was spying on us."

"Let him stay here," Peggy supplied, in her turn. "He's nothing to do with us."

Ferret had already drawn his weapon from his belt, but Pat's strong arm interrupted his gesture.

"Stop!" he ordered. "You're all forgetting that we owe him our salvation. Let's at least give him a chance, for in my estimation, we don't have the right to abandon him. Now, everyone get ready." He took up a position at the head of the group, and released the locks securing the heavy door of the warehouse himself.

Outside, the first glimmers of the spring dawn were setting the horizon on fire, and a fresh, light breeze was bearing unknown perfumes.

Fats squeezed Pat's arm. "Thanks," he murmured. Then, in his turn, he launched himself outside.

CHAPTER VIII

Within a few minutes, they had left the city. They took a street that extended through the ruins of the northern suburb and rapidly reached the city limits.

Around them, the hideous creatures were fleeing in terror, but it was evident that this violation of the law that had contrived to impose on humans for a century had awakened their suspicion and defied their comprehension.

Pat and his companions were quite familiar with the long multicolored tremors that originated abruptly within the globular mass of the *things* whenever a unexpected events disrupted their monotonous habits. It was their way of reacting to the effects of the external world.

Pat accelerated the pace further. He was in haste to see the city of men disappearing behind him, as he still had reason to fear the wrath of Greene and his acolytes—but the tension he felt at present was very different from that which he had felt before. Then again, there was the Sun, its blinding glare, and the mild heat that he was beginning to feel in spite of the fibers of his garments. What was going to happen later when the star reached its zenith? Would they be able to tolerate that burning radiation, and resist such an assault of heat?

The ground, in which clay mingled with soil, was soft underfoot, but the first vegetation was beginning to make its appearance on the sterile terrain, which was fissured in places and striped with broad brown bands formed by ashes that had accumulated over time. The plants seemed to have lost any green or greenish shade. They presented the appearance of hard, desiccated things.

When the escapees reached the summit of a small rise, Pat ordered a halt, and got his breath back. The intensity of the light and the heat was already tormenting them in an unbearable fashion, and he picked out a tall vertical rock that offered a shelter from the Sun's rays.

The air still seemed overheated to them, even in that shadowy corner, and made all of them feel intolerably ill, but the anguish of their flight through the subterranean tunnels had vanished, and the success of their enterprise, in spite of everything, filled their hearts with an enormous confidence—Pat's especially.

He did not experience any feeling of having acted stupidly or unreasonably in leading his companions away, and when he looked back in the direction of the city it was with an expression of incredulity. Over there, life was going on, miserably, without consequence, dedicated to an excessively cruel fate that nothing could any longer modify.

The *things* would continue to stand guard until the end, tracking the humans in their final refuges. But here and now they had disappeared almost entirely, having fled like figments of a nightmare.

He could not believe it.

He was snatched out of his reverie by Moustache's voice, which asked, with a note of anxiety: "What shall we eat from now on?" And he added, in a lower voice: "For my part, I confess that I'm beginning to get hungry."

"Doc took the precaution of bringing a few biovitamin tablets," Pat told him. "They'll help us get by until we find edible plants."

Peggy pulled a face. "Ugh! Vegetable nourishment—how horrid!"

"Disabuse yourself," Doc replied. "I've read that certain plants, in addition to their nutritive value, have a very pleasant taste. It will be sufficient for us to discover them and get used to them." He cast a glance around him and, as no one replied, he continued: "We'll also find water. I'm certain that we won't die of thirst."

"If only we knew where to find that miraculous region," sighed Mira, sweeping the horizon with her gaze.

Fats came forward and said, abruptly: "Why don't we try to reach the secret city?"

Everyone turned round, and hostile gazes shone within the gaps in the protective hoods.

"What do you mean?" growled Doc.

"Speak," said Pat.

"I've heard talk of it in my sector. Adults were discussing the subject, and I overheard their conversation. They were saying that a secret city exists, which escaped the catastrophe by some miracle, and that it's situated on a high plateau—which protects it from the *things* because the *things* can't live in regions poor in oxygen. It appears that they suffer from…"

"Anoxia," Doc interjected. "That's been known for a long time—and it's also a question of atmospheric pressure. But what proof do you have of what you're saying?"

Fats shrugged his shoulders slightly. "None, of course—but the Adults affirmed that it was possible to pick up radio messages transmitted by the mysterious city at regular intervals."

Ferret came forward and said: "It's true. I've also heard mention of that. But no one has ever succeeded in deciphering the meaning of those messages. What do you think, Pat?"

Pat remained lost in thought for a moment. What Fats had just revealed was surprising, and evidently offered an immense hope. He felt himself suddenly gripped by the enthusiasm that was already overtaking the group—but it still remained to find the true direction of this unlooked-for haven.

There, again, Fats proved categorical and affirmative. He knew the exact location that the Adults had ascribed to the secret city, by identifying the transmission-point of the radio signals geographically. With the aid of a flat stone, he rapidly traced the approximate limits of the region on the ground, marked the position of the city with a circle, pointed to the north-west and drew a cross.

"It's there," he said, "about 500 miles away."

"Five hundred miles!" exclaimed Karen. "We'll never be able to cover such a distance."

"We have all the time we need," said Pat. "We only have to walk in the right direction."

Fats judged it useful to declare: "I've learned the movements of the Heavens, and I can orientate myself without any difficulty."

"What?" said Moustache. "You can really say that you know how to read the stars?"

"Leave him alone," said Pat. "He must know what he's saying. I say we trust him. How about you?"

Doc was perplexed, but he knew how to interpret others. "You're the leader. Decide, and we're ready to obey. That's the law of the group."

Pat was about to give the signal to move off when an exclamation uttered by Mira made them turn round in unison.

She pointed to the rocky wall on which she had rested her hand. An expression of disgust was painted on her face. "How horrid!" she said, eventually. "I had the impression that it moved under my fingers. Look…here!"

They all touched it to make sure, and experienced the same strange sensation. The rock was soft and warm at that location, and seemed to retract under the pressure of numerous hands.

Doc shrugged his shoulders. "Probably a variety of rock whose properties are unknown to us," he concluded. "We certainly haven't finished with astonishment, and many things remain for us to discover. Now, let's go."

The heat was oppressive, but the young fugitives endured it without too much difficulty, guided by Pat, who had taken the lead.

They were now advancing into a more fertile and more welcoming region, and the vegetation, more abundant and more varied, aroused everyone's curiosity and admiration.

Around them there was a riot of stalks, leaves, brightly-colored—almost unreal—flowers, gnarled tree-trunks and slender branches, some of which were folded back on themselves in curious positions…and all of it was undulating and quivering under the caress of the wind, in a deathly silence. And yet, nothing could have been more alive than this nature liberated from all constraint. The smallest tuft of grass between the stones was bursting with life and reaching proudly into the spring air. It was simultaneously majestic, imposing and extraordinary—and also strange.

There was a strange little animal with two heads that suddenly appeared at a bend in the path, whose tail, like a long tongue, trailed along the ground, leaving behind it a long slimy wake.

Equally strange were the interwoven cacti incessantly tearing one another with their slender spines, releasing from their eternal wounds a reddish liquid that looked like blood.

Strange, too, were things reminiscent of membranous wings, which beat continuously and seemed to spring from a low scaly branch.

A little later, an even more astonishing event occurred. It was a fight between an enormous caterpillar with feet like a lobster and a flexible, sinewy root, which detached itself from a dwarf tree streaming with an almost-impalpable viscous material. It was a fight to the death.

The mimetic capability of the root permitted it gradually to take on the appearances of the caterpillar's body, painting itself with the other's multicolored patches, the symbol of a struggle more intense than the one that was going on everywhere else.

The attack was sudden and fierce. The lobster-feet cracked like whips and the indented pincers tried in vain to cut through the reptilian root, but the vegetable launched a surprise attack, arching itself abruptly and slicing pitilessly, like a blind scythe, through the round and pulpy mass of the caterpillar-lobster, slashing the flesh of its victim with extreme savagery.

Fascinated by this implacable duel, the humans stood still, as if petrified. Pat felt Karen's fingers clench on his am, and he became aware that she was shivering from head to toe, presumably from horror or fear.

Not wanting to witness the end of the combat, they all plunged into the bushes, fleeing the last atrocious echoes of the massacre, and soon reached an outcrop of rock surrounded by a broad belt of heavy and waxy plants.

The soil was spongy there, carpeted with fine adhesive moss that stuck to their feet: an insect-trap cleverly camouflaged by a cunning and clever nature—but Pat and his companions did not know that. They stumbled, slipped and fell in that viscous fringe, trying to avoid the redoubtable flora, and had a great deal of difficulty pulling Peggy out when she became trapped in the vegetal glue.

"This way!" shouted Moustache, pointing to a bare patch, which seemed to him to offer a safe retreat.

They all rushed forward, and let themselves fall heavily on the firm and dusty ground.

"I can't go on any longer," Mira whimpered. "I can't go on…"

"We'll never get out of this forest alive," said Peggy, breathlessly.

"Shut up," Pat commanded. "We're merely victims of our inexperience. We'll get used to it eventually."

Doc reflected, and affirmed after a brief pause: "An entire civilization developed right here. Our ancestors lived in these conditions. Why can't we?"

Only Fats' expression contradicted his words.

CHAPTER IX

Little ripples of fire were dancing over the lagoon. The sparkling disk of the morning Sun transformed the liquid surface into a dazzling cloth of gold, and Pat watched Mira's body capering in the luminous waves.

For a moment, he was tempted to undress in his turn and to feel the new sensation too—that of offering his body to the caress of the calm warn water, which Mira seemed to be savoring with visible pleasure—but he restrained himself, only consenting to take off his hood for the first time. Mira's temerity and insouciance frightened him.

"Come back, Mira!" he shouted. "That's an order!"

She saw him, stood up in the middle of the lagoon and marched regretfully through the clear water, causing thousands of sparkling drops to splash up in her wake.

Pat contemplated her, in the marvelous nudity that she displayed without restraint, until she had rejoined him. Then she let herself fall and roll in the fine sand, whose golden grains gathered on her velvet flesh like stardust sprung from the beginning of time.

"What you're doing isn't very prudent," he told her, gently. "Get dressed—the Sun's rays are becoming hotter and hotter."

"I took advantage of the fact that you were still asleep—I wanted to do it so much! You have no idea how god it is, Pat—and how marvelous it must have been in the olden days."

"Those days aren't dead—we can bring them back."

"No, Pat, we belong to a different race, and we shall never know those pleasures."

"Why do you say that?"

"Because we'll be dead before then." She rolled on to her side, stretched herself lazily and stared at him through half-closed eyes. "You don't desire me any longer, do you? Nor Peggy?"

"Get dressed, will you! The others might be getting anxious about our absence."

She got up and started laughing. "Karen?"

Pat did not have time to answer. He knew the two creatures that had just appeared abruptly over the lagoon only too well. "Look out!" he shouted, instinctively drawing his gun.

Mira howled in her turn as she recognized the *things*. Her bare flesh had attracted them, and only Pat's scarlet armor was still causing them to hesitate. The two spheres bobbed up and down in the calm and clear atmosphere, then skimmed the waves, finally stabilizing their position over the lagoon. All of a sudden, they launched themselves forward with unexpected violence.

With one bound, Pat threw himself on top of Mira to ward off the attack, making himself a protective rampart for her body.

He was just in time. One of the *things* passed only a few centimeters from their entwined bodies, whistling; then, mechanically, Pat squeezed the trigger of his weapon.

It was a puerile, absurd, insane gesture, for he knew perfectly well that thermic rays had no effect on the globular masses of those uncanny monsters. On the contrary, the blasts only served to inflame their combativeness, and they attempted a new assault, which was quickly stopped short again by the color that prevented them from reaching Mira's body.

Panting hard, Pat suddenly pointed to a crack in the rocks a few meters away. It was Mira's only chance. Slowly, he reached out his arm, grabbed the girl's garments and gave them to her. "Run to the rock," he told her. "I'll prevent them from getting in. Look out, it's time. Run!"

She broke free and ran, while Pat leapt to his feet in his turn and rushed forward. Mira plunged in and Pat's body blocked the crack, just as the filthy creatures dived.

There was a sharp whistle, and the air vibrated above the boy's head, while the others irrupted on to the beach.

The *things* did not persist then, fleeing and disappearing as quickly as they had come.

"By my eyes!" exclaimed Ferret. "What's happened?"

Pat waited for Mira to rejoin them, fully dressed. "Let that be the last time," he pronounced, dryly. "I won't tolerate such imprudence any longer."

Above them, the sky was beginning to darken, and thick black clouds were rising over the horizon. Immediately, the surrounding area seemed to emerge from its lethargy. The waters of the lake began to stir, and a fresh wind blew keenly over the beach, while the plants undulated behind the rocks, shaking their branches angrily.

A swarm of feline creatures with terrifying forms appeared, moving through the long grass, without taking any notice of the humans. In the air too, bulky insects fled northwards. Everything that was capable of movement started running, spurred on by fear.

A large eyeless wading bird had sprung forth from the bushes and was staggering along the beach, another victim of the general terror. In its blind course it crashed into the rocks, and the tumultuous waves swallowed its broken body.

"We have to take shelter!" Pat shouted, in order to be heard over the racket. "Behind the rocks, quickly!"

They fought against the violence of the wind on all fours, breathing with difficulty, splashing through the pools of muddy water that surrounded the rocks. There, they were obliged to dispute their shelter with a group of little animals with the heads of tortoises, whose bodies were covered with a fleece that seemed to be part-flaxen and part-vegetable—they could not tell, exactly. They were symbiotes, Doc declared—but no one was listening to him.

Around them, now, nature was unleashed in all its horror and power.

Suddenly, a warm sticky substance began to ooze from the rocky walls. It was Karen who noticed it first. Soon, the viscous gel soaked into the soil, and other tortoise-headed creatures emerged from a cleft, racing forward to fight over the nauseating mineral nourishment.

Stamping their feet in the sticky mud, the humans moved out of the way, horrified, stumbling over the bodies of the voracious animals that were jostling one another to gorge themselves on that unappetizing paste. Others were still arriving, blocking the passage. It was then that Pat felt that he had to make a decision if he wanted to preserve his authority. "This way!" He pointed, without really knowing what he was doing. His idea was to get out of the rocky shelter, at all costs—better to brave the tempest outside.

He climbed first on to a smooth rock, and helped the others to hoist themselves up. Then they leapt into the muddy pools, into the midst of transparent reeds that broke like glass beneath the weight of their bodies.

It was then that something emerged from a deeper pool and suddenly loomed up in front of the group. At the tip of a vegetable stem, formed of little scaly protuberances with yellow and black spots, an *almost*-human head was swaying feverishly.

It was unthinkable, astounding, at the very limits of possibility and horror.

The humans froze, as if fascinated by that atrocious, bloated head bristling with long, dull, flowing hair. It was half-way between human and animal, to judge by the expression in its large, almond-shaped eyes, and the powerful fangs that bordered a lipless mouth in the form of a sucker.

CHAPTER X

For a mortally long second, Pat felt fear twisting in his gut, but he conserved an absolute immobility when the head turned in their direction. His entire being was frozen, as if numb.

Suddenly, a voice resounded in his skull—a supernatural voice that expressed itself without the collaboration of any vocal cords. It penetrated, intensely, into the remotest recesses of his being, perfectly in accord with the harmonies of his own mind.

He realized immediately that he was not the only one to perceive the strange phenomenon, however. All his companions also heard the extraordinary silent voice, which said:

Miserable humans that you are, what are you still hoping for on this world that no longer belongs to you? By what miracle, then, can you move about in the open, in defiance of our laws? Is this the resurrection of your race?

"Who are you?" Pat demanded, speaking aloud.

I'm not unaware of the history of your race, human; I can perceive the thoughts of anything whatsoever in this world, combine them, assimilate them and organize them. It serves no purpose, alas, except to torment my poor brain. I listen, I hear, I discern, and I begin again, without respite, without rest, without end.... Eternally, I listen, I hear, I discern... I listen, I hear, I discern....

These words resonated like hammer-blows in Pat's skull, and he was obliged to react violently to interrupt the absurd monologue. "Stop! Speak more clearly. Where do you come from?"

I'm part of the new race. Don't you know, human? Yes, to be sure, you come from the human city... I can read your mind... I listen, I hear, I discern....

Pat sensed the creature's psychic tension weakening again. "Speak!" he cried.

Immediately, the silent voice resonated more clearly in his skull: *Once, your race dominated this world, I know—I've seen it. It reigned as master, and was ready to conquer the Universe. But for you humans, it was difficult to conceive that living beings could evolve in environments other than your own. That was the state of affairs before the atomic era, when your scientists affirmed the impossibility of any aquatic life in the marine depths, when, in reality, the abysses were swarming with animal life, nourishing itself exclusively on the organic mud of the great deeps. You also refused to believe in the micro-organisms polluting "stones from the sky." And the same faulty reasoning did not permit you to understand the new form of life that existed on Capella when your rockets traveled through space and landed on that unknown world. They ought to have reasoned by analogy and not limited themselves narrowly to laboratory experiments. Capella was, however, the very symbol of life.*

"What life are you talking about?" asked Doc.

Of that to which I belong.

"That's a lie—there was no creature of your species on Capella. I know—I've read about it."

But there were the spores. Capella was none other than the seat of universal panspermia, and no one suspected that the rockets were transporting the seeds of new life to Earth. No one. Evidently, the frightful war that divided you in that epoch did not permit you to interest yourselves in the phenomenon. Thank God—in those circumstances, the war was our ally. The spores had survived in the void, stuck to the metal hulls of your space-vessels, and they gradually spread over the surface of your planet, settling in lagoons and remote bodies of water, in order to accomplish their work of cellular proliferation in total tranquility. They developed, and, once their metamorphosis was accomplished, became what you call the things. *What an absurd word that is, denuded of meaning—isn't it?*

"What happened after that?" asked Pat, avidly.

They made their appearance in the four corners of the globe, and everyone understood that nothing could impede their progress henceforth. The outskirts of cities were infested. There was panic, and no one sought to understand where they came from. Already, numerous animals were dead, completely pulverized following contact with the things, *and it was soon the turn of the humans. They fell, petrified, strewing the streets and plazas, until the wind dispersed their disaggregated cells. All kinds of weapons were tried to fight against the* things, *but nothing worked and they continued to divide and subdivide, to give birth to other* things. *The process is unlimited.*

"What relationship can you have with that race?"

It created me, like everything else that now lives on this world.

"You mean that all the creatures that are alive now didn't exist before the catastrophe?"

No.

"And nothing any longer exists of the species of old?"

No, not any more. I've told you that I listen, that I hear, that I discern. I'm a relay. The things *don't lie.*

"How, then, have they been able to create these new species?"

By violating the laws of chance. The things possess a collective consciousness, and they're attracted by elementary living cells, thanks to their powerful magnetism. They're cellular catalysts, unable to conceive of a mode of life independent of any symbiosis. That's the very essence of universal life. Thanks to an organizing field that they possess, the things, *as you call them, reorganize the dissociated elementary cells, which have conserved, in spite of their appearance of death, an individual and independent life. Even the most complex substances of the vital world suffer the effects of the force-field. Every molecule is guided, directed and amalgamated, almost instantaneously, to form a new, better-constituted creature. Anyway, I know that your ancestors were quite familiar with those forces that oblige atoms and molecules to respect perfectly-defined trajectories even outside a vital organism.*

The Sun had reappeared in the sky; the wind had ceased howling, and silence reigned once again over the region. Pat suddenly realized that, while his mind was trying to comprehend the terrible revelations of the plant with the human head. Many things escaped him, and he privately cursed the ignorance that prevented him of getting to the bottom of the problem.

Even Doc, with all his knowledge, had difficulty conceiving the fantastic reality.

They reacted again when the creature spoke inside their heads: *What hope still remains to you, humans, after what I've just revealed to you?*

"That of living and fighting until our dying breath," Pat replied.

Karen suddenly seized Pat's arm and began to speak in her turn: "Since you're not unaware of anything, since you know everything, since nothing is impossible for you to know..."

I listen, I hear, I discern...

In their skulls there was something akin to a flood of confused thought, whose incoherence resembled a kind of monstrous laughter.

Then a unique thought-wave replied: *One of you knows the location of the secret city. It will suffice for you to continue to march in a north-westerly direction. Two hundred miles from here, you'll find the Temple of the Future, but above all, avoid going in. Also avoid the Valley of the Voracious Ones if you want to reach it. You aren't strong enough to fight them. Stay away from the Sound of Life—your ears can't resist it. Good luck, humans, god luck... and most of all, have courage.*

The same atrocious laughter echoed in the skulls of the humans; then the monstrous head, at the tip of its stalk, lashed the air with its long flaxen hair, and dived straight toward the liquid surface, disappearing abruptly with a curious gurgling sound.

Only a few bubbles, which gradually burst, revealed the traces of its flight in the direction of the lagoon.

"What did it mean?" asked Moustache.

"This place is hellish," said Pat. "Let's get out."

They left the lagoon and went into the forest,

As if their tribulations were not sufficient, a thick heavy mist rose, rendering their progress, under Fats' guidance, even more difficult.

CHAPTER XI

A sort of yelping was resounding here and there; luminous insects were blinking in dark corners, speckling the darkness with little multicolored lights, and unknown animals were modulating strange songs in the spiny thickets.

Stars were appearing in the sky, between the branches, and a yellow Moon rose in the east.

The group had run aground in a clearing through which a stream meandered, which had slaked their thirst—but Pat had sense the general distress and universal despair. "Let's try to envisage the question like an Adult," he never ceased repeating. "For the moment, you can't do anything except submit to the hostile nature whose enemy you've become."

He knew, however, that that they did not have a chance in a million of reaching the famous and mysterious secret city—and the atrocious laughter of the human-headed plant was still resonating in his skull.

He looked around before ordering a halt. In the darkness, the faults in the rock seemed to yawn like grimacing mouths. From time to time, large phosphorescent lizards turned away from the stream and went across the clearing to disappear into a nearby thicket. There might have been thousands of them between the flat stones along the stream.

Pat shivered involuntarily. In Karen's face he read an extreme lassitude and an insurmountable disgust. That was what he felt too.

"I can't do any more," she murmured, letting herself fall on to the short, coarse grass. "By the Unity, Pat, what's going to become of us?"

"We're going to go on till the end. Nothing will stop us."

"I admire your determination, but it's beyond my strength. Why such obstinacy?"

"Because I'm still trying to believe that things aren't as they seem to be. Because I want to continue to hope that our salvation lies at the end of our route. No, please, don't say anything—think of the others. This isn't the time to engage in a conversation of that sort."

Thy rejoined the group, built a fire, and restricted their evening meal to a few condensed-food tablets that were part of Doc's reserves. Then they lay down on the bare ground, leaving Ferret with the responsibility of supervising the first watch.

At first light, Fats set about waking the others up, and gave the thermic pistol that had been passed from hand to hand by the group's protectors back to Ferret. It was reassuring to know that they possessed such a redoubtable weapon, even if the dangers that menaced them were more redoubtable still.

Pat squeezed the butt of the weapon held in his own belt, which seemed to restore his confidence, and then went to quench his thirst in the stream that ran nearby. He had to crush a good 20 slugs as stout as liter bottles to clear a path to the stream, and was almost bitten by a furry decapod disturbed in the meal that it was making of a red-haired grasshopper.

Life was waking up along with the first gleams of dawn, sinister, cruel and hallucinatory.

When he came back, Ferret was just finishing putting out the fire and Karen was putting on her protective garments Peggy was massaging her ankles between Doc and Fats, and Mira, who was sitting on a rock, abruptly turned her head away at the sight of him. She had been treating him coldly since the previous day. Why? He had no idea, unless it was because of his indifference since their encounter on the edge of the lagoon. Yes, that must be it—but it was of no importance. Her contempt had only hastened the inevitable.

Suddenly, Pat noticed that Moustache was not in the group. "Where's Moustache?" he asked.

"I don't know," Doc replied. "He was here a moment ago."

A silhouette emerged from the shadows. It was Moustache, quite breathless. Anxiety was legible in his face. "Come and see," he said. "It's quite incomprehensible."

They all followed him to the edge of the clearing, where the forest's reign began. He showed them imprints in the dew-dampened soil, and they could not believe their eyes. They were the neatly-defined tracks of bare feet—human feet—with toes, soles and heels.

"They seem to be recent," Moustache declared. "They can't belong to humans, can they? Humans like us…"

"That's impossible," Doc murmured. "We're the only humans able to…"

"Perhaps it's an animal that resembles a human," Pat put in. "Yes, that must be it—an animal, for sure…"

"They must have been prowling around our camp last night," Peggy remarked.

"We didn't see anything," Fats replied.

"I definitely heard a slight noise, myself," Mira said, "but…"

Pat cut her off. "It's all right—let's get moving, quickly—that's the most prudent course of action."

They looked around, rapidly got their bearings, and then moved off into the woods.

The ground soon began to rise in a gentle slope between two enormous masses of vegetation. There were loose red rocks veined with black underfoot, and they had hardly recovered their breath when they entered a gully that seemed to extend far into the distance beneath the foliage.

It was then that a strange murmur seemed to rise up around them. It was reminiscent of wind blowing through reeds—but there was no wind…nor any reeds.

Then the single noise broke up, as if emitted from several different points. It was an association of sounds that was producing the unusual concert.

Pat accelerated the pace of the march without turning round; then, all of a sudden, something struck him. The voices had something human about them…terribly human.

He stopped abruptly, drew his weapon and gathered his companions together. "Let's get out of the gully," he said, "and hurry—the girls can go first and we'll bring up the rear."

Peggy was pale. "Pat…" she murmured.

He shoved her forward unceremoniously. "This is no time for whining. Go on!"

They were about to run forwards when the most unexpected and terrifying thing that a human brain could conceive occurred.

Behind them, at the end of the gully, the clamor became louder. Moustache was the first to see the frightful creatures surge forth. They seemed to have sprung out of the ground, as if by magic.

Nude, or nearly so, apart from the vegetal loincloths that swathed their pelvic regions, seemingly-human beings invaded the gully, accentuating the atrocious murmur that paralyzed the group, which was produced in chorus by thousands of gaping mouths.

Their bodies were covered with them. The thorax and the abdomen were crowded with horrible and menacing mouths, lipless but bristling with sinister, sharp-pointed fangs. And all those mouths were opening, stretching and chattering, making dreadful noises.

Pat felt his blood freeze in his veins, and a frightful nausea rising in his throat.

For an instant, he only wanted to look at their faces, refusing to admit the monstrous revelation—but there was even more ferocity in the globular eyes, ringed with a cartilaginous border, that each creature possessed.

The Voracious Ones, he thought, suddenly remembering the words of the plant with the human head. He hesitated, though, over firing and starting a battle. Perhaps there was another solution, which would avoid the worst.

Things happened with extreme rapidity, though. A dozen Voracious Ones launched themselves from the surrounding rocks and landed near the group like stones from a catapult, making guttural cries, sowing panic among the humans.

In a fraction of a second, Pat—who had pushed Karen against the rocky wall—saw Moustache, surrounded by the Voracious Ones, hurl himself into their midst, mingling his howls with those of the polybuccal monsters. The latter, howling all the louder, sent Moustache spinning from one to another as he cannoned into them in his panic.

Pat and Ferret understood that they had to make use of their weapons without the risk of hitting their unfortunate companion.

The incomprehensible game lasted a few more seconds; then, one of the Voracious Ones struck Moustache on the back of the neck with a scything blow of his hairy first, and projected his victim forwards. The boy lost his balance and stumbled into another Voracious One, who received him with open arms.

The howl of atrocious agony that rose over the din made the horrified humans understand what was happening. The creature that had gripped Moustache was in the process of devouring him alive, all its avid mouths biting with incredible ferocity, tearing the flesh away shred by shred.

Pat was about to launch himself forward, but the other monsters plunged in their turn and rushed to fight over Moustache's already atrociously-lacerated body. He was no longer screaming…

Pat squeezed the trigger of his weapon then. Ferret followed suit. They fired at hazard, blast after blast, scything down the first opponents, who were exploding in a filthy fountain of charred flesh within the gully.

The horde abandoned Moustache's remains and retreated slowly, while some, seriously burned, writhed in agony on the ground.

"Quickly!" Pat shouted to his companions. "Run for the forest."

"Impossible," said Doc. "We're surrounded."

Pat looked round momentarily and observed in his turn that it was too late to pull back to the exit from the gully. It had happened so suddenly that neither Pat nor anyone else had had time to realize it.

Another 20 Voracious Ones leapt down from the rocky ridge, falling upon the group of humans with unexpected savagery. Pat reeled, and fired almost at point-blank range at the one that hurled itself upon him. The creature exploded, blown apart, but another pounced and snatched away his weapon.

Pat cried out, and sank his foot into the monster's drooling abdomen, then smashed a face in the mêlée, while seizing another and thrusting it brutally aside in order to clear a path to Karen, who had just collapsed.

What happened next he did not understand. He was only aware of being firmly held by two hairy, terribly powerful fists. Around him, his companions were lying on the gully floor, utterly unable to fight. He waited, in anguish, for the avid mouths that he could see writhing a few centimeters away start biting, but nothing happened. There as a gesture from one of the Voracious Ones—the one that seemed to be the leader of the band—and a profound and discordant note issued from his entrails.

The monsters regrouped, lifting up the prisoners and shoving them into the middle of the column that they had formed. The voices became calmer and fell silent; then the column moved off, in deathly silence, and disappeared into the sinister grayness of a clump of trees.

CHAPTER XII

After several hours of an exhausting march, the column emerged from the forest and came into an immense clearing where there were primitive huts made of earth and interwoven branches.

Pat still had the nightmarish scene before his eyes in which the poor body of Moustache had been fought over while it was being devoured. He would never forget it. What would become of them now? At what vile feast were he and his companions about to be sacrificed? He dared not think about it—and when he examined the surroundings, he realized that an intense activity was under way in the clearing.

Round-faced females were running around with their multitudes of gaping mouths, dragging no-less-repugnant offspring behind them. In front of the huts, a few Voracious Ones were lying on their backs, with bloody joints of meat pressed to their bodies, which their multiple mouths were devouring gluttonously.

He noticed then that the leader of the horde had engaged in an animated conversation with a few plume-wearing individuals that had just appeared in the middle of the village. They were using a language that was more like roaring than speech.

"Look, Pat," whispered Karen. "He's showing them our weapons."

"I don't think they realize that they need to press the trigger to obtain a thermic rejection."

"What do they want?"

He pointed to the feathered creatures, which were heading toward them. "We'll soon find out."

The face of the big fellow who was advancing toward them wore a stupid expression that was both primitive and bestial. His globular eyes fixed themselves on Pat, and his multiple mouths joined in chorus to vomit forth a surprising tirade: "You... Great Moon Spirit... come bearing Eternal Fire to wretched Voracious Ones, who not understand... Great Moon promise Eternal Fire to tribe of Voracious Ones for cold seasons... but Voracious Ones not know... Have pity on poor, unhappy Voracious Ones... Have pity..."

A concert of lamentations went up around the humans, while Ferret whispered in Pat's ear: "What do they mean?"

Pat frowned. "Let me handle it—I think I understand. They think we're gods."

"Gods?"

The tribal chief resumed yapping loudly, with a pleading expression. "O powerful spirits with one mouth, do not bring down the wrath of the Great Moon upon us. Have pity... have pity..."

"It is difficult to speak of pity when one of our number has been devoured in a cowardly fashion by your brothers!" shouted Pat.

"We not know. We think evil red spirits come into land of Voracious Ones, but our hearts are broken and our sated mouths accursed forever, for having bitten the divine flesh of the Great Moon."

"What, then, do you want of us, wretched Voracious One?"

"That you lessen our distress by offering us Eternal Fire, as the Great Moon has promised, through all the millions of mouths that contemplate us every night through the Sacred Eye."

"Of what Eye do you speak?"

"Of the Eye found in accursed ruins, for contemplating the mouths of the Great Moon."

The language, though rudimentary, had something simultaneously poignant and hallucinatory about it. Fortified by the revelations of the plant with a human head, Pat and his companions guessed, to their amazement, that this caricature of a language was the only thing that still existed of the human race, which had served to create these absurd and incomprehensible beings. It was probably due to some atavistic memory buried in the depths of nerve-cells newly-fashioned by the strange process of metamorphosis. Scraps of human thought still subsisted, therefore, in these new creatures issued from the most terrible and demonic of geneses.

They allowed themselves to be guided by the Voracious Ones' chief, and went into the largest hut in the village.

Enthroned in the middle of a heap of bones and stinking refuge, aimed toward the exterior, was a most unusual and unexpected object: a sort of telescope, mounted on a tripod, which appeared to be the object of the most profound veneration on the part of the Voracious Ones. This, therefore, was the Sacred Eye. Pat understood immediately what had happened.

This telescope, presumably discovered in some ancient ruin, had been the instrument that had permitted these people to concoct a religion appropriate to them. They had needed a god, and they had found one in the pale disk peppered with countless round marks reminiscent of giant mouths, which was enthroned in the Heavens like an eternal promise.

Beautiful Diana, blonde Phoebe, benevolent Isis, charming Astarte—of what impious religion have you become the goddess? You, whom the Ancients made the queen of the night and the accomplice of their loves! What monstrous poets will you be able to inspire henceforth?

That was what Pat was thinking, when the Voracious Ones' chief added: "The thousand mouths of the Great Moon promise Voracious Ones Eternal Fire... Great Moon sends to land of Voracious Ones deceptive spirits with one mouth, to test loyalty of Voracious Ones... but Voracious Ones not know... little brains but big hearts... Must forgive... must... for we adore Great Moon."

While he was speaking, Karen had gripped Pat's arm. "To what eternal fire is he alluding?"

"Shhh!" Pat whispered. "Be quiet! At all costs, we mustn't awaken their suspicion. I believe I know what they want." Then, he turned proudly to the monarch and said: "I will grant the eternal fire to the tribe in return for our liberty."

"Liberty will be granted if you are the Spirit of the Great Moon."

"Don't forget," Pat replied, not taken aback. "Otherwise, the wrath of the Great Moon will destroy your brethren, to the very last."

His gaze had turned to the two Voracious Ones who were still holding the thermic pistols. Hurriedly, the chief ordered his brothers: "Let them be given the mouths of fire, and may our forever-broken hearts bleed with eternal gratitude."

Pat and Ferret recovered their weapons with a sigh of satisfaction; then Pat addressed a wink to his companions. "They want fire," he confided to them, in a whisper. "We're going to give it to them. Follow me."

They left the hut and, on Pat's orders, began to heap up all the dead wood they could find in the vicinity in the center of the village. When they had finally assembled a huge bonfire, Doc sprinkled the whole with a resin derived from a variety of plant that grew in profusion not far away. Then, without further delay, Pat pressed the trigger of his gun twice.

Immediately, an enormous flame sprang from the pyre, which began to crackle amid exclamations of joy uttered by thousands of mouths.

Indifferent to the general delight, Pat suddenly directed his companions' attention to the sky, which had just darkened abruptly above their heads. "I think we'd do well to take advantage of the only chance that remains to us to get out of this place. If it starts to rain, that will put an end to our prestige."

"Indeed," agreed Doc, peering at the somber masses that were rising above the horizon. "That's a bad sign, and I think it's entirely in our interests to make a rapid getaway."

They took their leave of the monarch, in spite of his pleas and prayers, promising him the eternal protection of the Great Moon, and left the valley of the Voracious Ones with great relief.

Black clouds were piling up in the sky, racing over the tops of the giant plants.

A heavy vapor rose from the overheated ground. Numerous spirals rose up and drifted slowly sideways in the nebulous brightness between the tall plants.

Overhead, the enormous plants were disappearing, drowned by threads of vapor that wound around the trunks and stems like long, flexible, moving tentacles.

They continued thus for a further hour, until the approach of night, at which time the mist lost its color and on a leaden hue.

They were all exhausted, and the efforts they had been obliged to make since they had left the Valley of the Voracious Ones had weakened their resistance. They were all in, especially the girls. Peggy nearly slipped into a muddy pool when a reptilian liana gripped her ankle as she passed by. She felt the terminal ramifications of the liana bite into her flesh, and screamed. Fortunately, Ferret was beside her at that moment, and he sliced through the horrible plant with a brief thermic discharge.

It was while they were hesitating as to whether to continue their advance in the semi-darkness that they saw a curious luminosity ahead of them. Intrigued by the origin of the light-source, they went forward cautiously, and soon witnessed as spectacle as magical as it was hallucinatory.

The low branches of a clump of plants were bristling with curious phosphorescent blisters, dispensing spectral light all around, which deformed the somber masses of the thorny thickets.

Karen's face was grey in the unusual lighting. "Look," she said, pointing with her finger at large insects that were emerging from shadowy corners and zooming forward, as if attracted by the luminous pockets. They were crashing into the vegetal jelly and disappearing, completely liquefied, inside the nocturnal traps, which presumably ensured the nourishment of the carnivorous plants.

"Be careful," said Pat. "Whatever you do, don't touch those pockets."

They bent down, skirting the traps and avoiding them as best they could, until they had reached the summit of an arid rocky hill drowned in darkness. They could not go any further, and rain had begun to fall in large drops.

Doc found a narrow opening in the rock and they all plunged into the precarious refuge, utterly exhausted. They intended to rest there until first light, until they noticed the lethargy that gradually invaded their limbs and brains.

Doc realized the danger. As he observed, it was definitely caused by emanations from the rock. There was a bitter, intoxicating odor in the crack, and they rushed outside, their heads heavy and their limbs numb, gluttonously breathing in the cool, keen air that whipped their faces.

The malaise dissipated, and Pat looked at his companions. For the first time, he understood what they were feeling. There was no longer the slightest glimmer of will-power or confidence in their tearful eyes, and when Peggy collapsed into Ferret's arms, he did not have the courage to intervene.

"I can't go on," she sobbed. "I can't go on. All this is too much for me."

Mira had advanced toward Pat. He sensed that she was at the end of her tether.

"I can't go on either. I'm exhausted.... exhausted and ill. I refuse to go any further. I'd rather die here."

"Have you gone mad? We must go on, no matter what the cost—it's our only chance."

"We'll never get there," Doc put in, in his turn. "The route is long, and must be swarming with unknown dangers. I don't think I have the strength to go on any longer."

"Troop of brainless monkeys!" cried Pat. "Think for a moment about what will become of you if you stay here." He turned to the others, and felt the same distress. He knew then that they had made their decision, and that nothing could change their opinion.

"We're going to stay here," said Ferret, "and wait for death. We no longer fear it now."

"Very well," said Pat, shaking his head. "As you wish. But for my part, I prefer to go forward to meet danger rather than wait for it. I'll continue alone."

"I'll go with you!" Karen exclaimed, running toward him. "I'm going too."

Only Fats had said nothing, and his eyes met Pat's momentarily. The hatred that he still divined around him surely tipped the balance of the decision. He knew that Pat would never betray his trust, and it was for him that he opted. "Me too," he said. "I'll go with you if want me to."

Pat shook the hand that was held out to him, and pocketed the three shares of food reserves that Doc handed to him without a word. Then he darted one last glance at his companions, and the trio set forth.

CHAPTER XIII

Every time that Pat felt nausea twisting his stomach again he lay down in the grass to vomit. He stayed there, lying on his belly, breathing like a damned soul and cursing all the plants in creation.

It was the same for Karen and Fats too, since they had consumed their last biovitamin tablets and had been forced, no matter what the risk, to begin to feed themselves on wild fruits and berries discovered by chance along their route. Their physiology was not adapted to that vegetal nourishment, and they had immediately fallen prey to atrocious sickness, as if their entrails were rebelling violently against the abrupt change in regime. They knew, though, that the sickness would be temporary, and that their stomachs would gradually adapt, for their physiological defense systems would work in that way.

The bouts of nausea became less frequent in the days that followed, and they were soon able to sustain themselves reasonably well with the vegetables they encountered, which Karen was able to locate with a sure instinct.

One morning, a large ocean presented itself to their sight, and, for the first time, they contemplated that enormous liquid expanse from the top of a cliff as a huge red sun seemed to emerge from it, its reflections dancing in the shape of a sparkling saber. There too, however, in spite of the beauty and the purity of the scene, Hell had its rights, so powerful was Hell's reign over the world that god seemed to have abandoned.

Unknown dangers were lying in wait for the three fugitives, and they discovered them along the beaches and cliffs, which were infested with marine creatures, the majority of them amphibious, engaged in an eternal battle outside the water.

Enormous rocks swarmed with intense life, bristling with long flexible tentacles that lashed the waves with an extreme violence. The trio observed with horror that they were dealing with long serpents, one of whose extremities was fixed to the rock by a multitude of suckers. All of them were parts of a single body, and seemed to be animated by a collective consciousness that had no other aim but to nourish the community by capturing an incredible quantity of strangely-formed fish.

Further on there were enormous crabs whose carapaces were covered in strands of green algae, which served them as camouflage between the reefs. The humans nearly fell into the trap. It was Fats who had a sudden intuition of it, at the moment when Karen set her foot on one of the monsters half-buried in the sand.

They left the coast and moved away from the shore to penetrate into an interminable steppe.

At dusk, vanquished by fatigue, they ate a few fruits, drank fresh water from a stream, and then—as they did every evening—lit a protective fire, which they took turns to feed until morning. That was sufficient to keep all the undesirable guests that haunted the region away from the camp.

At first light, Fats, who was certainly the most depressed of them, could not help saying: "All this is absurd and incredible, and I'm wondering how humans can still be living in this secret city that is our only objective and our only hope."

"Perhaps they've found means of combating this hostile nature," said Karen, thoughtfully. "Perhaps they've been able to protect themselves. Why shouldn't they be working to rid the world of the leprosy that's eating it away?"

Fats sighed deeply and murmured: "Perhaps, instead, they're awaiting a death that doesn't arrive—and that's the most terrible possibility of all." He lay down on the sand, half-closing his eyes, and added, as if to himself: *And in those days, men shall seek death and shall not find it, and shall desire to die, and death shall flee from them.*

"What's that you're saying?" asked Pat.

Fats looked at him, and the red flames that were still dancing in the dying fire were also dancing in his pupils. "It's a verse from the Bible," he said. "Forgive me for the quotation—it was involuntary."

"What does it mean?"

"That for us, there is no death more atrocious than living until the end of our days...if they are to have an end."

Pat shrugged his shoulders, and his face moved closer to Fats'. "The Apocalypse, eh? That nonsense imagined by the prophets of your religion. Sadism, that's what it is."

"It is, in any case, a prediction that has been verified."

"But after all, Fats, how can you believe such a thing, when no one, even the cruelest, should be able to imagine it? And even if this God of whom you speak really exists, what ignominy could the human race possibly have committed to merit such a fate? No, I refuse to believe it—all this is purely accidental. Do you remember what that plant with a human head said about Capella, spores, and the form of life that surpasses human understanding? We're simply victims of the duality that exists throughout space, and which sets all dominant species at odds. A war is lost or won, that's the law of nature—but in the end, hope always remains. Do you understand?"

"The only hope that I possess is in my heart and in my soul."

"Because you reason like a Christian and, quite simply, lack realism, Listen, Fats, and try to understand. The material reality of a fact is one thing, but its psychological reflection is another. You've been subject to that reflection for centuries, and you don't seek to know the truth because that truth scares you. Why? Because the dread of a supernatural force has never ceased to haunt the human mind since the beginning of time. Alas, I lack sufficient knowledge in that domain to speak with precision, but I know that our remotest ancestors worshipped material idols. Later, every phenomenon of nature was considered as a divinity. With the assistance of evolution, belief in a unique god displaced paganism, further fortifying that absolute dread. But all your theological philosophers had to collapse one day, and that's what happened on the day when people came to consider the problem of overpopulation. I've heard it said that was necessary to develop effective procedures for the regulation of sterility and fecundity, in order to be able to control the reproduction of our species. The nurses taught us that, Fats, do you remember? After that, your religions were done for, because they were conceived in a time that was ignorant of the enormous menace hanging over the human future." Pat nodded his head and continued, lost in thought: "Yes, it was necessary that they should die, in order that humans might finally glimpse the truth."

"By creating the Unity!" Fats replied. "How can you prove that *that*'s the truth?"

"Because the Unity is a reality, simultaneously scientific and spiritual, and because it has permitted us to abolish dogmatic rigidity and ritual to make way for a superior kind of faith."

In the dust, Pat negligently traced a V inside a circle. "There," he said. "The very foundation of our thought." And he did his best to render that thought as clear as possible.

According to him, the Unity grew in parallel with the universe whose fabric it was, evolving *incessantly* toward increased consciousness. It was, in sum, the axis of evolution. To put it another way, the Unity had been created at the same time that all the matter composing the universe had been created, or every particle contributed to the general edifice. Everything resonated with the whole. No particle was inseparable from the cosmos itself, which implied a perpetual communion of the Individual with the Whole, and the Whole with the Individual. And it was the same for the mentality that animates our miserable material carcasses. Each of our deaths reinforced the power of the Unity and contributed to its total perfection. That would continue until the universe had attained its full development. At that moment, the Unity would reach a phase of complete consciousness and absolute perfection on a cosmic scale, and would destroy itself in order to engender a new universe, which would follow the same phases of development in its turn—and from death, life would be reborn, in the incessant cycle that, for Pat, symbolized Infinity and Eternity.

Fats, who had listened attentively, could not help shaking his head. "In sum, if I understand correctly, your materialism shelters you from divine wrath, since you have no fear of it? In that case, what can prevent you from doing evil?"

Pat frowned. "Our conscience and the love of knowledge. Humans are capable in themselves of knowing what is just, true and good, without the collaboration of any religion. I'm certain that virtuous people existed even before humans offered themselves to the first divinity." Then, challenging Fats with his gaze, he said in a dryer tone: "And that materialism of which you speak also shelters us from hypocritical prayers of a god from whom one always demands, but to whom one never gives."

Fats stood up, his fists clenched. "I can't tolerate such an insult, Pat. You don't have the right."

Karen leapt between them. "No—have both of you gone mad?"

She did not have time to say another word. A long and flexible sinewy liana that had sprung from the ground nearby thrashed the air furiously, and abruptly liberated all its ramifications.

Pat leapt backwards, dragging Fats and Karen with him. In his haste, however, the thermic pistol had slipped from his belt. It lay on the ground a few paces away.

As he was about to launch himself forward, Karen held him back. "Look out, Pat!"

He realized the danger then. Something had just opened up in the rough cortex at the tip of the principal branch. It was a globular mass, reminiscent of a huge eye. A demonic gleam shone in the eye, whose unique and inhuman gaze was staring at the trio with an extraordinary intensity.

It swayed at the end of the vegetal stem, registering Pat's slightest gestures—and when the latter tried to bend down, all the other ramifications beat the air urgently, blocking his action.

Pat recoiled.

"Be careful," breathed Fats. "Try to deflect its attention to the right. I have an idea."

Pat obeyed without asking any questions. He moved away from the others, attracting the monstrous eye's attention to himself.

Fats acted then with lightning rapidity. He drew his knife from his belt and plunged forward, gripping the master liana with his free hand. It immediately began to writhe, trying to coil itself around him with a rapid reptilian movement—but Fats had calculated his blow perfectly, and his blade plunged into the round eye twice, then drilled into the gelatinous mass.

Thick greenish blood spouted forth, splashing the boy, while Pat, who had succeeded in picking up the thermic weapon, fired at the dangerous plant at point-blank range. Two blasts of force cut the branch in two, and it collapsed, killed outright, dragging Fats down as it fell.

Pat and Karen leapt forward and helped him disengage himself from the vegetal tangle, still animated by its final twitches.

Fats wiped the blade of his knife with a handful of grass and looked at Pat. "Well, I'm hot," he said.

"Me too," said Pat." Then he smiled, nudged the other in the ribs and said: "Let's be on our way. I'm beginning to get seriously hungry—I suppose that's a good sign."

Scarcely had they reached the top of the ridge that barred their route than they stopped dead before the most unexpected spectacle that could have offered itself to their gaze. In front of them, on the other side of the hill, confused pieces of metallic debris were shining in the ardent sunlight: disemboweled, rusty, dismantled carcasses, some fragmentary items of which were reminiscent of the ancestral silhouettes of the terrible engines of death of the time of the Catastrophe. It was a veritable cemetery of rockets.

CHAPTER XIV

A few long-tailed birds took flight, frightened by the arrival of the humans, uttering little cries. Then a heavy silence fell.

In front of the trio, a metallic carcass loomed up, half-buried in the sand, with large gaps through which the wind blew, and large climbing plants reminiscent of long petrified snakes extended.

Pat, Karen and Fats had stopped, unable to believe their eyes. All this was definitely the work of humans, of an extinct race whose true history would probably never be known. But it was obvious that a terrible and implacable battle must have taken place here, a century before, to judge by the still-visible traces of a hail of fire hat had smashed and disemboweled the rockets' hulls.

Not far away, Karen spotted an immense cupola that seemed to be emerging from the sand, and whose glittering mass seemed to be intact.

In his turn, Fats discovered an opening at ground level, half-blocked by stones and vegetation. They made haste to clear a passage, and soon reached a sort of tunnel slanting downwards at a gentle gradient—but the air deteriorated rapidly, and they were obliged to enlarge the opening in order to be able to breathe normally.

Almost at the same time, they perceived the creature. It seemed to be staring at them, from a moist and shiny protuberance haloed with a thin, decorative veil, which was confused with the sands of the surrounding desert. It was crouching in a hollow of the tunnel, and was formed like a grotesque furry ball bristling with gelatinous pseudopods. It uttered a slight squeal, and raced away through the opening, bouncing with incredible rapidity.

"I'm scared," Karen moaned. "It's dark and cold."

"Come on," Pat ordered, paying no heed to her lamentations. He led the way, and all three of them continued their advance into the arched subterranean corridor. They did not understand what the two gleaming tracks might be that extended into the depths of the corridor, nor what the hard, cold material of which they were might be, whose solidity seemed able to withstand anything.

Karen stumbled over a stone and exposed a skull that crumbled under her foot. A few more scattered bones were lying a little further away—probably the remains of a human being like them.

There were others at intervals within the tunnel, which prompted Fats to say: "Men died in this place in hundreds, perhaps thousands. I'm certain that there are surprises still to come."

They had to overcome a thousand difficulties in order to reach the interior, but finally emerged beneath the enormous transparent cupola.

To begin with, they found a vast hall, a veritable labyrinth of twisted beams and bricks. After having finally come to a heavy batten that pivoted on its axis, grating lugubriously, however, they found themselves in a room whose ceiling was constituted by the transparent vault, which allowed the daylight to filter through, in spite of the dust and earth that the wind had been accumulating outside for a century.

Nothing moved. A heavy, ancient silence saturated the atmosphere. Objects strewed the floor, depleted by time to a greater or lesser extent, some of them falling apart beneath their feet.

There were also all kinds of strange and unknown apparatus: long tubes with tapering ends, standing upright on their bases, as well as gleaming spheres, arranged in a long sequence that ended at the rim of the transparent dome. They were placed on   four-wheeled carts of a sort, which seemed to be designed to move along two long rigid rails giving access to the outside of the building, without appearing to end anywhere.

Suddenly, they made out four lifeless bodies lying in grotesque poses. Humans! Two of them were lying on their backs, at the foot of a heap of scrap iron, another was hunched in the middle of the room, and the last had collapsed on a low chair in front of a wall-panel cluttered with a multitude of switches and buttons, his hand still set on a massive lever.

As Pat and his companions stepped over the body lying in the middle of the room, Karen's foot collided with the inert mass, which resulted in the cadaver coming apart, as if by the effect of a magic wand. A few ashes floated around the three humans, then dispersed without leaving any trace.

The displacement of air occasioned by Pat and Fats—who had stepped back abruptly, moved by an identical reflex—had provoked the disintegration of two other bodies; the only one that remained intact was the one at the control panel. Pat pointed at it. "That one must have been the last to die," he said. "I wonder what he was trying to do at that apparatus."

"Perhaps it's a radio-post." Fats suggested.

"Yes, I was wondering that."

Pat had come to a halt in front of the wall-panel and looked with interest at the innumerable dials and buttons. Then his attention was attracted by a concave screen in front of the cadaver, at head-height. It could not be anything but a television screen. Mechanically, piqued by curiosity, Pat lovingly manipulated the articulated knobs whose disposition reminded him of the old visiophones that he had known since infancy, with which the city of men was provided.

He uttered a sigh, abandoned the screen, and turned to his companions. As he was about to speak, he suddenly interrupted himself, and abruptly turned his head. A faint noise, as soft as a murmur, was emanating from the wall-panel, and a few needles began to flutter nervously over their dials. A few red and green lights began to flicker, and fugitive flashes striped the screen of the visiophone.

"By my spirit!" Pat swore. "These machines are still working. That's incredible."

He headed for another wall-panel, and was feverishly inspecting the rows of switches and the amplification circuits when a voice suddenly rang out behind him: a well-modulated voice, which said: "Men and women of Eurasia, unite in bad times as you have in the good. Fight against the saboteurs of the government of free Eurasia."

Pat wheeled around and stared.

Within the concave screen, the image of a human clad in a curious uniform had appeared. He was almost an old man. Tall, severe and stiff, he spoke with authority and emphasis, punctuating his speech with broad and measured gestures.

"These people employ the worst sort of politics, and such intrigues cannot justify the astonishing accusations contained in the note from the African government. I know...yes, I know...that these politics have received the approval of several States, which see them—falsely—as a guarantee of peace and security..."

"What's happening, Pat?" asked Karen, fearfully. "Do you know who that man is?"

"How should I know?"

"It resembles the mysterious speeches that the Adults have picked up in my sector," Fats replied, after reflecting. "I recognize the voice."

"Does this transmission originate from the secret city, then?" Pat murmured.

"I don't know."

"What does it mean?" Karen asked. "What is he talking about?"

The man's voice continued: "The government of free Eurasia must similarly call attention to the inaccuracy of criticisms leveled at the clause of the treaty providing for the extension to Timbuktu of non-military dispositions. And I give you my personal guarantee, men and women of Eurasia, that the clause in question..."

The rest of the sentence was lost in a scream uttered by Karen, to which another exclamation from Pat replied.

In the middle of the room, between the sparkling spheres, an imposing creature of steel was standing.

CHAPTER XV

One might have thought that the metal monster had sprung from the ground, as if by magic. It was motionless, and seemed to be watching the humans with large round eyes, in which strange gleams were shining.

Suddenly, it took a step forward, and Pat sensed that it was ready to attack. He wanted to make sure, though, and leapt to his right in order to trust the reactions of the robot, whose mysterious and sudden appearance he still did not understand.

Immediately, the metal man changed direction, and continued to advance toward him.

Pat felt his stomach clench as he saw that three more robots had just emerged from the back of the room, with jerky and methodical movements that directed them toward Fats and Karen. What was happening? With what mysterious senses might these vulgar masses of iron be equipped, which seemed to be so jealously guarding the ruins that had been abandoned for a long time?

Indifferent to everything, the voice was still ringing through the hall. "Never—yes, never, I affirm—will the government of free Eurasia tolerate such an insult, and never..."

"Run!" Pat howled at his companions. Then he drew his weapon and fired, instinctively, at the nearest aggressor. Struck squarely, the robot shuddered, at the same time as a gaping incandescent opening appeared in the middle of its body. Molten metal ran out of it like blood from a wound and splashed the floor, while a steel fist came down violently on the back of Pat's neck and caused him to totter.

"...because Timbuktu persists in the critical attitude that it has continually adopted..."

Semi-conscious, Pat felt his legs give way beneath him, but he succeeded nevertheless in avoiding the worst. He turned round to face a new aggressor, paying no heed to his injury or to the swelling voice that now drowned out the sound of the battle.

He retreated toward the back of the room and, in a flash, saw Fats at grips with the two other steel monsters. The boy was smashing the massive heads as hard as he could with an iron bar that he had picked up.

Karen was also defending herself with the energy of desperation, doing her best to evade the furious and implacable attack of the nightmare creatures, which were arriving in ever-greater numbers through a large opening that presumably communicated with a back room.

Pat felled two more robots, stepped over the incandescent debris, and raced toward his two companions. He was just in time. Overwhelmed by numbers, Karen and Fats, backed up against a wall, were only defending themselves with the greatest difficulty.

"We shall fight to the end, with the unbreakable faith that animates…"

Thermic blasts destroyed several more robots, and while Pat directed the murderous beam of his weapon at the compact group, there was a veritable hecatomb. Molten debris spattered the walls as the robots collapsed like broken puppets, horribly mutilated, with sinister cracking, grating and clicking sounds.

With one bound, Fats had closed the door and jammed the locking mechanism. His face was covered in sweat and blood, which were streaming on to his scarlet clothing. He spat disgustedly, and let himself fall to the ground, while Karen, in tears, threw herself into Pat's arms.

"Oh, Pat, Pat! I can't do any more. I can't go on!"

"Come on, Karen, calm down. It's over. There's nothing more to fear."

"But what happened?"

The voice had died away, and the image of the old man had disappeared from the screen. Only a few blinding flashes were still dancing in the luminous rectangle. Pat clenched his fists and replied. "It's possible that it was my fault. All those buttons I pressed, perhaps. Truly, I shouldn't have done it. Let's get out of here—I still prefer fighting in the open air."

"What's happening?" Fats exclaimed. "Look!" He pointed at three shiny spheres enthroned in their cart in the middle of the room. The strange machines had suddenly started humming, agitated by long quivers that made the ovoid carcasses sparkle with a thousand gleams.

Through the narrow portholes, they saw something then that they had not noticed when they came in. Robots identical to those they had destroyed were at the controls and we beginning to move with slow but precise gestures, obedient to some mysterious will. Soon, the humming grew louder, while Pat, Karen and Fats retreated instinctively, prey to a keen anxiety.

Jets of fire abruptly flooded from the base of the machines, while a frightful noise echoed throughout the building. With bulging eyes, they watched the three spheres slide toward the exterior with a thunderous roar, borne by the carts on the metallic rails, then break through the compact transparent material of the dome, which shattered into smithereens around them.

"By my spirit!" stammered Fats. "Is that possible?"

"I think I understand," said Pat, frowning. "We're obviously in a fortified base, of the sort the Ancients had at the time of the Catastrophe. I've heard of them. It's possible that the people occupying it died before being able to close down the operation of their offensive system."

"But that implies indestructible armaments," Karen objected.

"Everything encourages that supposition."

"There must, however, be an energy source to fuel these machines."

"Unless they found a means to capture it directly from the atmosphere or the ether. In that case, the motive force might be regenerated indefinitely. Unfortunately, we'll doubtless never know."

"How, then, do you explain the visiophonic transmission that we witnessed?" asked Fats, not entirely convinced.

Pat shook his head pensively before replying. "That was merely accidental. In any case, it's good evidence for the existence of the secret city. We also have proof that humans like us still populate the globe, retaining their mastery of countries that the scourge must have spared. We must get there, at all costs." Radiant with joy, he added: "I told you…I told you that salvation was at the end of our journey. Come on—I think we've lost enough time. Let's get out of here."

They left the hall and succeeded in regaining the exterior without sustaining any harm. Then, after taking a few steps, Karen pointed up into the sky, at a shining, slowly-moving dot that was describing a broad curve overhead.

They recognized one of the ovoid machines piloted by the redoubtable robots.

"This time, we've gone too far," Pat groaned. "Come on, let's not linger here."

He drew his companions behind him in the direction of the blue-tinted hills that marked the horizon.

In the sky, the machine visibly increased in size and plunged toward the steppe with amazing rapidity.

A few meters from the ground, jets of flame emerged from the luminous hull and solid projectiles swept the space in front of the three fugitives, causing rocks and stones to explode and tracing profound grooves through the grass and dust. At the same time, the sphere soared into the blue again, like a gigantic ball hurled by some invisible force.

Without pausing for thought, Pat had shoved Karen and Fats in front of him, obliging them to press themselves against a heap of stones. Then he dived in his turn, without knowing why.

He understood immediately, when a second sphere dived toward the ground, in a blind and crazy course, raising whirlwinds of pebbles and dust with its explosive blasts.

Further away, the murderous and destructive rage of the engines of death were similarly manifest against the deserted steppe, with a demented fury that nothing seemed able to stop.

The mad machines, diving and soaring aloft again, spitting torrents of flame that ignited immense fires in the four corners of the plain, awoke echoes in the ancient solitude of the atrocious battle that had once destroyed more than half the human race.

In a brief but hallucinatory vision, the probable issue of a few atavistic memories buried in their subconscious, the three young people suddenly had before their eyes the image of the most terrible slaughter that humankind had ever known. The sky was peppered by the destructive machines surrendered to indifferent and insensible robots...also peppered was the ground, but by the dead, the dying and the wounded. Peppered too, but with machine-gun fire, were the dismembered and mutilated bodies that comprised the horrible abattoir...

Horror, horror, horror...

Pat was the first to chase way these visions and recover contact with reality, as the sounds of the hail of fire faded away in the distance.

He raised his head and glimpsed the three machines, left to their own devices, continuing their mad excursion. It was time to go. They had to flee, to find shelter, to run—to run no matter where, but not to see or hear any longer.

They plunged on at hazard, stumbling at every step, without paying any heed to the mad monsters that crossed their course, running away from a fire encouraged by the wind, splashing through a muddy pool and ignoring the inhuman screech uttered by a plant with a human head that surged forth abruptly in front of them.

Its demonic laughter drilled into their feverish brains and died away in a gurgle that stirred up the entire pool, ready to swallow anything: Pat, Karen, Fats...and perhaps the world along with them....

Such, at least, was the impression of the three unfortunates, now exhausted and vanquished, dead on their feet, at the extreme limit of their strength. They let themselves fall into the narrow opening of a cave and lost control of themselves entirely.

CHAPTER XVI

A dull and regular sound brought Pat back to reality.

It was beating with metronomic regularity, and his ear, laid on the ground, registered the obsessive, monotonous, almost captivating rhythm, which seemed to him to be coming from the very bowels of the Earth.

He sat up. The throbbing sound faded away, leaving his head.

Fats pointed into the depths of the cavern. "That light…there might be a passage through the mountain."

Pat shook his head. Solar light did indeed seem to be reflected at the far end of the gorge, forming a sort of halo at the point in question.

Perhaps there was another exit—and given that the fire outside the cave was increasing in intensity, Pat thought it preferable to verify that hypothesis before making a decision. He helped Karen to her feet, hugged her momentarily, then helped her to move into the narrow passage, bristling with sharp and trenchant protrusions that rendered their progress even more difficult.

As if that were not enough, the ground beneath their feet became slippery, and they had to redouble their precautions, for the slightest false step risked precipitating them against the razor-sharp rocky projections.

The tunnel soon widened, while the luminous halo became more intense.

At that moment, an awkward fall on Karen's part made her two companions lose their balance as they tried to catch her. All three rolled on the damp and sticky rock, and the filthy contact made them cry out.

The ground had taken on the consistency of gelatin, and long shudders suddenly commenced beneath the humans' fingers. With a desperate thrust, Pat tried to crawl in order to extract himself from the viscous matrix, but it was too late.

Every movement that he made was a complete waste of effort, for, at the same moment, a current of undulations formed in the moving mass, which caused his body to slide toward the depths of the cavern, nullifying his efforts.

"I'd rather have been burned alive," moaned Karen, likewise trying in vain to crawl. "This place is hellish."

"Get up!" Pat shouted. "Get up, quickly!"

He set an example, tearing himself away from the glutinous liquid that was beginning to stick to his clothing, and the trio waded through the noxious slime until they reached the middle of the luminescent cavern.

They realized that they were in a cul-de-sac, and that the soft phosphorescence prevalent around them came from the walls that rounded out above their heads like an enormous pocket with moving folds, from which the sticky liquid was oozing, running down in thin trickles.

They understood the frightful reality then. This cave was nothing but a gigantic stomach, whose one and only function was to attract and swallow anything that had he unfortunate idea of taking shelter in the passage. Furthermore, the debris and nauseating putrescence that the humans stepped over in their panic testified to that monstrous organic activity. In their turn, they too were going to be digested, to serve as nourishment for the mineral stomach, whose everlasting appetite would never be satisfied.

Prisoners of that insatiable ogre, Pat, Karen and Fats felt the deepest despair. At any moment, the cavern's secretions would attack their flesh and they would begin to dissolve under the action of the corrosive acids in which they were in the process of wading. They had to do something—even something crazy, utterly insane. It did not matter what—anything rather than the atrocious death that was lying in wait for them.

The air was becoming unbreathable, and sickening gurgling sounds were emerging from the walls, as if the mineral monster were already delighting in contact with the providential nourishment that had just been granted to it.

Horrified, Karen pointed to the orifice of the evacuation tunnel, toward which the peristaltic movements of the gut were automatically directing the debris of the digestive process. It was the only exit available to them, and Pat, without pausing for thought, was the first to venture into it, trying to master the nausea that rose up in his own stomach.

He drew his weapon and shouted to his companions: "Let's try this way—follow me."

They advanced, holding their breath, wading calf-deep through the thick dark jelly that was running through the tunnel. Pat immediately realized that symbiosis lost its empery a few meters further on, in favor of a normal mineral structure that revealed uneven rocks extending as far as an opening large enough to permit the passage of a human body.

In a few bounds, he passed through the nauseating mire that a friable and porous soil was sucking up avidly, reached the rocky entablature and let himself slide through the opening.

In front of them, another immense space gaped like an abyss, and the dull throbbing sound that they had already heard drummed in their ears, this time with greater clarity.

They made their way down along the rocky wall, helping one another, and soon found themselves on firm damp ground, dazzled by the fabulous surroundings into which they had just emerged.

Fabulous... supernatural... unreal... beyond human reason.

Faint shadows were moving along the rocks, which one might have thought sculpted by some accursed hand, working outside time and space, so forcefully did the forms seem to emerge from the depths of centuries, seemingly parading all the impious symbols of creation, shamelessly. A bitter, fetid odor floated in that sinister décor, recalling that of tombs.

The humans went past several solid blocks, avoiding looking at the unknown grimacing faces carved into the stone, fixed in their eternal and demonic expressions. They had only one objective: to quit this terrible place and find an exit that would be their salvation, bringing them back into the open air—but they had the impression of moving through an immense self-enclosed labyrinth. They realized that when they observed that they had returned, after multiple efforts, to their point of departure.

They attempted a further flight in a different direction, however, and a hectic course brought them to the foot of a granite wall colored with strange gleams. In front of them, fantastic statues were standing on their pedestals.

For a moment, they refused to believe what their eyes were showing them. Living matter and inert matter were uniting in a new symbiosis to form hallucinatory caryatids perched on their podia, who were moving their heads and arms to the monotonous and sensual rhythm of the dull beat whose origin still remained mysterious.

The legs were made of stone, and conserved in their mineral prolongation all the grace and femininity radiated by the entire body, terribly alive, whose nacreous flesh palpitated in the multicolored light emanating from the vault.

Petrified with fear, Pat, Karen and Fats discovered, to their horror, that the flesh fused with the stone, confounded with it without any possible separation. These creatures were pinned to the wall, of which they were the eternal prisoners.

The mysterious ballet of heads and arms ceased, then recommenced more ardently; then, finally, nervous laughter sprang from the full lips and shook the magnificent throats, immodestly and extraordinarily human.

"It's impossible," Fats murmured. "I'm dreaming. It's enough to drive one mad."

Pat looked at him. "We shall indeed go mad if we continue to deny the laws of this symbiosis, which escape us."

"I can't believe it."

No, Fats could not believe it. He could not understand that the contagious blight that had come from Capella had not spared the Earth its mysterious laws. The *things* had turned the world upside down and given birth to *another* life, the only one they knew and were capable of imagining and ordering, as an alchemist brings together several elements in his alembic to create a new element, unknown to and ignored by Creation.

The *things* had made use of the animal, mineral and vegetable kingdoms that nature, on Earth, had been ingenious in differentiating and confining narrowly, without any possible linkage, and they had accomplished these extraordinary unions that surpassed comprehension. They had modified, decomposed and recomposed organic cells and also metamorphosed inorganic molecules, paying no heed to terrestrial laws, thus giving free rein to the craziest and most inconceivable of geneses.

For Pat, this was perfectly comprehensible, and did not give rise to any supernatural terror. The danger was still tangible, concrete, material, and whatever expression his face wore, he was one of those who felt the strength and the courage to fight, without the shadow of any spiritual dread whatsoever.

A god, even if he were a devil, could not engender such infamies.

CHAPTER XVII

The mocking laughter invaded the hall again, reflected with a frenzy of echoes by the long crystalline stalactites suspended from the vault.

Around the humans, the odor became more and more intoxicating.

It reeked of death and love.

But what love and what death could dispute those caryatids of flesh and stone, fixed for all eternity in their virginal and inaccessible presence?

Then, in the midst of the odor, the laughter and the obsessive rhythm, a creature of flesh—and nothing but flesh—appeared, whose entire nudity could not arouse the slightest indignation or the slightest revulsion.

It was an absurd, sexless creature: a living abstraction that denied all masculinity and all femininity.

Its cranium was smooth—as was its entire body, devoid of navel and breasts.

It had appeared in a long swirl sprung from the ground, which had raised up millions upon millions of dazzling particles, like a nova in the void.

The creature looked at the humans with interest, then pranced momentarily on its slender legs, as if prey to a violent excitement.

It spoke, saying: "Humans, what folly is guiding you? To delay transfiguration is not good. What are you still doing on this reorganized world? You no longer have a place here. You're lost... lost. You're alien to us... do you understand? No one will help you, no one can help you any longer... do you understand... understand...?"

Pat advanced, threateningly. "Who are you?"

"I have no name, if that's what you want to know."

"And this place? What is it?"

The creature smiled with amusement as it replied: "It's the Temple of the Future, whose guardian I am."

"The future!" Pat growled. "There is no future for the accursed races that you represent. Humans will expel them, destroy them, and you will return oblivion." His voice grew louder to add: "*To oblivion... all...*"

A cascade of echoes unwound in the hall, repeating: "*To oblivion... all...*"

Immediately, mocking laughter sprang from the caryatids of flesh and stone, dominating the racket. Then the termagants' voices began to howl in unison, like a demonic and demented choir, rising and falling in cadence with the dull, incessant beat...

"It has sounded... sounded... the knell of humankind. The reign of men is forever consummated."

In a fit of rage, Pat drew his weapon, ready to fire—but Karen leapt to interpose herself. "No, Pat—look out!"

As if it had read his thoughts and anticipated his gesture, the guardian of the Temple had abruptly disintegrated, to leave nothing but a swirl of sparkling dust animated by a violent and rapid rotation. It reconstituted itself a few meters further away, as if by the effect of a magic wand, recovering at a stroke all the cells of its body. In a fraction of a second, the admirable and extraordinary cellular architecture had been reconstituted, obedient to unknown laws that were more extraordinary still.

"Poor lunatics!" murmured the composite being. "You ought to be punished for daring to profane our Temple thus."

Fats stepped forward and spat in disgust. "To what miserable god is this Temple devoted, then?"

The creature's gaze wandered over the three humans, briefly. "As if there could be several gods in a single universe! Absurd... nonsense... and as if every species could boast of possessing a unique god! Folly! Stupidity! What is a god? What is the Unity? Fantastic concepts to depict the One who reigns over life and matter, and who makes no distinction between a fish, a larva, a human or a symbiote. Why would the Creator overwhelm or protect such and such a species? For what reason would he help one at the expense of another? Insanity! Mindlessness! And your humankind has died without ever finding a face for him. Merely names, suppositions, theories... and nothing more."

A sardonic smile lit up the creature's face. "The same fate awaits the new species that populate this world. They will become extinct one day, like your own, having exhausted the entire vocabulary to discover the appropriate Name, and imagined all sorts of the most improbable hypotheses without ever crossing the forbidden threshold... Never... never..."

"In that case, why this Temple, since you know your failure in advance?"

A burst of monstrous laughter filled the hall, and the caryatids began agitating on their pedestals, while the absurd creature volatilized, to reconstitute itself above an enormous block sculpted with strange and grimacing figurines. One might have taken them for thousands of pink, green and black faces, similar to carnival masks heaped up pell-mell on the eve of Mardi Gras. And all of them were glittering, scintillating, dazzling, with reflections of sardonyx, jasper, onyx, topaz and carbuncle.

"Human," the voice replied, "that question is prohibited. It's a question that one never asks... never... never..."

It extended an arm, and the rock obeyed. An opening appeared between two massive blocks and a cliff appeared, as if the creature possessed the extraordinary power of controlling matter by will-power alone.

"Go," it ordered. "Flee outside this Temple, and offer the Sound of Life the sacrifice of your impure and abject flesh."

"Impure... abject..." intoned the caryatids, frenetically. "It has sounded, the knell of humankind. The reign of men is forever consummated."

In their panic, Pat, Karen and Fats rushed into the gaping opening, while the nameless creature disappeared from its perch and a heavy silence fell once more in the immense hall.

Outside, it was dark. The night was just coming to an end, still cool and scintillating with distant stars, charged with light and intoxicating perfumes.

But there was the sound.

Dull, insinuating and incessant, it dominated the darkness and the glare of the stars.

Like an immense clock beyond all logic, it beat out the flow of time, dividing the seconds as if to hasten its fall.

The three fugitives ran until they were out of breath, until the sound in their ears became bearable.

The continual hammering beat their eardrums with extreme violence, and Pat felt that his skull was about to burst. It was untenable, intolerable.

He tried to get his bearings, but could see nothing around him but an uninterrupted chain of rocky peaks with sharp and jagged ridges.

They found themselves in the interior of a vast circus, whose depths descended in a gentle slope toward a central point, which the first glimmers of dawn did not yet permit them to distinguish clearly.

That was, however, *it*: the source of that strange and dangerous sound. They were certain of it.

"Let's go around the cliff," Pat advised. "Perhaps we'll find an exit."

They moved off rapidly, but lost their momentum after a few steps. They could not bear it any more, for it was now in their flesh, in their blood, that the terrible sound was resonating. It was necessary to go on, though, to get out of that infernal region before sinking into madness.

In spite of the intellectual confusion in which they were struggling, they realized then that they were not alone in the circus.

The yellow gleams that appeared between the jagged crests were now projecting enough light to reveal the presence of slight, supple, almost human forms not far away, which were dancing and moving in step, in an incessant and monotonous ballet.

They took a few more paces, and found themselves in the midst of a nightmare.

The creatures that were dancing to that accursed rhythm were transparent, almost fluid, and were moving like serpents of smoke, scarcely touching the ground. There were thousands of them, agitated by the same movements, and the infernal dance continued around a confused enormous mass that occupied the bottom of the basin. It was then that Pat, Karen and Fats howled, unable to conquer their terror.

That mass, all palpitating, all quivering, which the red fires of the star rendered even more abominable, *was nothing but a heart*: a giant, enormous, colossal heart, each pulsation of which was like a stroke of a gigantic, shattering gong, which swept the expanse like a tempest.

CHAPTER XVIII

It was the Sound of Life.

The symbol of Sound and Life united in that mass of flesh, the inconceivable aggregation of living cells forming the monstrous organ that beat...beat...beat for the damnation of all eternity.

All around, in a demonic ballet, the transparent creatures were dancing...dancing...dancing to the pulsating rhythm of the sound waves, without ever pausing.

Hell now had a face, bathed in darkness and fire, through the smoky shadows of the moving creatures: the hell of an anticosmos emergent from the depths of time, through the smoky shadows of the moving creatures; the hell of an anti-cosmos emergent from the depths of time, through darkness and the void.

For a moment, the three humans succeeded in overcoming their terror and suffering to contemplate a further detail.

A river of blood was running down the mountain, rolling with the consistency of dough toward the giant heart, which sucked up the scarlet flux with continuous avidity. Along the banks, the grass was red, and it was easy to imagine it sipping the foul liquid that poured out of the mountain like a profound, incurable wound. In a few obscure gorges on the heights, the *things* had obviously found the means of synthesizing all the elements of the sanguine liquid, and the reserves were undoubtedly inexhaustible.

What infernal pact might they have sealed with this impious blood that aliments the Sound of Life? That thought occurred to Fats, inevitably, but he refrained from voicing it aloud. The others could not understand. For them, still, this could not be anything but accidental, organized, material and devoid of all malevolence.

It might also be waging war against itself, destroying itself, effacing itself from the surface of the world, and nothing more...

"A way out—there!" Pat's voice suddenly exclaimed.

Fats looked. Already, his two companions were launching themselves into the midst of the dream-creatures, cutting through the incessant dance, lunging toward a narrow defile. In his turn, he set off and raced between the tormented rocks, through a world that no longer had any color.

Pat led the way, pulling Karen behind him, paying no heed to the heavy and acrid vapors that floated in the passage—but they were far from being out of trouble.

The canyon broadened out further on and branched into a multitude of corridors, every one of which opened on another circus bathed in phosphorescent vapors, which seemed to be delimiting the world. How many secret marvels and horrors might these unknown places still be sheltering?

On the brink of panic, the three humans scaled a rocky slope, rolled in the dust and the stones, and found themselves once again on a narrow ledge swept by a fresh and beneficent wind.

The sound...the frightful sound...diminished in intensity, giving way now to a long plaint—that of the wind rising from the plain, where wheat grew that seemed eternal, and which no scythe ever cut.

The golden ears were undulating under the gentle caress of the breeze, like a sparkling sea devoted to a few fabulous sirens. Their presence was divined rather than seen, moving lightly, slyly and malicious over the bed of that fantastic ocean, which no Ulysses had ever had the audacity to affront.

"Don't listen!" cried Pat, his eyes bulging. "Don't listen, if you want to save your lives."

They threw themselves over the steep slopes to reach the other side, but the incantation grew in strength. The notes were running into one another, striking the cliff, then exploding in arpeggios and reverberating in the sky like some gigantic firework display.

Hand in hand, Pat and Karen ran at top speed, and when they turned round, they could not see Fats at all. He had disappeared. Before their eyes, the notes of the song were transforming into slow polymorphic vibrations and falling on to the rocks. They were sliding, deforming, breaking and twisting in frightful dodecaphonic convulsions.

Momentarily, they envisaged being submerged by that sonorous avalanche, which was ready to swallow them body and soul, and they raced to escape the monstrous musical assault, which the Heavens seemed to echo.

Soon, it was like a long serpent coiled around the cliff, which formed a moving gilded chain of notes, shrill and loud, bass and sharp, rolling over one another in a frightful crescendo.

The *things* had not spared anything—not even sound. It too had its symbiosis and its hallucinatory reality in this new state of matter that surpassed human understanding.

Pat and Karen never knew how they escaped the empery of that infernal melody, or how they came to find themselves at the foot of the cliff again, on the far side, out of breath, haggard and ready to howl or commit any folly.

A stream quenched their thirst and they drank like animals. Then they lay down in the grass, rolling around without finding rest or relaxation in their flesh. The agitation was both physical and moral, beyond reason and consciousness. A blind, brutal and uncontrollable force united them in a wild embrace, and their first kiss was nothing but a cruel bite.

Then, at the water's edge, they were swallowed up, and became oblivious to the world.

CHAPTER XIX

Three times, Pat plunged his head into the fresh, clear water; then he heard the rustling behind him. He turned round abruptly, gun in hand, and immediately recognized Fats, who was dragging himself through the grass, out of breath.

The poor boy had got out of it too, and, guided by his companions' tracks, had reached the bank of the river. Pat and Karen saw a long trickle of blood striping his forehead, but the wound seemed to be superficial. They helped him as best they could, and judged it politic to wait until the following day before resuming their enterprise. It was still a long way to the secret city, and Fats needed to recover his strength.

They spent the night beside the river, huddled between stones and rolled up in a ball beneath heaps of leaves. It was good to be together again, all three of them, and each one's presence reinforced the hope and security of the others.

They resumed their march at dawn, after making a meal of wild fruits, and quit the river bank, which had become the domain of large birds with menacing beaks curved like scimitars, to go into a desert region burned by the Sun, which extended before them as far as the eye could see.

They pressed on resolutely, and, after two days of exhausting marching, discovering a long rectilinear strip bordered with ditches, which extended to the horizon. Fats reached it first, and examined the hard and compact coating, strewn with cracks and crevices invaded by a meager vegetation. There, too, life continued, stubbornly reclaiming its rights.

"It must be an ancient road," said Fats. "One of the communication routes that once permitted the passage of vehicles from one city to another."

"Highways," Karen added. "That's what Doc called them."

"It's possible that this one will lead us directly to the secret city," Fats went on. At any rate, it seems to lead in that direction. The best thing to do is follow it."

Courage and confidence seemed to be returning gradually, and a new ardor took hold of the three humans at the thought that their long calvary might be approaching its end. They had eventually contrived to forget their torments and the thousand dangers that lay in wait for them in this new world, but the appearance in the sky of mysterious entities, twice over, brought them back to reality.

Things were passing over their heads, simultaneously hesitant and excited by their presence—but the trio's protective clothing repelled them rapidly, and they disappeared in the distance, as they had come.

Fats did not hide his doubts and apprehensions. "We can't be far from the secret city now," he declared. "What troubles me is the presence of *things* in the region."

Pat reflected, and replied: "Didn't you say that the city was built at high altitude, and that it was out of their range?"

"Those were only suppositions. There's nothing definite in what I heard said. Then again…" He pointed to the horizon in front of him.

Apart from a few undulations, nothing suggested that they were heading toward a mountainous region. It was equally possible that Fats' estimations were erroneous, and that the distance they still had to cover was even greater than they had imagined.

The latter hypothesis permitted them to conserve an ultimate hope, and, during the days that followed, they continue to progress along the cracked road, which was now meandering through a regions strewn with verdant trees and striped by limpid streams.

One morning, they made a brief halt to refresh themselves on top of a small hill.

This time, the horizon seemed promising. In front of them, the green slopes of hills came together gently to form the foothills of a mountain chain that seemed to surge forth abruptly from the ground. No more was needed for the three young people to let their joy overflow, and they were already preparing to launch themselves on to the verdant slope when Karen made a gesture.

"Get down," she whispered, "and look!"

Pat and Fats obeyed instinctively.

In the valley, at the foot of the hill, a band of humanoid creatures was moving nervously along the grassy bank of a watercourse. There were at least 100 of them and it was impossible to tell whether they were running or jumping, so imprecise and jerky were their strides.

The trio continued to observe them attentively—and what they eventually discovered froze them in amazement.

Details that had previously escaped their attention revealed to them that the creatures, whose bodies were somewhat human in appearance, had heads that were purely animal, with a canine aspect. That, at least, was the term employed by Karen, who had had the opportunity to get close to a few rare specimens of the canine species in the zoological reserve of the city of men.

But were they *really* dogs? The comparison, made because of the unhuman conformation of the muzzle, became increasingly inadequate, inasmuch as the creatures appeared to be behaving like beings endowed with intelligence. A few were fishing in the river with the aid of lines that others were preparing or hastily fabricating on the bank. Others were cleaning or carving up large fish on flat stones and lighting fires in order to cook them.

An almost-equal percentage of males and females were living in perfect harmony, either in couples or in groups, making themselves busy in almost total silence. From time to time, a voice carried as far as the attentive humans, a combination of mock-roaring and muffled growling, utterly unintelligible, but which could be interpreted as brief and laconic orders: a kind of sonorous symbolism avoiding any unnecessary eloquence.

Pat shivered involuntarily. What might these half-human, half-animal creatures be, which populated the region in the vicinity of the mysterious secret city?

They went around the valley to continue on their way, but came across others further on, occupied in hunting large animals armed with lances and arrows. They avoided them skillfully and reached the crest of a ridge, where they spent the night, with the hope of finding the slumber and repose of which they had so much need—but the long and terrible night was nothing but a concert of sinister howls, which echoed from the slopes of the mountains that loomed abruptly over the plain.

CHAPTER XX

Late in the morning, a most unexpected spectacle presented itself to the trio in the green basin of an idyllic valley that had suddenly appeared.

An immense metallic tower, shining in the sunlight, stood up proudly, its height dominating the tenebrous ruins grouped around it: the ruins of half-collapsed buildings and houses, still supporting a few portions of aerial track, which resembled streamers caught in the city's hair.

In the avenues, strewn with debris of every sort, the omnipresent creatures that continued to trouble the humans were circulating. The monsters with doglike heads were going back and forth among the ruins. They were emerging from everywhere—every hole, every fissure, every gaping orifice—and the humans saw that they were grouping in ever-increasing numbers around the immense circular building that seemed to have miraculously resisted the total destruction of the ancient city.

What could all this signify? What was happening?

Pat, Karen and Fats did not have time to wonder, for the sound of footsteps behind them, accompanied by mocking barking, made them turn around in unison.

A group of gaudily-clad creatures had just appeared on the hill, heading toward the tower. Viewed at close range they all bore a similar resemblance to an image of Anubis emerged from some ancient Egyptian fresco. They came to a halt, fixed the humans with their keen and mobile little eyes, and then began growling duly, drawing back their chops to expose their terrible fangs.

Mechanically, Pat had bought out his thermic weapon, and his gesture made the dog-headed creatures hesitate. He took advantage of that to say to his companions: "These beings are intelligent enough to realize that we possess a powerful weapon, capable of destroying them. Let's try to profit from our superiority."

"What do you intend to do?" asked Karen, without taking her eyes off the group of monsters.

"I want to know what's happening here. If they're not as ferocious as we suppose, they might be able to help us."

"Pat's right," Fats put in. "All this doesn't mean anything to me. We might as well get to the bottom of it right away."

Pat pointed to the tower and the curious procession that was in the process of being organized in the valley.

"Follow me," he ordered. "Walk slowly—and whatever happens, stay calm. I have the impression that we're going to need a powerful dose of it."

He set the example, setting forth to go down the slope of the hill in the direction of the tower.

When they had reached the valley, Pat stopped and glanced behind him. The group was still mid-way down the slope, following the humans at a respectful distance.

Other groups were already forming up in the valley, and the slow procession had come to a stop at the foot of the tower, mute and motionless. Thousands of eyes were directed at the humans, who had resumed their slow and regular march, their senses alert in the wind and the silence.

By the Unity, Pat thought, *why don't they react? Something absolutely has to happen—it doesn't matter what, but it has to.*

Yes, it had to. It had to, before they reached the ruins of the tower. It had to, before they lost their assurance completely or committed some imprudence that would precipitate their ruination in an irremediable fashion. He wished for anything whatsoever—anything, rather than the silence and extraordinary tension that he sensed in the rigid and impassive crowd.

They came through the first ranks of the procession, and Pat, for a brief moment, felt a mad desire to squeeze the trigger of his weapon—anything to hasten events and give a direction to the situation, as absurd as it was untenable. He controlled himself, however. No, perhaps that was the trap that was being laid for him—and he shuddered at the thought that these creatures might be even more intelligent than they had supposed...unless that was only fear and stupidity....

He no longer knew.

It was then, inevitably, that the desired event occurred.

A creature bounded in front of the humans and blocked their way, ears pricked and chops quivering. It emitted a series of yelps and strident squeals, and then succeeded in articulating a few words, at the cost of a violent effort.

"Ouaaouh... grrrr... You have come to join us... Long-Muzzle people welcome you with joy and gratitude... We offer your admirable sacrifice to the Voice, in order that the Visage may remain unique and eternal... Grrr..."

Overcoming his repugnance. Pat seized the creature by the neck and held it firmly. "We care nothing for your gratitude and that of your brethren. What is this city that is no more than ruins? What do you know about it?"

The Long-Muzzle growled dully, and replied in a guttural tone: "It's the city of the Voice... Grrr... Don't you know that?"

"Speak more clearly, ignoble brainless larva, if you want to avoid my wrath." He pointed to the gigantic tower, in front of which the monstrous creatures were still assembled. "What happens inside this tower? What's in there?"

"The Voice! Glaaap... Ouahou... The Voice that speaks in our hearts and in our flesh... The Eternal Voice..."

Pat was about to speak again when Fats' hand clenched on his shoulder. "Look out, Pat! This idiot is trying to distract us. Look!"

Pat turned round and he too saw a group of dog-men, who had deployed themselves in a circular arc behind them, armed with menacing daggers whose sharp blades were flashing.

"They want to sacrifice us, and nothing more," Fats added. "Fire, damn it, fire!"

"Yes, Pat, fire," Karen growled in her turn. "Kill them... just kill them!"

Pat had no time to reply, because, at that moment, the creature confronting him uttered a terrible howl that chilled the blood in their veins. "Ouaaaouh... let your heads be offered to the Eternal Voice... Ouaaaouh... And let the Unique Visage bless your blood!"

It made a gesture. Behind it, the crowd stood aside with a mass movement, abruptly evacuating the surroundings of the tower. At the very foot of the colossal edifice stood a black marble altar that had been hidden from the humans' view until now. It shone with a strange gleam: the gleam of the blood that was running abundantly from the three hideous heads that had been placed upon it: three human heads, whose extinct gazes seemed still to reflect the last rightful vision they had had: those of two men and one woman...

Doc! Ferret! Peggy!

CHAPTER XXI

The scream uttered by Karen awoke echoes in the numerous and overexcited crowd, and that was perhaps what enabled Pat to react and to overcome the terror and sickness that overwhelmed him.

He was raising his weapon, ready for anything—even the worst—when two dog-men cleaved through the crowd, dragging a human creature whom the three young people recognized immediately.

It was Mira!

The girl was shoved brutally on to the bloody altar, and a long heart-rending plaint emerged from her bruised lips as she recognized her former companions in her turn.

What happened then was so incomprehensible and unforeseen that the humans stood there petrified by amazement.

First of all there was the raucous baying of the Long-Muzzle that was directing the ceremony, which resounded in their ears, in the midst of the sinister howls uttered by its fellows.

"Grrouaaaouh… Houaaah… Blessed be the Eternal Voice that watches over our people… The Voice awakens in our flesh and the Unique Visage rules the world… Ouaaaouh…" It was the first to fall on its knees facing the tower, its long head pointing toward the summit of the imposing edifice. It had forgotten the humans.

Before the altar, those surrounding Mira did likewise, as did the crowd filling the esplanade.

Suddenly, silence reigned, total, complete and absolute, among the strange creatures. One might have thought them mummified, paralyzed or thunderstruck, beyond even rapture and ecstasy—as if their senses had been abolished by a beatific, indescribable vision, whose source surpassed human understanding.

With one bound, Pat rejoined Mira; no one opposed his action. He helped her down from the altar, and when they were all together again in front of the tower, he said to Mira: "You can tell us your story later. For now, I don't understand what's happening at all, but we have to take advantage of the unexpected opportunity, or we're doomed."

"They'll catch us," Mir moaned, "and I have no strength left. Oh, if you knew..."

Karen was also at the end of her resources. Pat knew that. He had to act, though, before the monster recovered consciousness. That might only be a matter of minutes...or even seconds.

Then, he saw the two battens of a monumental door open in the base of the tower. "Follow me!" he shouted to his companions. He launched himself resolutely into the interior of the metal edifice.

They all found themselves in an immense hall, in the center of which was the foot of a huge spiral stairway, which extended into the imposing mass of a luminescent vault. They rushed to it without pausing for thought, spurred on by fear but guided by an inexplicable curiosity, which momentarily overwhelmed all other sentiments.

What was this place? What might it represent for that race of dog-men, simultaneously capable of ecstasy and cruelty?

They reached the first floor, having to manipulate various mechanisms to reach a heavy and massive door, and hesitated momentarily before going into the transparent cabin that presented itself to them. Fats pressed a button, and the plastosteel cage slid within its supports, carrying the humans toward the summit of the tower at a vertiginous speed.

They emerged into an immense hall, cluttered with machines and apparatus of the most various sorts. Pat was the first to realize that the majority were working mutely in a silence that might have lasted for centuries.

In a massive transparent box, two voluminous reels were turning on their axes, and a slender plastic ribbon was sliding slowly between two magnetic heads.

"A sound-image recorder!" Fats exclaimed. "What's happening?"

Pat did not reply, and feverishly manipulated the mechanisms controlling the visiophonic screens with which the huge room was fitted.

What happened then left them flabbergasted. The screens lit up, and the image of the tall, stern old man they had already seen in the refuge of the robots suddenly appeared,

It was the same face, the same voice. It was also the same incomprehensible speech.

"I know... yes, I know... that these politics have received the approval of several States, which see them— falsely—as a guarantee of peace and security... Men and women of Eurasia, have confidence..."

Pat had gone pale, and he cut the contact with an angry gesture. Abruptly, he had just realized the frightful and cruel mistake that he and his companions had made. The secret city entertained by legend, on which they had founded all their hopes, *did not exist*.

They all knew, now, the source of those obscure and mysterious messages picked up by the Adults. It was a matter of a recorded voice on a vulgar magnetic strip, which had continued unrolling and rolling up again on its reels for more than a century. By virtue of what strange phenomenon? No one could tell, and doubtless no one would ever be able to explain it. Perhaps it had been sufficient for nothing to cause an interruption of the automatic transmission circuits. A trivial thing, to be sure, to maintain the last illusions of a doomed race.

But how cruel the deception of Pat and his companions had been! For a long moment, they forgot the critical nature of their situation inside the tower that had just yielded its terrible secret to them.

Then, finally, Pat crossed the room and let his gaze wander over the numerous and compact crowd still massed and prostrated around the edifice.

What was happening in the brains of those creatures was even more terrible and hallucinatory. Unconsciously, they were receiving he sounds and images broadcast by the tower, as if their brains had been designed and tuned to react to electronic vibrations. That explained the almost total absence of language, in favor of mass telepathy, especially the ecstasy and indescribable bliss to which the dog-men had been subject during the broadcasting of the incomprehensible speech.

It was certainly incomprehensible to them too—but the voice and the image that their subconscious registered had assumed for the monsters a divine, even sublime character, which surpassed their understanding. It was the Voice, the Unique Visage…the concretization of an Ideal on the frontier of the Absolute and the Absurd! A new religion had been born, with its rites, its customs and even its sacrifices.

At that thought, Pat felt himself shudder.

"We came to regret your departure and our cowardice," Mira explained, "and had decided to join you when we strayed into the Valley of Echoes. Then Doc, who was lost, climbed up a large rock and started hailing you. He shouted for some time, hoping that the sound of his voice might reach your ears—but the echo was unexpectedly powerful, and must have been received by the Long-Muzzles, for we were just on the point of coming back together when they appeared. I witnessed the massacre. It was horrible…" She uttered a sort of hoarse sob, and continued: "Then I tried to run away, but they eventually caught me. I was absolutely exhausted."

"That's what awaits us, too," Pat sighed, "when we emerge from this tower." He pointed through the large bay window at the crowd that was gradually emerging from its bliss state and coming to its senses.

Behind them, the reels in the box had stopped turning, and the machine had switched itself off.

Pat turned his head. He could see Mira, who was huddled in Fats' arms, weeping silently, but he frowned as he said: "Where's Karen?"

A door at the back of the room was open, and they all ran toward it. Karen was in the middle of another room, calling out to them.

"Come and see," she said to them. "I still can't quite believe it."

In her extended, wide open hand, she showed them pills and nutritional tablets that she had extracted from the interior of an automatic distributor. There were incalculable reserves, disposed in several rows all around the room.

The same idea occurred to them all then, and Pat summarized it feverishly in a few words. "That's not all. We still need to make certain that…"

His heart beating ready, he dragged his companions behind him.

On the lower floors they found other store-rooms, medicines of every sort, piles of magnetic tapes and abundantly-furnished lecture-rooms—as if humankind, on the eve of the Catastrophe, had designed this inviolable refuge to assist the survival of a few select individuals. But there the mystery still remained complete, and no one would ever know the final word of the story. They could only suppose that the Ancients had not had enough time to bring their project to its conclusion, and that the trumpets of the Apocalypse had sounded the death-knell of the human race too soon.

Yes, that might be the explanation—but what did it matter now, since the tower was finally going to fulfill its true role?

At the base of the edifice, the monumental door was still wide open, but the Long-Muzzles outside the entrance did not move a muscle when the humans appeared. Supernatural dread prevented them from crossing a threshold that was forbidden to them.

Then Pat turned to his companions, his heart full of delight, and said to them: "There was, after all, hope at the end of our journey." He activated the closing mechanism himself, and the heavy battens closed again, with a dry click.

Bibliography

(*All titles published in the Anticipation imprint of Editions Fleuve Noir, Paris.*)

Les Conquérants de l'Universe [*The Conquerors of the Universe*] (Anticipation 1, 1951) *Conquérants 1*

À l'Assaut du Ciel [*To Assault the Sky*] (Anticipation 2, 1951) *Conquérants 2*

Retour du Météore [*Return of the Meteor*] (Anticipation 3, 1951) *Conquérants 3*

La Planète Vagabonde [*The Wandering Planet*] (Anticipation 4, 1952) *Conquérants 4*

Croisière dans le Temps [*Time Cruise*] (Anticipation 6, 1952)

Sauvetage Sidéral [*Interstellar Rescue*] (Anticipation 37, 1954) *Conquérants 5*

SOS Terre [*SOS Earth*] (Anticipation 55, 1955) *Sydney Gordon 1*

Vingt Pas dans l'Inconnu [*Twenty Steps into the Unknown*] (Anticipation 60, 1955)

Feu dans le Ciel [*Fire in the Sky*] (Anticipation 64, 1956)

Objectif Soleil [*Target: The Sun*] (Anticipation 69, 1956)

Altitude Moins X [*Elevation Minus X*] (Anticipation 75, 1956) *Sydney Gordon 2*

F. RICHARD-BESSIERE
les Conquérants de l'Univers
ANTICIPATION
Editions
"Fleuve Noir"

Route du Néant [*Nether Road*] (Anticipation 81, 1956) *Sydney Gordon 3*

Cité de l'Esprit [*City of Mind*] (Anticipation 85, 1957) *Sydney Gordon 4*

Création Cosmique [*Cosmic Creation*] (Anticipation 89, 1957) *Sydney Gordon 5*

Planète de Mort [*Death Planet*] (Anticipation 93, 1957)

La Deuxième Terre [*The Second Earth*] (Anticipation 97, 1957) *Sydney Gordon 6*

Via Dimension 5 [*Via Dimension 5*] (Anticipation 101, 1957) *Sydney Gordon 7*

Fléau de l'Univers [*Universal Scourge*] (Anticipation 105, 1958)

Carrefour du Temps [*Time's Crossroad*] (Anticipation 111, 1958) *Sydney Gordon 8*

Relais Minos III [*Relay Minos III*] (Anticipation 117, 1958)

Bang! (Anticipation 121, 1958) *Sydney Gordon 9*

Zone Spatiale Interdite [*Forbidden Space Zone*] (Anticipation 126, 1958)

Panique dans le Vide [*Panic in the Void*] (Anticipation 129, 1959) *Sydney Gordon 10*

Le Troisième Astronef [*The Third Spaceship*] (Anticipation 135, 1959)

Escale
chez
les Vivants

**F. RICHARD
BESSIERE**

★

ANTICIPATION

Editions
"Fleuve Noir"

Ceux de Demain [*Those from Tomorrow*] (Anticipation 139, 1959)

Réaction Déluge [*Reaction Flood*] (Anticipation 144, 1959)

On a Hurlé dans le Ciel [*They Screamed in the Sky*] (Anticipation 148, 1959)

Terre Degré 0 [*Earth Degree 0*] (Anticipation 153, 1960) *Harry Stewart 1*

Générations Perdues [*Lost Generations*] (Anticipation 157, 1960) *Harry Stewart 2*

Les Pantins d'Outre-Ciel [*The Puppets from Beyond the Sky*] (Anticipation 162, 1960)

Escale chez les Vivants [*Stop-Over Among the Living*] (Anticipation 166, 1960)

Les Lunes de Jupiter [*The Moons of Jupiter*] (Anticipation 169, 1960)

Destination Moins J.-C. [*Destination Before J.-C.*] (Anticipation 175, 1961)

Plus Égale Moins [*Plus Equals Minus*] (Anticipation 179, 1961) *Sydney Gordon 11*

Légion Alpha (Anticipation 183, 1961)

Les Mutants Sonnent le Glas [*The Mutants Bring Down the Curtain*] (Anticipation 188, 1961)

La Guerre des Dieux [*The War of the Gods*] (Anticipation 192, 1961)

INVERSIA

RICHARD BESSIÈRE

FLEUVE NOIR

ANTICIPATION

Les Poumons de Ganymède [*The Lungs of Ganymede*] (Anticipation 198, 1962) *Sydney Gordon 12*

Les Derniers Jours de Sol 3 [*The Last Days pf Sol III*] (Anticipation 201, 1962)

Les Sept Anneaux de Rhéa [*The Seven Rings of Rhea*] (Anticipation 205, 1962)

Micro-Invasion (Anticipation 210, 1962) *Sydney Gordon 13*

La Mort Vient des Étoiles [*Death Comes from the Stars*] (Anticipation 214, 1962)

Visa pour Antarès [*Visa for Antares*] (Anticipation 222, 1963)

Les Jardins de l'Apocalypse [*The Gardens of the Apocalypse*] (Anticipation 228, 1963)

Planète à Vendre [*Planet for Sale*] (Anticipation 232, 1963) *Sydney Gordon 14*

Pas de Gonia pour les Gharkandes [*No Gonia for the Gharkands*] (Anticipation 238, 1964)

Alerte en Galaxie [*Galactic Alert*] (Anticipation 244, 1964)

Un Futur pour M. Smith [*A Future for Mr. Smith*] (Anticipation 250, 1964)

La Planète Géante [*The Giant Planet*] (Anticipation 255, 1964) *Sydney Gordon 15*

N'accusez pas le Ciel [*Don't Accuse the Sky*] (Anticipation 259, 1965)

LES MAITRES DU SILENCE

RICHARD BESSIÈRE

FLEUVE NOIR

ANTICIPATION

Les Pionniers du Cosmos [*The Pioneers of the Cosmos*] (Anticipation 264, 1965) *Pionniers 1* (refried version of *Conquérants*)

Le Chemin des Étoiles [*The Path to the Stars*] (Anticipation 268, 1965) *Pionniers 2* (refried version of *Conquérants*)

Les Maîtres du Silence [*The Masters of Silence*] (Anticipation 279, 1965)

Je m'appelle... Tous [*I'm Called... All*] (Anticipation 280, 1965)

Les Mages de Dereb [*The Wizards of Dereb*] (Anticipation 289, 1966) *Sydney Gordon 16*

Agent Spatial No. 1 [*Space Agent No. 1*] (Anticipation 293, 1966) *Dan Seymour 1*

Cerveaux Sous Contrôle [*Brains under Control*] (Anticipation 300, 1966) *Dan Seymour 2*

Inversia (Anticipation 306, 1966)

Cette Lueur Qui Venait Des Ténèbres [*That Light Which Came from Darkness*] (Anticipation 320, 1967)

L'Enfer dans le Ciel [*Hell in the Sky*] (Anticipation 329, 1967) *Dan Seymour 3*

Chaos sur la Génèse [*Chaos over Genesis*] (Anticipation 335, 1967)

Ne Touchez Pas Aux Borloks [*Don't Touch the Borloks*] (Anticipation 342, 1968) *Sydney Gordon 17*

LES MAGES DE DEREB

RICHARD BESSIÈRE

FLEUVE NOIR

ANTICIPATION

Tout Commencera... Hier [*It All Began... Yesterday*] (Anticipation 359, 1968) *Dan Seymour 4*

Des Hommes, des Hommes et encore des Hommes [*Men, Men and Forever Men*] (Anticipation 365, 1968)

La Machine Venue d'Ailleurs [*The Machine from Beyond*] (Anticipation 372, 1969) *Sydney Gordon 18/Machine 1*

Cauchemar dans l'Invisible [*Nightmare in the Invisible*] (Anticipation 380, 1969) *Dan Seymour 5*

Les Marteaux de Vulcain [*The Hammers of Vulcan*] (Anticipation 400, 1969)

On Demande un Cobaye [*Guinea-Pig Wanted*] (Anticipation 406, 1970)

Les Prisonniers de Kazor [*The Prisoners of Kazor*] (Anticipation 422, 1970) *Dan Seymour 6*

Quatre Diables au Paradis [*Four Devils in Paradise*] (Anticipation 438, 1970) *Sydney Gordon 19*

Concerto pour l'Inconnu [*Concerto for the Unknown*] (Anticipation 461, 1971)

La Loi d'Algor [*The Law of Algor*] (Anticipation 473, 1971) *Dan Seymour 7*

Variations sur une Machine [*Variations on a Machine*] (Anticipation 482, 1971) *Sydney Gordon 20/Machine 2*

Le Vaisseau de l'Ailleurs [*The Ship from Beyond*] (Anticipation 501, 1972)

ANTICIPATION
FICTION

RICHARD-BESSIERE

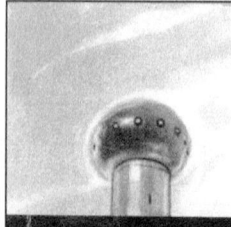

CETTE LUEUR
QUI VENAIT DES TENEBRES

FLEUVE NOIR

Energie -500 [*Energy -500*] (Anticipation 516, 1972) *Dan Seymour 8*

Quand les Soleils s'éteignent [*When the Suns Die*] (Anticipation 531, 1972) *Dan Seymour 9*

1973... Et La Suite [*1973... And the Rest*] (Anticipation 555, 1973)

Les Seigneurs de la Nuit [*The Lords of Night*] (Anticipation 591, 1973)

Les Ruches de M.112 [*The Hives of M112*] (Anticipation 615, 1974) *Dan Seymour 10*

Les Sources de l'Infini [*The Sources of Infinity*] (Anticipation 636, 1974)

Quand la Machine s'emmêle [*When the Machine Meddles*] (Anticipation 646, 1974) *Sydney Gordon 21/Machine 3*

Les Portes du Futur [*The Gates of the Future*] (Anticipation 696, 1975) *Donald Greene 1*

Et La Nuit Fut... [*And Night Fell...*] (Anticipation 700, 1975) *Donald Greene 2*

Déjà Presque La Fin [*Already Almost the End*] (Anticipation 773, 1977)

Cette Machine est Folle [*That Machine Is Mad*] (Anticipation 809, 1977) *Sydney Gordon 22/Machine 4*

L'Homme Qui Vécut Deux Fois [*The Man Who Lived Twice*] (Anticipation 852, 1978)

ANTICIPATION

FICTION

RICHARD-BESSIERE

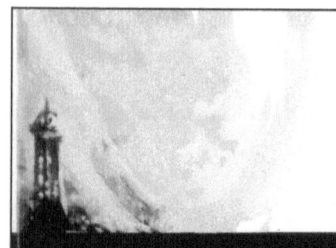

DES HOMMES, DES HOMMES. ET ENCORE DES HOMMES

FLEUVE NOIR

Tout Va Très Bien, Madame La Machine [*All's Well, Mrs. Machine*] (Anticipation 903, 1979) *Sydney Gordon 23/Machine 5*

Les Quatre Vents de l'Eternité [*The Four Winds of Eternity*] (Anticipation 964, 1980)

Quand la Machine Fait Boum! [*When The Machine Goes Boom!*] (Anticipation 1032, 1980) *Sydney Gordon 24/Machine 6*

N'Aboyez Pas Trop Fort, Mr. Benton [*Don't Bark Too Loudly, Mr. Benton*] (Anticipation 1114, 1981)

Les Survivants de l'Au-Delà [*The Survivors from Beyond*] (Anticipation 1136, 1982)

Avant les Déluges [*Before the Floods*] (Anticipation 1214, 1983) *L'Histoire des Hommes 1*

Après les Déluges [*After the Floods*] (Anticipation 1228, 1983) *L'Histoire des Hommes 2*

A La Découverte du Graal [*Searching for the Grail*] (Anticipation 1261, 1983) *L'Histoire des Hommes 3*

Les Maîtres de l'Horreur [*The Masters of Horror*] (Anticipation 1293, 1984) *Coburn 1*

Les Pierres de la Mort [*The Stones of Death*] (Anticipation 1346, 1984) *Coburn 2*

Silence... On Meurt! [*Silence... People Are Dying!*] (Anticipation 1370, 1985)

ANTICIPATION

FICTION

RICHARD-BESSIERE

LES MARTEAUX DE VULCAIN

FLEUVE NOIR

Cadavres à tout faire [*Handy Corpses*] (Anticipation 1411, 1985)

ANTICIPATION
FICTION

RICHARD-BESSIERE

LES SEIGNEURS DE LA NUIT

fleuve noir

SF & FANTASY

Guy d'Armen. *Doc Ardan: The City of Gold and Lepers*
G.-J. Arnaud. *The Ice Company*
Aloysius Bertrand. *Gaspard de la Nuit*
Richard Bessière. *The Gardens of the Apocalypse*
Félix Bodin. *The Novel of the Future*
André Caroff. *The Terror of Madame Atomos*
Didier de Chousy. *Ignis*
C. I. Defontenay. *Star (Psi Cassiopeia)*
Charles Derennes. *The People of the Pole*
Harry Dickson. *The Heir of Dracula*
Georges T. Dodds (anthologist). *The Missing Link*
Jules Dornay. *Lord Ruthven Begins*
Sâr Dubnotal *vs. Jack the Ripper*
Alexandre Dumas. *The Return of Lord Ruthven*
J.-C. Dunyach. *The Night Orchid. The Thieves of Silence*
Henri Duvernois. *The Man Who Found Himself*
Henri Falk. *The Age of Lead*
Paul Féval. *Anne of the Isles. Knightshade. Revenants. Vampire City. The Vampire Countess. The Wandering Jew's Daughter*
Paul Féval, *fils. Felifax, the Tiger-Man*
Arnould Galopin. *Doctor Omega*
Nathalie Henneberg. *The Green Gods*
V. Hugo, Foucher & Meurice. *The Hunchback of Notre-Dame*
Michel Jeury. *Chronolysis*
O. Joncquel & Theo Varlet. *The Martian Epic*
Gérard Klein. *The Mote in Time's Eye*
Jean de La Hire. *Enter the Nyctalope. The Nyctalope on Mars. The Nyctalope vs. Lucifer*
André Laurie. *Spiridon*
G. Le Faure & H. de Graffigny. *The Extraordinary Adventures of a Russian Scientist Across the Solar System* (2 vols.)
Gustave Le Rouge. *The Vampires of Mars*
Jules Lermina. *Mysteryville. Panic in Paris. To-Ho and the Gold Destroyers*
Jean-Marc & Randy Lofficier. *Edgar Allan Poe on Mars. The Katrina Protocol. Pacifica. Robonocchio. Tales of the Shadowmen* (anthos.; 7 vols.)
Xavier Mauméjean. *The League of Heroes*
John-Antoine Nau. *Enemy Force*

Marie Nizet. *Captain Vampire*
C. Nodier, Beraud & Toussaint-Merle. *Frankenstein*
Henri de Parville. *An Inhabitant of the Planet Mars*
Polidori, C. Nodier, E. Scribe. *Lord Ruthven the Vampire*
P.-A. Ponson du Terrail. *The Vampire and the Devil's Son*
Maurice Renard. *The Blue Peril. Doctor Lerne. The Doctored Man .*
A Man Among the Microbes. The Master of Light
Albert Robida. *The Adventures of Saturnin Farandoul. The Clock of*
the Centuries.
J.-H. Rosny Aîné. *Helgvor of the Blue River. The Givreuse Enigma.*
The Mysterious Force. The Navigators of Space. Vamireh. The World
of the Variants. The Young Vampire
Brian Stableford. *The New Faust at the Tragicomique. Frankenstein*
and the Vampire Countess. The Shadow of Frankenstein. Sherlock
Holmes & The Vampires of Eternity. The Stones of Camelot. The
Wayward Muse. (anthologist) *The Germans on Venus. News from the*
Moon
Jacques Spitz. *The Eye of Purgatory*
Kurt Steiner. *Ortog*
Villiers de l'Isle-Adam. *The Scaffold. The Vampire Soul*
Philippe Ward. *Artahe*
Philippe Ward & Sylvie Miller. *The Song of Montségur*

MYSTERIES & THRILLERS

M. Allain & P. Souvestre. *The Daughter of Fantômas*
Anicet-Bourgeois, Lucien Dabril. *Rocambole*
A. Bisson & G. Livet. *Nick Carter vs. Fantômas*
V. Darlay & H. de Gorsse. *Lupin vs. Holmes: The Stage Play*
Paul Féval. *Gentlemen of the Night. John Devil. The Black Coats:*
The Cadet Gang. The Companions of the Treasure. Heart of Steel.
The Invisible Weapon. The Parisian Jungle. 'Salem Street
Emile Gaboriau. *Monsieur Lecoq*
Steve Leadley. *Sherlock Holmes: The Circle of Blood*
Maurice Leblanc. *Arsène Lupin vs. Countess Cagliostro. Lupin vs.*
Holmes: The Blonde Phantom. The Hollow Needle.
Gaston Leroux. *Chéri-Bibi. The Phantom of the Opera. Rouletabille*
& the Mystery of the Yellow Room
William Patrick Maynard. *The Terror of Fu Manchu*
Frank J. Morlock. *Sherlock Holmes: The Grand Horizontals*
P. de Wattyne & Y. Walter. *Sherlock Holmes vs. Fantômas*

David White. *Fantômas in America*

SCREENPLAYS

Mike Baron. *The Iron Triangle*
Emma Bull & Will Shetterly. *Nightspeeder. War for the Oaks* Gerry
Conway & Roy Thomas. *Doc Dynamo*
Steve Englehart. *Majorca*
James Hudnall. *The Devastator*
Jean-Marc & Randy Lofficier. *Royal Flush*
J.-M. & R. Lofficier & Marc Agapit. *Despair*
Andrew Paquette. *Peripheral Vision*
R. Thomas, J. Hendler & L. Sprague de Camp. *Rivers of Time*

NON-FICTION

Stephen R. Bissette. *Blur 1-5. Green Mountain Cinema 1*
Win Scott Eckert. *Crossovers* (2 vols.)
Jean-Marc & Randy Lofficier. *Shadowmen* (2 vols.)
Randy Lofficier. *Over Here*

HEXAGON COMICS

Franco Frescura & Luciano Bernasconi. *Wampus*
Franco Frescura & Giorgio Trevisan. *CLASH*
L. Bernasconi, J.-M. Lofficier & Juan Roncagliolo Berger. *Phenix*
Claude Legrand, J.-M. Lofficier & L. Bernasconi. *Kabur*
Franco Oneta. *Zembla*
L. Buffolente, Lofficier & J.-J. Dzialowski. *Strangers: Homicron*
Danilo Grossi. *Strangers: Jaydee*
Claude Legrand & Luciano Bernasconi. *Strangers: Starlock*

ART BOOKS

Jean-Pierre Normand. *Science Fiction Illustrations*
Raven Okeefe. *Raven's L'il Critters*
Randy Lofficier & Raven OKeefe. *If Your Possum Go Daylight...*
Daniele Serra. *Illusions*